Tybee Island
H-Bomb

Tybee Island
H-Bomb

Michael Houtchen

Seventh
StarShadow

Cover design: Stephen Zimmer

Cover design in this book copyright © 2019 Stephen Zimmer & Seventh Star Press, LLC.

Editor: Holly Phillippe

Published by Seventh StarShadow

ISBN: 978-1-948042-78-9

Seventh StarShadow is an imprint of Seventh Star Press

www.seventhstarpress.com

info@seventhstarpress.com

Publisher's Note:

Tybee Island H-Bomb is a work of fiction. All names, characters, and places are the product of the author's imagination, used in fictitious manner. Any resemblances to actual persons, places, locales, events, etc. are purely coincidental.

Printed in the United States of America

First Edition

ACKNOWLEDGMENTS

They say you should always save the best for last, but not me. In my mind, the best should go first. So, I want to thank Stephanie, my muse, who also happens to be my wife, for all her encouragement. When I doubted, she was the one who said I could. Throughout the years, she has supported me in all my crazy endeavors. A special thanks to Charlotte 'M'. Yes, the same Charlotte as in the book. When she reads, the Pages are covered in blood, a.k.a. red ink. Finally, and definitely not the least, my publisher, Seventh StarShadow, especially my new friends, Holly and Stephen. I'm honored and privileged to be a member of the Seventh Star family. Thank you.

Dedication

To my grandkids: Caleb, Isaac, Ella, Natalie, Gavin, Miles, Shane, and Shyanne.

Prologue

Homestead Air Force Base, Florida.

February 5, 1958

Today's mission: Drop one hydrogen bomb on a remote, sleepy little village somewhere deep inside the Soviet Union. Upon completion of said assignment, Captain Samuel Rice in his B-47 bomber, is to evade the Soviet Air Force on his way out...Simple task. Looking at his watch, Rice noticed they were already four minutes late in departing.

"Captain here," Rice said, speaking though his handset. "What seems to be the holdup down there?"

"Sorry boss, but Kim's being a bitch. She doesn't want to be strapped in."

"Kim?"

"Yes, sir. Kim Novak. That's the name we painted on the side of the bomb. Did you see her in *Bell, Book, and Candle*; the one where Jimmy Stewart was her co-star?"

"I did see the movie, but I think Jimmy Stewart was the star, and Kim was the co-star."

"Whatever Captain, but you'll have to agree, Kim Novak is a bomb shell...Bomb shell, get it?"

"No argument there, guys," Rice replied, rolling his eyes, "but Jesus, how much longer?"

"Hold on a sec . . . There. All done. You can close the bomb-bay doors."

Rice nodded to his copilot who flipped a switch. They could hear gears grinding and hydraulic levers engaging. Soon a red blinking light turned green, indicating the bomb-bay doors were being closed and latched.

Kim Novak, a 7,600-pound Mark 15 hydrogen bomb, was twelve feet long and about two feet in diameter. It looked like a huge black dart with its pointy nose and tail fins, a dart containing four hundred pounds of conventional high explosives and an unknown large amount of highly enriched uranium. The pointy nose was the plutonium trigger, which would initiate the explosives on impact and start the nuclear reaction. The bomb's destruction power – one hundred times greater than the Hiroshima bomb dropped on Japan in 1945, would incinerate everything within a five-or-six-mile radius. The radioactive fallout alone would be deadly for a radius of a hundred sixty miles from the point of impact.

The ground crew watched as the big bird taxied away and finally took off. With his part of the mission complete, a sandy haired boy from Ohio lit up a cigarette and took a long drag.

"What's his problem? Four minutes late, my ass. He knows this is just a simulation. Nothing's going to go bang. No one's going to die. And, there's no reason to get all worked up."

His buddy agreed. "You know those guys. Always by the book. Let's get the hell out of here and get us a late-night snack. I'm starving."

"You're always starving," the boy from Ohio laughed, slapping his buddy on the arm.

The B-47 rose in the cloudless, moonlit, skies above and turned north. Today the small Soviet village being destroyed was Reston, Virginia. If the plane stayed on course and the wind speed held steady at 36,000 feet, the Bombardier would locate the target and press the disabled release button. The bomb would not be released. Instead, onboard instruments would log the current position of the plane, the planes air speed, current heading, altitude, and wind direction. Later the number crunchers back at Homestead would calculate the bomb's flight path to determine if the target had been destroyed.

Everything went according to plan. With the bomb "released," the B-47 was now hightailing it back to the friendly skies over North Carolina.

"Navigator to Skipper," a voice squelched over the headset.

"Go ahead Fred," Captain Rice came back.

"We've got four birds on our tail sir. Probably F-86 fighters out of Virginia. "

"Roger that. Keep a close eye on them."

"Roger that, sir."

Samuel loved the B-47. Its cool aluminum skin sparkled in the sunlight. Slick and compact, it sliced through the sky and flew more like a fighter plane than any bomber and Rice would know. During World War II, he had piloted more than thirty missions into Germany and two on D-Day. On every mission, he dodged German fighters before reaching safe air space.

At 2 a.m., the B-47 crossed over into the friendly skies of North Carolina...Mission complete. Captain Rice leaned back in his seat, took a deep breath, and gave a thumb's up to his copilot. They were cruising at 36,000 feet, air speed two hundred knots. The mission had gone off without a hitch and Rice was relieved it was over. With the current strong tail wind, they would even make up the lost four minutes. He turned to his copilot, about to say something, when the plane shook violently, rolling to the right. Grabbing the controls, Rice brought the plane back to level, but it took all his strength to keep it that way.

"What the hell just happened," he yelled.

"We just had a collision," his copilot yelled back.

"You've got to be shitting me."

"No, sir. I wouldn't shit you about something like that. It's hard to see, but it looks like one of the F-86s clipped our starboard wing."

"You've got to be kidding ... are you sure?"

"Yes, sir. In the moonlight, I can see an F-86 going down. It's missing a wing . . . The pilot just bailed out because I can see his parachute opening . . .It's now fully open, looking like a white mushroom cap. That's a beautiful sight. He should be fine."

"Thank God for that," Rice exclaimed. "But, someone back at HQ is going to be pissed losing a fighter during a simulation . . . how's our damage?"

"Looks like our starboard wing is intact but spewing a ton of fuel. I can just barely make out the outer engine hanging on by a few wires. I'm not sure if we're going to be able to land safely."

Because of the combined weight of the plane, its payload and the loss of one engine, the B-47 was slowly losing altitude. With the drag on the disabled engine, keeping the plane level was almost impossible.

"We got to do something Skipper and very soon," the copilot remarked coldly.

"You don't think I know that," the Captain snapped back. Rice took another deep breath and slowly exhaled. *God, I wish I had a cigarette right now.*

"Sorry about that Tom. I'm a little on edge right now."

"No shit. I wonder why?" the copilot laughed.

The six General Electric J-35 turbojet engines of the B-47 creates 3,970 pounds of thrust. With the loss of one engine, the plane can still be flown safely, however engine number six was causing too much drag. The Skipper didn't know how much structural damage had been done to the wing. In other words, the drag on the wing could cause it to tear off at any moment.

"Homestead, this is Captain Rice, looks like we have a situation."

"Come back, Captain. We didn't quite hear you."

"I said, it looks like we have a situation. We were just clipped by an F-86, and engine number six is dangling by a thread. I can't tell how much damage there is to the fuselage, but we're losing fuel. Homestead, I'm not sure we can land this bird."

"Affirmative, Captain. What's the condition of your payload?"

"Intact, but if we try to land, she could lose her mind."

"Understood. Can you head out over the ocean and jettison her?"

"Negative. We don't have the fuel necessary to get far enough out for a safe jettison, let alone to get back. We've got, maybe, just enough fuel to try a couple of landings. That's all . . . Guys, I don't want to go belly up with a raw egg onboard."

"Understood. Let me contact HQ and get their take."

"Don't take long."

For the crew, time seemed to drag, but Captain Rice was too busy to notice. Further analysis revealed their navigation system was disabled. As bad luck would have it, the electricity necessary to power the navigation equipment came from the generator attached to engine six. They knew where they were in the grand scheme of things but could not narrow down their location to more than a couple of miles. With no clouds in the sky and a full moon, Rice brought the plane down to 7,600 feet. He would try to fly by sight.

Banking to the east, he headed towards the coast. At the coastline, he turned south. With the moonlight reflecting off the waters of the Atlantic, Rice knew he would be able to pick out a few known landmarks. Up and off to the west should be the lights of Savannah and the lights of Tybee Island dead ahead. After a few breathtaking minutes, Rice could see the lights of both cities.

"Homestead to Nighthawk, over."

"Nighthawk here," Rice replied.

"What's your current location?"

"The best we can tell, about ten miles north of Savannah, which is to our Southwest. We should be coming up over Tybee Island in a few."

"Perfect. Now listen carefully. About five miles south of Tybee Island is Wassaw Sound. It's huge. The waters there are five to forty feet deep, and the bottom is soft mud and silt. The key point here: the bottom is soft mud and silt. HQ thinks you can drop the egg there . . . Without it bursting."

"They think? What do you mean, they think? Listen, do you know how many people will die if it goes off? Tybee Island would disappear, and Savannah would become a radioactive ghost town."

"Captain! Guard your words. We're on an open channel. And yes Captain, sadly, they do know. Damnit Rice, those are my orders and now yours."

"Affirmative," Rice replied, pissed off. Turning off external communications, he looked over at his copilot.

"Okay, Tom, here's where we earn our keep. We have to make sure we hit the Sound. If we don't, a lot of people won't be waking up this morning."

Quickly calculating the wind speed, direction, and their altitude, Tom came up with the best time to let her go. Captain Rice found no reason to disagree with him.

Rice had a sick feeling in the pit of his stomach as he listened to the bomb-bay doors opening.

Good God, what are we doing? Do I know anyone who lives down there? Holy Mary, Mother of God, I pray I don't. Jesus, forgive me.

The bomb silently fell away.

Holding their breath, both men waited, counting the seconds. Then . . . Nothing happened; no massive explosion; no mushroom cloud; nothing.

"Thank you, Jesus," Rice whispered.

"Amen," his copilot added. Thankfully, the loss of the bomb's weight made the plane easier to handle.

Captain Rice flicked the external communication switch. "Homestead, the egg has been dropped, and all's quiet. Repeat, the egg has been dropped."

"And?" Came a nervous reply.

"And it didn't crack."

"Good work, Captain. Damn good work. The military will be sending someone to pick it up. Now, let's get you guys down."

The B-47 was redirected to Hunter Air Force Base just outside Savannah, where it took three attempts before Captain Rice was able to safely put the bird on the ground. Captain Samuel Rice would be awarded the Distinguished Flying Cross for his role in saving the B-47 and his crew.

The next day, a search and rescue team consisting of 1,000 military personnel headed to Savannah, Georgia. For six weeks Wassaw Sound and the surrounding area was combed. The Forrest Sherman, a US destroyer, plowed the Atlantic coastline from Hilton

Head Island to Sapelo Island. PT boats cruised the surrounding rivers and creeks searching the banks, divers scanned the murky waters, soldiers waded through the salt marshes, and several blimps flew overhead looking for an impact crater.

One day, for no apparent reason, the search was called off.

Chapter 1

Joe Ray "Bubba" Henry, was a six foot three African-American, close to three hundred fifty pounds, proportionately huge, hated everything and everyone. If it walked or crawled, it needed its legs broken. If it flew, it needed its wings clipped. If it breathed, it needed to be smothered. If not for the color of his skin, Bubba would be the spitting image of Hoss Cartwright from the television show *Bonanza*. While Hoss Cartwright was jovial, Bubba was not. While Hoss cared for others, Bubba cared only for himself. Bubba liked hurting things: small dogs, cats, squirrels, and the occasional girlfriend. Bubba, by all accounts, was a loser and blamed everyone – upper-class, middle-class, lower-class, Whites, Blacks, Hispanics, Catholics, Protestants, and Muslims – for his lot in life. He had two burning desires: getting rich quick, and hurting those responsible for his miserable existence, which meant just about everyone.

For the last five minutes, he'd been watching (from the safety of his carport) a skinny, white girl standing on the cross-over bridge to the mouth of the Savannah River and the Atlantic Ocean. He was sweating bullets from the humidity and not in the best of moods.

When you going to get your scrawny ass back over to your damn condo, he thought as he lit another cig. *I've got some big-time shit coming, and I don't want you anywhere around when it gets here. You're going to fuck up everything, and girly, that would piss me off royally.* Bubba stood there in a rage, clinching his hands, wondering how they would feel around her scrawny neck.

Months ago, Bubba started searching the internet looking for hate groups, any hate group that would give him a reason for living. Just for the fun of it, he checked out the Ku Klux Klan, founded by Confederate veterans at the end of the Civil War. The group sought to restore white supremacy to the United States. They felt the country was going to Hell, and this downfall was caused by Blacks, Homosexuals, Catholics, Jews, Mexicans, and now, Muslims. From the beginning, they assassinated prominent African Americans, immigrants, politicians, and religious figures. Bubba wished there was a Black version of the KKK.

He found a group called The Phineas Priesthood, a Christian based terrorist organization that used violence to promote its hateful message. Supposedly built on Christian roots, the Priesthood preached hate to virtually anyone that differed from them. They protested homosexuality, abortion, Judaism, and taxation. They wanted a Christian nation composed solely of white Americans. To Bubba, these guys were assholes and small time. Not once had he seen their names on TV or in the papers.

One organization made him laugh out loud. They call themselves The Animal Liberation Front, or ALF for short. These vegetarians consider themselves a modern-day underground railroad for all creatures. They free animals from laboratories, farms, and factories. They claim to be non-violent, but these terrorists caused millions of dollars of damage every year to innocent farmers and scientists, all the while, harming the animals they are attempting to save. It turns out, many of the rescued animals can't survive in the wild without proper care, and as a result, are left to die.

Bubba heard rumors of a secret group responsible for kidnapping the President's wife last year, even though the White House denies it. *Conspiracy Magazine* says a group called *Citizens for a White America* had taken the First Lady into one of the State Parks up in New York State and held her there for a month before she was rescued.

Pussies, Bubba thought. *All these guys are nothing but a bunch of pussies. What happened to the good old days of Al-Qaeda, and their desire to get a bomb? Osama bin Laden was dead, but there was still a hornet's nest of bad asses out there. Imagine the damage a dirty bomb could do to those white-ass , snub their noses at you, my shit don't stink, big-shot mother-fuckers.*

Bubba, though big, was not a brave man, nor did he want to die. He wanted only to get rich, no matter what, no matter who got hurt. What's wrong with that? Wasn't that the American dream? Didn't your status in life depend on how many "toys" you had and how much money was in the bank? Growing up in eastern Georgia, and spending weekends on Tybee Island, he had heard the stories about the hydrogen bomb the Government had lost. Even if the bomb were waterlogged and useless, the radioactive material would still be good enough to make a dirty bomb. The locals say it's only a tall tale, and the bomb didn't exist. Bubba searched the internet and had found a story entitled – *Tybee Island H-Bomb.* Along with the story were pictures of the bomb, the plane after the collision, and the pilot.

How much money could I get if I found it? Shit, it's going to take money to make this happen; money I don't have. But it will be worth it if I can find that damn bomb.

The only people close enough to be called Bubba's friends were Pete Franklin and Frank Beasley, though the word "friends" would be a misnomer. They were more like servants at his beck and call; his "yes" men. In Bubba's mind, Pete and Frank reminded him of the Warner Bros. Looney Tunes cartoon about Spike the Bulldog and Chester the Terrier. Bubba was Spike the burly, gray bulldog who wore a red sweater, a brown bowler hat, and a perpetual scowl. Pete and Frank were like Chester, the terrier who was just the opposite of Spike, small and jumpy with yellow fur and brown, perky ears. Chester idolized Spike and would do anything for him. As long as Spike needed Chester, Spike would put up with him. As long as Bubba needed Pete and Frank, he would put up with them.

Peter "Pete" Franklin grew up in the Midwest before moving

11

to Macon, Georgia, at the age of ten. He was the only child of Marlene and Herman Franklin; hard working, blue-collared and God-fearing Southern Baptists. Marlene spoiled and pampered Pete in his younger days, but in his late teens, he became a handful; a redneck as his dad called him. His mom couldn't count the number of times she had been called to school because Peter had busted the nose of someone who had used his first name in some derogatory remark about a certain body part. Peter was highly intelligent and kind. In his younger days, he wanted to go to college, but his dad said they couldn't afford it. Now in his early twenties, Pete had enrolled at the local vocational school, taking welding classes. He enjoyed being active, using his hands, getting them dirty. Herman was relieved his son was learning a trade, not ending up a bum, and mooching off of him and Marlene for the rest of their lives.

At first, Marlene was overjoyed her son had taken an interest in his future. But now she wasn't sure. Peter was beginning to hang out with two "men" his age from his welding class; two men, whose names seemed to be in the paper way too often. Every day Marlene would scan the police reports, looking for Peter's friends. More days than not, she found them there. Most of the crimes they were arrested for were small time misdemeanors, ending in a slap on the hands, fines, and community service. She dreaded the day she would find Peter's name in print.

She prayed her son would someday meet a nice girl, a girl who could set him on the straight and narrow. Peter was a nice-looking kid; average height, slim, short brown hair, blue eyed, nice smile, and always sporting a dark two-day old trimmed beard. But the girls Peter met were only sluts from the bars where he and his two friends spent most of their free time. Marlene felt if she could get Peter away from his two friends, Frank Beasley, and "Bubba" Henry, he would straighten his life out.

Francis Beasley was a dark complexion Caucasian, with long jet-black hair, which he kept in a ponytail most of the time. He was five-five, if he tip-toed, because of this, he had what is called "the small man" syndrome. Any comment about size, his or something else, would piss him off. And if he'd been drinking, could send him over the edge. Dozens of times, Pete or Bubba, would come to his aid, keeping Frank from getting a butt kicking.

To make matters worse, Frank was a little slow. It was said, it was due to him being dropped on his head as a baby. When he was a youngster, he struggled in school, with the kids making fun of him. Later on, drunks in bars would call him names. The day he met Pete and Bubba all that stopped. He went by Frank because Francis was a girl's name.

For Bubba, it had been easy talking Pete and Frank into his grand scheme. If they found the bomb, they would be millionaires. Hell no. Trillionaires. Screw getting their hands dirty from welding. Fuck Uncle Sam. Fuck the American people. What had anyone ever done for them? They deserved to be happy. Didn't they? They wouldn't build a dirty bomb, nor would they set it off. They weren't murderers. They would only be acting as the middlemen, suppling the necessary raw materials. It would never be used on American soil, he promised them. Even though secretly, Bubba didn't give a shit if it was. He reminded Pete and Frank if they didn't find the bomb, someone else would. Others were searching for the bomb, even as he spoke. This was the opportunity of a lifetime, an opportunity to better themselves. They could move to Argentina. Uncle Sam couldn't fuck with them there. They would live like kings. Besides, what's the worst that could happen – they would spend a few weeks on the beach, ogling girls in their string bikinis, drinking beer, eating pizza, and getting laid. The other two laughed and punched each other when Bubba said, "getting laid."

Yeah, just like Spike and Chester, Bubba thought.

"Damnit to hell," Bubba exclaimed under his breath. Not only was the girl still on the fucking bridge, but another bitch had just joined her.

Chapter 2

Charlotte Knott, sweaty and exhausted from her late afternoon stroll on the beach, stood in the shade of the turtle-bridge gazebo catching her breath. *I need to start slowing down. Physically, I'm not the woman I used to be.* From her calculations, she had walked nearly three miles this evening, through the strength sucking sand of the riverbank, past the townhouse double swing at the foot of the dunes, and to the coastline. She couldn't wait to relate to the others the "almost" shark attack she had witnessed over on the beach a few minutes ago.

She'd just passed the breakers at the river, walking along the coast toward the pier far off in the distance, when she heard someone scream, "Get out of the water." Scanning the ocean, she noticed three people frantically trying to get out of the surf. They were about twenty yards offshore in neck deep water and even at that distance, Charlotte could see the panic in their eyes. Charlotte could also see the reason why. About ten yards south of them, a black dorsal fin broke the surface, only to disappear a second later. The dreadful music from *Jaws* flooded her mind. *Duh-Dun . . . Duh-Dun . . . Duh-Dun.* The fin appeared, closer this time. *Duh-Dun, Duh-Dun, Duh-Dun.* The man who screamed was bringing up the rear, and the fin was zeroing in on him. Covering her mouth with her hand, Charlotte fought back a cry. She expected to see bloody foaming bubbles any second. *Come on,* she thought. *You can make it.* Three feet from the man, the fin disappeared, only to re-appear seconds later three feet past him. The fin continued bobbing in and out of the water, as it made its way up the coast. The victim crawled onto shore, rolled over on his back, and started laughing.

"It was a dolphin," he said, coughing out a mouthful of water. "I thought I was going to die, and it was only a dolphin."

"I could have told him that," a woman said, standing behind Charlotte. "That's Sandy. He comes through here this time every day, on his way to his favorite feeding hole."

"Why didn't you tell them?" Charlotte asked.

"Do you think they would have heard?"

"I've had enough of the beach for one day," the victim said, regaining his feet. "Let's head in. I think I need a drink." The others in his party agreed.

The lady standing behind Charlotte had seen enough and was going in too. In a matter of minutes, Charlotte was alone on the beach. *Duh-Dun . . . Duh-Dun . . . Duh-Dun.*

The glare of the setting sun was starting to give Charlotte a headache. Fanning the lower end of her tank top, she hoped to relieve herself from the discomfort of the dreaded boob sweat, something men never seemed to worry about. She couldn't wait to get back to the condo for a cool refreshing shower. Hopefully, the crew would have the cards shuffled and a blender of Brandy Alexanders waiting.

Halfway across the turtle-bridge, was a young teenage girl leaning over the rail watching the turtles. She looked to be around fifteen or sixteen, wearing a two-piece swimsuit, tall and skinny with long raven hair, sparkling eyes, and a beautiful smile.

"What're you doing?" Charlotte inquired, walking up.

"I'm feeding them pieces of bread."

"Oh my, look at all of them," Charlotte laughed, leaning over the rail beside the girl.

The pond beneath the bridge was foaming with hundreds of turtles fighting for the scraps being dropped to them. Most were about a foot in diameter, but there were some Goliaths measuring in at around two feet.

"Look how the larger ones are stealing from the smaller ones," the girl exclaimed in amazement. Turning to Charlotte, she asked, "Are you staying in the blue condo?"

"We are."

"I'm in the condo across the street. I saw your license plate. You're from Kentucky. So are we. We're from Bowling Green."

"We're from Franklin. That's only twenty miles from Bowling Green. Funny. You come all this way down to Tybee Island just to run in to someone from home. My name's Charlotte by the way."

"I'm Sara, Sara Sinclair."

"Nice to meet you, Sara Sinclair. Have you been to Tybee before?"

"Nope. This is our first time."

"This is our sixth. We love it here. Sara, you don't find it boring? There's not a lot of things for young people to do. I mean, like there are in Gulf Shores and Destin. Stuff like go-carts, putt-putt, those kinds of things."

"No," Sara replied. "I love the sun, sand, and water. It's nothing like back home. (Charlotte nodded in agreement.) And there are things people my age can do. You have to know where to look. My dad lets me have my own golf cart. So, I've been driving my little brother Shane back and forth to the beach and pier. That's fun in itself. Dad gives me money so Shane and I can run over to *Lighthouse Pizza*, all by ourselves. We all run into Savannah most days, shopping for souvenirs." Charlotte laughed. "It sounds like you're having fun . . . Look over there at our condo. You see that woman on the patio holding up the tall glass in her hand. That's Stephanie, and she's letting me know the Brandy Alexanders are ready. I better get going before they melt. It was nice meeting you Sara. Maybe we can take a walk on the beach together sometime."

"I'd like that."

As Charlotte turned to go, Sara grabbed her arm. "Can I ask you a question?"

"Sure."

"Look over my left shoulder, but don't make it too obvious."

"Okay. What am I looking for?"

"Is there a big black man looking at us?"

"There's a guy over there under a carport, but he's talking on his cell phone. Why?"

"He's been staring at me."

"You sure?"

"I started out feeding the turtles on the other side of the bridge and noticed him staring. My backs to him on this side, but now and then I look toward my condo, and out of the corner of my eye, I can see him staring."

"I'm sure it's okay, but maybe you need to go in. Oh, wait. He's going inside."

"Good. I know how it must sound. I'm sure it's nothing. I think I'll go ahead and take a walk on the beach."

"Be careful, the sun will be going down soon, and you don't want to have to make your way through the dunes in the dark."

"Will do Charlotte. Thanks."

Chapter 3

Sara, huffing, and puffing from her walk on the beach, paused midway across the bridge to check on the turtles. A few were swimming in the murky water. Some were walking on the mud flat below the bridge, and a few were coming out onto the bank to eat grass. The sun was setting casting everything in deep shades of grey. Even the foul green pond water was now a dark grey shade of foul. There was barely enough light to see by. And in the faint light, she noticed something odd. From the condo on the corner, it looked like one of the men, the black man again, had just dropped a gun. He had an armload of what looked like rifles, and one slipped out of his hands. Sara froze, not knowing what to do.

Why does he have guns, and what's he going to do with them? Better yet, did he see me? What would he do if he had? I need to get back to my condo.

Sara knew, if she tried to make a dash for her condo, she would come within a few yards of the big man. The end of the bridge was on the corner of his lot, near his building, and he could easily grab her. Turning back toward the beach and hoping he hadn't noticed, she slowly began walking away. She felt a cold chill run down her spine. She would cross the dunes and make her way down to another walk-bridge further down the river near the townhouse complex on the corner of Van Horne and Captain's View. Stealing a look over her shoulder, her heart sank. She had been seen. Already the man was on the bridge running full out.

Sara being young and thin, could easily out distance the man, but she was already tired and out of breath. Exiting the bridge and entering the dunes, she stumbled twice in the loose sand before making the beach. She could hear heavy breathing behind her, gaining on her.

The last rays of the dying sun shone on the flowing waves of the river, casting dancing shadows of pink and orange on the now deserted beach. A loaded cargo ship, with a few running lights, silently made its way down river toward the ocean. In the darkness, anyone standing at its rail would miss seeing her. Any scream for help would go unnoticed. The labored breathing behind her was getting louder.

Sara began running parallel to the river, up close to the dunes, but the loose sand was slowing her down. Changing her course, she cut across the beach to the water's edge. The wet, packed sand made running easier. A few seconds later, water was splashing the back of her calves and legs from the man's feet splashing in the surf behind her. He was close, too close, and something told her she mustn't get caught.

Taking a deep breath, she turned sharply toward the dunes. Maybe she could lose him there. The loose sand sucked at her feet again, slowing her down even more. But she knew the sand would be doing the same to the big man. Maybe even worse. His weight would cause him to sink deeper into the sand, slowing him down even more than she. This encouraged her and gave flight to her feet. The townhouse walk-bridge was ahead, and she could hear music and laughter. She could see the faint glow of lights from the sliding-glass doors in the apartments. If she could make it to the bridge, maybe then a scream would be heard. If Sara could make it to the bridge, then maybe she had a chance. If she could just make it to the bridge.

Suddenly, pain shot through her shoulder blades, traveling up her neck, exploding in her head. Face first, she dove to the sand. She tried to raise up, but a great weight held her down, pressing hard on her back. She heard and felt ribs snapping. If only she could raise her head to catch a breath, but strong hands refused, pressing her face deeper into the sand. She couldn't breathe without taking in a mouth full of sand. *Can a person drown in sand?* Holding her breath and struggling as hard as she could, she still couldn't shake him off. The last thing Sara Sinclair remembered in her short-lived life – her mom's warm eyes, sweet wet kisses, and her gentle smile; her dad's strong protecting arms cradling her when she got hurt; her little brother, Shane, teasing the pee out of her; her dog Tony, who at fifty pounds, still thought he was a lap-puppy; the weight bearing down on her back; the pain of broken ribs; the agony of breathing sand.

Bubba knew the girl was dead, but to make sure, he held her face buried in the sand for an extra few minutes. He had hurt things in the past, even to the point of torture, but he had never killed a human and something about this moment was exciting and arousing. He had nothing against the girl, but she had seen; seen him and the guns. Would she have told someone? Sure, she would have, and that would have ruined everything. She would have kept him from bettering himself, kept him from getting what he wanted, what he needed, what he desired. God knows he deserved it. No, she had to die. It was the only thing to do, and it was the right thing to do.

Rising on trembling legs, he scanned the surrounding area. No one was out that he could tell. *Thank God*. But what to do with her? He couldn't leave her here on the beach. Could he? The early morning walkers would surely find her. Bubba almost panicked.

"Calm down and leave her," he told himself, as he wiped the sweat from his eyes.

They will find her anyway. Best to get away as quickly as he could. The longer he stayed here, the more likely he would be seen. All he needed now was star-struck lovers out on a moonlit stroll along the beach. Panic made him look around again.

Jesus Christ. Get ahold of yourself.

Grabbing her arms, he dragged her across the dune beside the bridge. She was light and limp, like a ragdoll. Under the bridge and in the dark, as best as he could, he covered her with sand.

Walking back to his condo, Bubba felt a pleasant stirring in his chest. He'd done it. He killed a person. And, it wasn't hard at all. He felt powerful.

Chapter 4

Rising slowly from the bed, to not wake Margaret, his wife, Ray slowly made his way to the bathroom. *What time is it?* The illuminated face of the alarm clock on the bedside table told him it was midnight. *Let's see. We played cards till ten, and then all went to bed. I know I went to the bathroom then. God, my bladder ain't what it used to be. I wonder if my prostate is getting larger.* During his last visit to the doctor, he was told that if his prostate got any larger, he would be put on medication. Ray hated taking medicine. Most of the time, his excuse was he just "forgot" to take it.

Slowly making his way around the end of the bed in the dark, he froze. A streak of red and blue lights was dancing on the wall beside the dresser. Looking for the source, he noticed it coming from the edge of the shade covering the window. Something was happening outside. *Holy shit. Aliens?* Pulling the shade away from the window, Ray saw a Tybee patrol car with its lights flashing, parked at the condo across the street. Returning to the side of the bed, he fumbled in the dark locating his shirt, pants, and sneakers.

Heading into the bathroom, he slowly closed the sliding door behind him. The bright overhead lights blinded him when he flipped the switch. *You talk about bed-hair*, he thought. Grabbing his brush, he dragged it through his thinning hair. Laying the brush aside, he went about what he had come in here for.

Returning to the bedroom, he located the metal box in the bottom drawer of the nightstand. Inside was his Colt 45 and holster. The holster he attached to his belt. Retrieving a small leather wallet, he checked to make sure his badge and credentials were in place.

Raymond Harris was sixty-nine, a survivor of a triple bypass, a little over-weight, five nine with thinning white hair. Ray, as his friends called him, had been a sniper in Vietnam. Even at sixty-nine, he could still shoot the stinger off a bee's ass at a hundred yards. If you don't believe it, just ask him. Once he mustered out of the service, he got into law enforcement. Raymond wore many hats: a loving husband, father, grandfather, and great granddad. This morning, his hat had been that of a tourist, but with the patrol car outside his bedroom window, he was now a police officer, the Sheriff of Franklin, Kentucky.

Once in the hallway, he slowly closed his bedroom door. Turning to go, he almost ran over Charlotte.

"Shit, Charlotte," he whispered. "What in the hell are you doing up?"

"I was reading Ray," she whispered back, "and I noticed flashing lights coming from the window. There's a police car across the street."

"I know."

"Ray, that's where Sara, the girl I told you all about last night, the girl on the turtle-bridge, that's where she's staying."

"I know . . . I remember . . . That's why I'm going over."

An officer was leaning against the patrol car as Ray walked up. The officer looked to be in his early thirties, slim, and heavily bearded.

A Duck Dynasty fan, perhaps.

"What can I do for you?" he asked.

"The name's Raymond Harris," Ray replied, showing him his badge and credentials.

"Again, what can I do for you, Raymond Harris, Sheriff of Franklin, Kentucky?"

"I saw your lights from my bedroom window and wondered if we could be of any help. We know the girl, Sara, that's staying here. Is everyone okay?"

"What do you know about Sara?" the officer asked, interested now.

"Me? Nothing."

"Then how do you think you can help?"

"One of the ladies in our group talked with her late this afternoon and was worried. That's all."

"Where's this woman now?"

Ray looked over at the condo. "She's standing in the doorway."

"Why don't you mosey back over there and join her. I'll check with the Police Chief and get back with you." With that, the officer turned and went inside the building.

Charlotte could hear Ray muttering under his breath, "Mosey my ass. I'll show him mosey."

"Well, what did he say?" Charlotte asked when Ray had joined her.

"Not much. *Duck Dynasty* said he'd get back with us. I think he'll have some questions for you." Charlotte was about to ask what *Duck Dynasty* meant when FJ poked his head around the corner of the stairway.

FJ, a.k.a. Milton Frederic Johnston – not his real name, but one given to him by child services – was born with achondroplasia, a common form of dwarfism, with a normal-sized head and torso but shortened limbs. This condition is caused by a genetic or nutritional disability. He used to brag that what was in his pants more than made up for his shorter arms and legs. Abandoned at birth by his mother because of his "condition", he ran away from several foster homes before finally ending up in a traveling circus.

At first, he was in a troupe of clowns with adults laughingly pointing him out to their children. "Look at the midget," they would shout, not knowing the word midget was considered derogatory and offensive. In truth, the word midget refers to a person who is very short, but with normal proportions. Today, the term has given way to "short person" or "little person." FJ preferred to be called what he was, a dwarf. As the years progressed, FJ's circus talents increased. He went from clown to animal trainer, to human cannonball, to knife thrower, to acrobat, to escape artist. He would amaze Ray and the others by having Ray lock him up in handcuffs and, every time, escape from them. There wasn't a lock he couldn't pick.

"What's going on?" FJ asked from the stairwell corner.

"What are you doing back there?" Ray asked. "Hiding?"

"No, I'm not hiding. I'm naked."

"Jesus, FJ."

"Ray, I always sleep in the nude. I told you guys that. And I also told you, I sleepwalk."

"Too much information. Go and get some clothes on, and while you're at it, you might as well wake up Mike, Stephanie, and Margaret."

"Hell no. I'll wake up Mike and Stephanie, but I'm not waking up Margaret. You go and wake up Margaret. She's your wife."

"And that's why I'm not waking her up. She'll kill me. You, on the other hand, are too little and cute for her to kill."

It was true. In the beginning, Margaret treated FJ like one of her grandchildren, which pissed FJ off. One day he'd had enough. He told Margaret he was a grown man; he had hair down there, he wasn't a virgin, he smoked pot, got drunk and watched porn. Margaret never treated him like a child again.

"Screw you," FJ whispered, turning to leave.

"FJ."

"What Ray?"

"Put some clothes on before you wake them."

"Screw you . . . again."

Five minutes, five slow minutes, passed before *Duck Dynasty* and another police officer came across the drive. The others in the condo were up and waiting with Ray in the hallway. Thank goodness FJ was wearing clothes.

"I'm Police Chief Aaron Rogers, and before you ask anything, not that Aaron Rogers. Deputy Brown says one of you might have information for us about Sara Sinclair."

"That would be me," Charlotte said, raising her hand.

"Tell me what you know Mrs. . . ."

"Charlotte Knott. I met Sara this afternoon, over on the turtle-bridge."

"Okay Mrs. Knott, what time was that?"

"I don't know. Around seven o'clock, I think. Right before we played cards."

"It was seven," Mike confirmed.

"What did you two talk about?"

"The turtles."

"Anything else?"

"We talked about where we were from and how much she liked Tybee. And then she told me she was going for a walk on the beach."

"Did she act like she was in a hurry? Like she was in a hurry to meet someone?"

"No, not really."

"Okay. Did she seem nervous or anything?"

"She seemed a little nervous."

"Why's that?"

"She said a man in the corner condo was staring at her."

"What man?"

"A large African American man. I guess he's staying there."

"Okay, I'll talk with him. Anything else?"

"No, that's about it."

"Okay, Mrs. Knott. You helped us tie down the time frame. You guys going to be around for a while?"

"All week," Ray answered.

"Good. If we have any more questions, we'll stop back by. And Mrs. Knott, if you think of anything, call us."

"Has something happened to Sara?" Charlotte asked.

Chief Rogers looked back at Sara's condo as if he was struggling with answering that question.

"Mrs. Knott, we don't know if something has happened to Sara. She didn't come home since she left for her walk."

"Oh my God," Charlotte exclaimed.

"What?" Ray and the Chief asked simultaneously.

"I told her to get back before it got dark, and now look. She's missing. I bet it was the man at the condo." Charlotte went back inside the condo before anyone could reply.

"I promise, I'll talk with him when I'm through here," Chief

Rogers assured Ray.

"Are you keeping something from us?" Ray asked, staring after Charlotte. "Have you found the girl?"

"No. Right now, she's just a missing person. We've had people wander off before and get lost."

"We're not talking about a little child. We're talking about a teenager."

"We got the call an hour ago. So, we've been checking out down by the pier, talking with the local teenagers she might have met. Could be she was hanging out somewhere and forgot about the time. Maybe she got drunk and is afraid to come home. No luck so far. We were getting ready to search the shoreline."

"You think she drowned?"

"Well, it was getting dark, and these waters can be dangerous for those not used to them."

"You need some help?"

The police chief gave Ray the once over. Here was an old man, probably in his seventies and overweight. He didn't need him tagging along, getting in the way. Hell, he could have a heart attack wandering out there in the dark.

"That's okay Sheriff," he came back. "I think we can handle this by ourselves."

"Bullshit. That's the stock answer everyone gives. As one officer-of-the-law to another officer-of-the-law, I'm offering my help."

"Okay, Sheriff. But, if you slow us down, I'll have your ass."

"Too late Chief. My wife's already chewed mine off."

"That's not funny Raymond," Margaret said sternly from the hallway.

"Not funny, but true," FJ whispered to Stephanie.

While Ray hunted around the condo looking for a flashlight, Chief Rogers went to talk with the large African American man.

"Well?" Ray asked when the Chief returned.

"He admits seeing them, Mrs. Knott and Sara, on the bridge earlier, but he said, he went inside. He hasn't seen Sara since."

"And you believe him?"

"I have no reason not to. Do you have anything that says he's lying?"

"No."

"Are you ready then?"

Ray nodded.

With a dozen officers, Ray crossed the turtle-bridge. Beams of light played across the still pond disturbing some of the turtles. Beams scanned the banks on both sides showing turtles grazing on grass.

"You know," Chief Rogers said. "I think I've seen your little friend before . . . I know. He looks like that little person who's on *Game of Thrones*."

"He does that on purpose," Ray laughed. "The way he wears his hair and beard, people come up to him asking for autographs, thinking he's Peter Dinklage, and most of the time he signs it that way – Peter Dinklage. But no selfies. Never selfies. He says selfies would give him away." The Chief laughed.

Flashlights danced around the dunes, like searchlights at the Academy Awards.

"Okay. Half of you split up and work your way upstream," Chief Rogers whispered. "The rest will go with the Sheriff and me downstream. Look for anything out of the ordinary. Give a holler if you find anything."

"Hold on Chief," Ray said, running his light across the sand.

"What?"

"Look closely here," he said, pointing at a set of tracks.

"Yeah. You walk on the sand; you leave tracks. Sheriff, there're millions, billions of tracks on this beach."

"But notice. Here's a set of prints of a person with small feet, running toward the water. And following is a set of a person with large feet."

"That doesn't mean a damn thing. A dad could have been playing tag with his kid. He could be trying to scare him or her with one of the crabs he caught in the dunes. Hell, they could have been made at different times. There could be a dozen reasons for those footprints. Sheriff, I think you're way out of line, and you're slowing us up. We're going to continue searching along the dunes. When and if we have to, we'll turn our attention to the water. But you go and do whatever you want, just don't slow us up."

The Chief set off alone to the beach next to the dunes. Ray made his way, following the tracks, toward the water.

"They disappear here," Ray hollered. "Maybe she got on a boat."

"Sheriff, waves always wash away footprints, and besides, you don't know if they were hers anyway," the Chief hollered back.

Which way? Upstream or downstream? Ray asked himself. *Sara, which way would you run?*

Upstream, for dozens of miles, was only the river and the marsh. Downstream were the townhouses and their walkways.

Turning downstream, Ray shined his light along the waterline. About a hundred feet, Ray picked up the tracks again. This time heading for the dunes and a walk-bridge. Coming to the base of a dune beside a bridge, Ray froze. *Good God,* he thought. *How could you guys have missed this?*

"Chief," Ray called to the group that just passed this very spot.

"What is it now, Sheriff?"

"You need to come look at this."

"You better not be wasting our time. What is it now?"

"What do you see here?" Ray asked, fanning his light around the sand.

"I see a kid making sand angels. You see it all the time on the beach. Hell, I bet I could show you a hundred of them in less than an hour."

"That's not what I see," Ray commented.

"Then please, by all means, tell us what you see."

"Someone, someone small, face down, flailing their arms trying to get up."

The Chief rolled his eyes. "I see someone, someone small, lying on their back, flailing their arms making angels wings. How in the world would you say he or she was face down?"

"Right here. Look at the impressions here and there. Those

are knees pressing into the sand. If a person were lying on their back, those wouldn't be there."

"Alright. You have a point."

Shining the beam of his flashlight here and there, Ray made his way to the top of the dune. Pointing back down the slope of the dune, he said, "See how the sand has been disturbed. It looks like someone was trying to smooth out any marks. But he or she missed some. Look there. Those look like drag marks." Shining his light on the other side of the dune, up under the bridge, he sat down heavily in the sand.

"I think I've found her."

"Where?" the Chief asked, climbing up beside Ray. Ray shined his light in the valley of two dunes to a spot below the bridge, to a small pile of sand; a small pile of sand the length of a small person.

"There."

The Chief slid down the side of the dune and ducking his head under the bridge, kneeled beside the end of the pile. Taking his hand, he slowly brushed away the sand. Suddenly he stopped. He had touched something, something fleshy. Gritting his teeth, he brushed again, uncovering a small foot.

"Holy Mother of God," he exclaimed.

Chapter 5

Mike walked into the kitchen craving coffee and a cigarette. It had been four years since his last cig, but he still wanted one. Every day since quitting he'd wanted one. At five-ten, Michael Roach was overweight, in his mid-sixties, balding and physically challenged from a childhood accident that left only twenty-five percent use of his left hand. He was also missing the two middle fingers on that hand. But, his messed-up hand he counted as a blessing. In 1970 he had won the government lottery, the Military Draft. His number had been 90, and the cutoff was 130. If not for his hand, he would have found himself slushing through the rice patties in Vietnam. He had retired as a computer analyst two years ago and now spent his time reading, painting, and writing adventure novels. Thank God for his computer analyst's 401K. His paintings and novels weren't selling.

It was nine o'clock in the morning, and Mike was still sleepy. It had been a long night. Charlotte had kept them up all night retelling her story of how she met Sara. Ray retold how he found Sara. Each telling hadn't lessened the pain or sadness.

Margaret and Stephanie were busy preparing breakfast. Margaret, Ray's wife, was a retired Judicial Assistant, sixty-three, slightly overweight, but as she put it, "I carry it well." With help from Miss Clairol, she sported dark auburn hair. She stood five-foot six and had a respiratory condition. She was a saint, having to put up with Raymond Harris day in and day out.

Stephanie Roach was the youngest of the group at fifty-eight. Her salon enhanced blond hair was beautifully streaked with gray that sparkled in the sun. Her warm blue eyes and smile made her an instant friend to everyone she meets. She stretched her five foot six, plus sized body, trying to get plates off the top shelf. Two years ago, she retired from the City of Franklin as an accountant and was now enjoying writing children's books. Her first book was doing well on *Amazon*.

FJ was sitting at the dining room table sipping coffee, and Ray was in the living room reading the latest *Jack Reacher* novel. He always pictured himself being the *Jack Reacher* type, if he was thirty years younger and a foot and a half taller. Mike went over and poured himself a cup.

"Need some help?" he asked the ladies.

"They always need help," FJ replied for them.

"You know, if you were taller, you could help cook," Mike spat.

"If you had ten fingers, you could help shuffle cards," FJ spat back.

"Are you two ever going to stop doing that?" Stephanie asked, turning sausage in a frying pan.

"No," they both answered.

"Charlotte been down?" Mike asked, changing the subject. Charlotte Knott was sixty-five, and a retired Media Specialist from the Franklin Middle School. At a petite five-foot one, she enjoyed reading, bike riding, walking, and exercising. She was the healthy one in the group. She was proud to be the grandmother of four, disliked sausage gravy, but liked anything chocolate. Being the last one to have seen Sara alive hurt her to the core. For some reason, she felt responsible. Ray tried to ensure her; she was not the last person to see Sara alive. The murderer was. That hadn't helped.

"Not yet, that I'm aware of," Margaret answered, filling glasses with orange juice.

Stephanie had just placed the platter of sausage patties on the table when her cell phone rang.

"I wonder who'd be calling us this early," she said answering it. "Oh hi, Samantha. What's up? You're kidding." After a long pause, "No. Take him to the emergency room."

"What's up?" Mike inquired. Stephanie held her hand up for

him to wait.

"I wouldn't mess around Sam," Stephanie said. "I'd take him there right now. Okay, call me when you get done."

"Well, what's up?" Mike asked again.

"That was Samantha. She -"

"I know who Samantha is."

"She said the baby just stuck a crayon up his nose." Everyone laughed.

"Oh, it's not funny," Stephanie said, seriously. "She's nervous."

"She can't pull it out?" Mike asked.

"It wasn't the whole crayon, smarty, just a piece, and, no, she can't pull it out. She's afraid she'll push it further up his nose."

"So, why did she call you?"

"I'm her mother of course. (Everyone laughed.) No, she didn't know whether to take him to Convenient Care or the Emergency Room. I don't think Convenient Care is open this early, so I told her to take him to the Emergency Room."

"What color was it?" FJ asked, taking a sip of coffee.

"What?" Stephanie asked puzzled.

"What color was the crayon?"

"How in the hell would I know?"

"You should have asked her." It was then that the front door opened and in walked Charlotte.

"Where have you been?" Ray asked from the living room.

"I was over visiting Sara's parents, and then I went for a walk on the beach along the ocean side," she replied, all sweaty. "It's going to be another hot day."

"How are they feeling?"

"As you would expect, losing a child."

"And how are you feeling this morning?"

"Better. I feel so sad for Sara and her family. Sara had a little brother, Shane. He's taking it hard. I hope they catch the one responsible soon." Charlotte went over and poured herself a cup of coffee. "This may sound horrible, but what happened shouldn't stop us from enjoying our vacation. So, what do you need me to do?"

"After you take a quick shower to get rid of the sweaty ocean smell, you can make the gravy," FJ said.

"Gravy? Are you out of your frickin' mind?" Charlotte exclaimed. "You know I can't even stand the smell of gravy. Just the sight of it makes me want to puke."

Everyone laughed. That's what they all needed right now, a good laugh.

"After breakfast, I think I'll walk down to the police station and see how things are going," Ray said, walking into the dining room.

"You want me to come with you?" FJ asked.

"You think you can keep up?"

"With the way you walk, a snail could keep up," Mike answered for FJ.

"Screw you, Mike."

***

"I still can't believe you killed her," Pete exclaimed for the thousandth time. "Were you out of your frickin mind? My God Bubba, she was only sixteen years old."

Bubba raised his head from the bowl of *Fruit Loops* he was eating. "How ya know she was sixteen?"

"Because we asked around," Frank answered, sternly.

"You guys shouldn't be asking around."

"You think? Everybody's talking about it. Everybody's asking questions. Everyone's curious, as you would expect. How do you think it would look if we're the only ones not asking questions? The only ones not concerned? Bubba, you screwed up big time. She was just a kid. She had a mom and dad, a little brother. I talked with her the other day on the turtle-bridge. Hell, I heard she had a dog, for Christ sake."

"You think I wanted to kill her? Hell, I didn't even know her. But she saw the guns. I panicked, alright? Is that what you want to hear? It was a spur of the moment thing. Damnit, Pete, she left me no choice."

"Bubba, nobody was supposed to get hurt," Frank whispered.

"Frank, she saw the guns."

"Who said we needed guns anyway?" Pete yelled.

"Shut your damn mouth," Bubba said, slamming the top of the table with an open hand, making the bowl of *Fruit Loops* jump. "You want the neighbors to hear you?"

Pete shook his head and whispered, "Damnit Bubba, she was only a kid."

"What's done is done. Yes, I killed her, and I can't bring her back. Pete, I did it for us. Besides, can you imagine the number of people who're going to die when we find the bomb? What's one more person?"

"The difference is . . . I haven't ever met them," Pete commented sadly, sitting down across from Bubba.

"Don't go soft on me, you two," Bubba said, throwing the nearly empty cereal bowl in the sink along with the other three days' worth of dirty dishes. "You've been screwed your entire life, and now you have the opportunity to do something about it. You want to get rich, don't you? You want to live like kings, don't you? You deserve it. You deserve to be happy. Imagine everything you ever wanted. The girl would have ruined everything. And remember this my friends, you're in this as much as me. If I go down, so do you."

Pete rubbed his forehead. "How can we forget?"

***

"While FJ and I are visiting the police station, why don't you call and make a reservation at the Sundae Café," Ray said, opening the front door.

"What day?" Margaret asked.

"Doesn't matter to me," Ray replied.

"Me either," FJ added. "Mike, what day is good for you?"

"We'll try and make it for Friday night," Mike answered, filling the dishwasher. "Yuck."

"What happened?" Ray asked.

"I just got gravy on my hands," Mike said, running his hand under the hot water.

"It's funny," FJ commented.

"What is?"

"Five minutes ago, you were eating that same gravy, almost licking the plate. But now, it's disgusting because it's garbage."

"You know Sundae Café is one of the hidden gems of Tybee," Margaret said, ignoring FJ. "Located between a liquor store and a convenient store, passerby's think it's an ice cream parlor. This is one time you shouldn't judge a book by its cover."

"It used to be an ice cream deli," Mike agreed, "but once you step inside today, you'll see it's something extraordinary. With its fancy cloth covered tables and fine china, its superior wines, mixed drinks, and beer, down to the six eating utensils around each plate, you know you're in for a real Southern treat. I love their Pan-Fried Pecan Chicken. Every year, FJ gets the Parmesan Fried Calamari. Stephanie won't leave the island without getting their Crab Cakes."

"Don't forget the Seafood Cheesecake as our appetizer," Margaret said. "People have questioned me about it, thinking Seafood Cheesecake sounded weird. I tell them it's shrimp and lump crab with a hint of smoked Gouda in a garlic butter crust, served over mixed field greens and a drizzle of balsamic syrup."

Amazed, everyone stared at Margaret. "I looked it up on their website," Margaret added. "It's worth dying for!" Margaret instantly regretted saying the word, dying.

"You're making my mouth water," FJ chimed in, lightening up the situation. "See if that girl who waited on us last year is working. You remember her name?"

"No," Mike replied.

"She was the tall girl with -"

"All girls are tall to you," Mike barked.

FJ pitched him a finger. "You know the tall one. Short blond hair pulled back into a ponytail. Nice figure, warm eyes, good sense of humor."

"If I ask – the tall girl, short blond hair pulled back into a ponytail, nice figure, warm eyes, and a good sense of humor – you think they'll know who I was talking about?"

"Screw you, Mike."

The Tybee Island Police Station occupied a new building on Van Horne. The group had watched it being built over the last few years. It looked clean, modern and up to date. To get there, Ray and FJ elected to walk past the large townhouse complex on Van Horne.

"Look there," Ray said pointing.

"Is that the same guy?"

"Looks like him."

The guy they were talking about was a man who fed the cats every morning at the complex. They saw him last year when they stayed in a condo across the street from the townhouses. They watched him every morning, stopping his bike on Van Horne beside a trash dumpster belonging to the townhouse and emptying a shopping bag full of cat food. Three or four cats would come out later to eat.

"Excuse me," Ray said. The man turned around. He looked to be in his early fifties, short, bald, oriental and wearing a Hawaiian Shirt decorated with bright Parrots, Bermuda shorts, sandals and glasses with thick lens. *Must be a Dead Head,* Ray thought.

"Yes. What can I do for you?" he asked, staring at FJ.

"We saw you here last year. Do you always feed the cats?" Ray asked.

"I try."

"Everyday?"

"Not every day," he replied, not taking his eyes off FJ.

Take a picture. It will last longer. FJ thought.

"Do these cats belong to the complex?" FJ asked, giving the man a reason to stare at him.

"Oh no. These are feral cats. Tame cats that have gone wild."

"I know what feral means," FJ came back. "Seems like a lot of work."

"We at the IFCP -"

"IFCP?"

"IFCP, Islands Feral Cat Project. We believe that all animals deserve to live, even feral cats. They can't help their predicament. Some were born in the wild. Some were put out by their owners simply because they don't want them anymore. Still, others wander into our area because their owners have moved and couldn't find them during the move. Regardless, they no longer have human contact or compassion. If they make their way to our stations, they find food, clean water, and a kind word."

"We do spay and neuter these cats to eliminate the repopulation of unwanted cats, and it has helped the colonies to dwindle. Each cat 'fixed' gets an ear notch. That way, we can keep track of which ones have been fixed and which ones need to be fixed."

"Can feral cats or colonies be relocated?" Ray asked.

"No. Cats are creatures of habit, like most animals. Where a cat lives is its home; whether it's behind a building, dumpster, wooded area, or someone's back yard. Cats have sometimes traveled hundreds of miles to get back to where they were moved from."

"Every year at *Fannies on the Beach*, we have a Pajama Pub Crawl. Everyone comes wearing their bedtime clothes. *Fannies* offers drink specials, and there are games, prizes, raffles and a bunch of other stuff. All proceeds go to IFCP."

"That's humane," Ray said.

"Yeah. humane," FJ added.

Chapter 6

Ray held the door open for FJ as they entered the police station, and both were instantly hit with a blast of arctic air.

"God, this is wonderful," FJ whispered.

"We may hang out here for a couple of hours," Ray added.

They stood there letting their bodies cool down, staring at the ceiling with their eyes closed.

"Excuse me," a warm, female voice said. "Can I help you?"

"In a minute," Ray answered.

"A minute, hell. Come back in fifteen," FJ corrected.

"Gentlemen. Is there something the Tybee Island Police Department can help you with?"

"Oh, I'm sorry," Ray said, opening his eyes. "It's just that your AC is awesome."

The officer stood there staring.

"Yes," Ray continued. "We'd like to see Chief Rogers, please."

"The Chief is busy right now. Is there someone else that might be able to help?"

"Okay. How about Deputy Brown?"

"The Deputy is busy right now. Anyone else?"

"They're the only two we know," FJ said, staring up at the attractive officer. She stood five foot five, short curly hair, large brown eyes, African American, her skin a silky mocha, shaped like an hourglass, nice boobs. All the things FJ lusted for in a woman. "Maybe you could help us," FJ continued.

"In what way could I help you, sir?"

FJ rolled his eyes. He had an answer but couldn't say it. Not here, anyway.

41

"We're here about the Sara Sinclair murder," Ray said, interrupting the staring contest between FJ and the female officer.

"Yes, Sir. Do you have some information for us?"

"No, I'm sorry we don't. We were hoping you had some information for us."

"I'm not authorized to give out any details about the case."

"Then who can?" Ray asked, getting a little pissed.

"That would be me," a familiar voice said behind Ray.

"Deputy Brown. I heard you were busy," Ray said, looking at the female officer.

"I was, but now I'm free. What can I do for you?"

"I, we, were wondering if anything new had turned up on Sara?"

"Very little I'm afraid. The ME's report says —"

"What the hell is going on here?" another familiar voice barked.

"Chief Rogers," Ray said, offering his hand, which the chief didn't take. "Deputy Brown was bringing us up to date on the Sara Sinclair murder."

"The hell he is," exclaimed Chief Rogers, his eyes burning holes in Deputy Brown. "Sheriff, as of this minute, you will have nothing to do with this case. You will not visit us. You will not call us. You will not stop us on the street. You will not question me. You will not question Deputy Brown. You will not question any member of the Tybee Island Police Department. Hell! You won't even ask the dog catcher anything about this case. You are dismissed and free to leave. Do you understand Sheriff?"

"Clearly," Ray replied, starting to heat up.

FJ had seen that look on Ray's face before. "Ray, I think we need to be going. Ray! I'm sure the Chief is a busy man, and we don't want to take up any more of his valuable time. Thanks, Chief, Deputy and you my dear officer . . . "

"Grace. My name's Grace McClure," she replied, taking FJ's hand.

Outside, the heat didn't help Ray's mood.

"Asshole," Ray spit. "I wonder what got his panties in a wad."

"I think she liked me," FJ said, ignoring Ray.

"Who does he think he is? Talking to me like that."

"She told me her name. Grace. What a beautiful name."

"I ought to go back in there and tell him to bite my ass."

"She took my hand. Her hand felt soft."

"He dismissed me. Can you believe that? He dismissed me."

"Her eyes were hypnotic."

"I'm free to leave, he said. I'll leave his ass."

"She gave me this when we shook hands."

"What are you talking about?" Ray asked, coming back to the moment.

"She gave me her card. It has her cell phone number on it."

"Jesus, FJ. Only you would hit on a police officer in a police station."

***

"Son-of-a-bitch," Frank exclaimed. "You guys need to come and look at this."

"What is it?" Bubba asked, hurrying into the living room.

"Look on the monitor," Frank replied, getting out of the computer chair. Bubba sat down, with Pete looking over his shoulder.

"You looking at porn again?" Bubba laughed.

"Not this time Bubba. Look."

The webpage was of a news outlet with a picture of a man, in scuba gear, swimming next to what looked like a bomb. There was also a picture of a young man and woman, both smiling. The headline read – TYBEE ISLAND BOMB FOUND.

"Holy shit," Pete shouted. "All this and the bomb's been found already. You know what that means? The girl died for nothing. She should be alive today. Christ, what are we going to do now? There's no earthly reason to stay here any longer. We should leave and pray to God they don't figure out we had something to do with her death. We'll go about business like nothing's happened. We'll get back in class. We don't have long to graduate. Unless you left your DNA, they wouldn't know it was us."

"Shut the hell up and let me read," Bubba cursed. "This morning a Canadian couple, while on their honeymoon on Tybee Island, was scuba diving in Wassaw Sound and discovered the bomb the government lost back in 1958. The area is now off limits, and this afternoon, the federal government will be sending experts to the scene to determine better how to remove the bomb."

"Well that settles it," Frank whispered, flopping down on the couch. "Can we go home now?"

"Shit. Shit. Shit," Bubba yelled, rolling his eyes toward the ceiling.

"Yeah Frank's right," Pete added. "Now can we go home and try to forget this whole shitty mess?"

"Wait a minute," Bubba demanded. "Wait a damn minute. Let me think."

Bringing up *Google*, Bubba typed in "Snopes." The first item in the list was the homepage of *Snopes*, a website dedicated to discerning rumors. In the *Snopes* search field, he typed – Tybee Island Bomb found. After a minute, the same article appeared on the screen like the one they had just read. At the bottom of the page, in a big bold red font, was the word – HOAX.

"It hasn't been found," Bubba exclaimed. "Hot damn. Boys, we're still in business . . . Look. I think we need to take a break. We've been cooped up here too long. Tonight, we'll run down to *Fannies on the Beach* and celebrate. It'll help us clear our minds. Tomorrow we load our gear on our boat, and our hunt begins."

"We have a boat?" Frank asked. "Cool."

Chapter 7

All night, music from Taylor Swift, Lady Gaga, Mark Ronson & Bruno Mars, Katy Perry, and a dozen other popular artists filled *Fannies on the Beach.* Currently, Lorde's song, *Royals* oozed through the bar, spilling out onto the sidewalk, making its way across the street and ending up on the beach. College-age women, wearing miniskirts and spiked-heels or string bikinis with shear wraps draped around their hips, swayed with their arms raised above their heads, snapping their fingers to the sexy beat. Half priced-drinks, margaritas and draft beer fueled the testosterone enhanced studs standing at the bar, each eyeing the flirting goddesses, trying to determine which one would be his reward for the night or even for a few hours. Like speed dating, the wannabe models made their way up and down the bar, searching for the right man who would spend his money on them and tell them how much prettier she was compared to the others.

For the last half hour, one of the mini-skirt divas had been talking with Pete, eyeing him up and down. He'd been feeding her drinks and snacks, making her happy, making her feel important and desirable. For the last five minutes, she'd been rubbing her erect nipples against his arm, telling him how handsome he looked.

"I have a car parked in the beach parking lot, across the street," the redhead whispered in his ear, trying to be heard above the music. "You want to go?"

"Go where?" he answered back, in her ear.

"To the backseat of my car," she replied, licking her red lips with her tongue.

"Sure," Pete replied, his testosterone pounding his loins.

Placing his arm around her waist, he led her to the top of the stairs leading down to the main level. "Shit," he whispered, releasing her. "You need to excuse me a minute, Sweetie. I need to talk with my friend over there," he said pointing to Frank. "Wait for me here."

"Okay, but don't take too long. The buzz is starting to wear off."

"Oh, I'll be right back."

Frank was standing near the door leading out onto the upper deck, talking with a beautiful blond wearing a two piece. It looked like she was sipping on a coke.

"Excuse me," Pete said, interrupting. "I need to talk with my friend."

"Not now, Pete," Frank said, pulling away from Pete's hand.

"Now Frank," Pete demanded. "He'll be back in a second. I promise."

Together, Pete and Frank forced their way through the crowd, out onto the upper deck, overlooking the dark water. A string of multicolored lights was strung along the railing, casting an eerie glow on those standing there talking and drinking. The music was less noisy, and they could hear the surf crashing against the shore.

"What do you want, Pete," Frank asked, eyeing, smiling and waving back at the blond in the doorway.

"Who is she?" Pete asked.

"I don't know, just some girl I met."

"Frank, I think her name is Jill Bates."

"No, it's not. Her name is Susie."

"You don't get it, do you Frank? Jill Bates is another way of saying jailbait."

"Jailbait?"

"How old does she look to you?"

"She told me; she was eighteen."

"Eighteen, my ass. She's sixteen if that old. Frank, you have sex with her, and you'll end up in jail for rape."

"Jesus," Frank whispered to himself. "She looks older."

"They all do."

"Excuse me," Susie said stepping up. "Frankie, when are you

going to show me your guns?"

"Guns?" Pete exclaimed, almost pissing his pants.

"Frankie said you guys have guns."

Pete laughed, thinking quickly. "You must have misunderstood him. Probably the loud music and all. We do have guns, but over at Hunter Air Force Base. We're testing out a new military weapon for the Navy Seals. It's Top Secret, and Frankie could get his ass in a sling for even talking about it."

"I could?"

"Yes, you could."

"I didn't know," Susie said. "He didn't tell me. I don't want Frankie getting into any trouble. If it helps, I promise I won't tell anyone."

"Thank you. That does help," Pete said, smiling. "It's getting late Frankie, and I think we need to call it a night. We're supposed to be out on the firing range first thing in the morning. Maybe Frankie will see you tomorrow night."

"I don't want to go," Frank said, stepping away.

"That's an order, Private Frankie," Pete said, sternly.

"Okay. Damnit."

The redhead wasn't at the top of the stairs, and Pete couldn't see her anywhere. "Oh well," he sighed. "The buzz must have worn off. Maybe another time."

"Are we coming back tomorrow night?" Frankie asked. Pete rolled his eyes.

They found Bubba smoking on the sidewalk outside *Fannies on the Beach*. This late in the evening, *Fannies* allowed smokers to take their drinks out on the sidewalk.

"I remember watching that rerun with my dad on the *Western Channel*," a beautiful mocha skinned woman was telling Bubba. "I don't remember the name of the show, but it was about a dad raising his two or three older boys on a ranch. If I remember right, their mother was dead, and they had a Chinaman housekeeper and cook. And I tell you Bubba; you look just like one of the brothers."

Bubba smiled, nodded his head. "It was called -"

"We need to be leaving," Pete interrupted.

"I'm busy here," Bubba snapped back.

"We need to be leaving, Bubba," Pete said, leading Frank away by the arm.

"What did he do this time?" Bubba asked joining them.

"I'll tell you on the way back to the condo."

***

"Gosh Damnit," Ray said, slamming his cards onto the tabletop. "I love getting my ass kicked by the girls. Don't you, Mike."

"Ray, it's just a game, a simple card game."

"How much did they beat us by this time?"

"5,000 points and they didn't beat us. We said uncle."

"That's the same thing. They've beaten us three times in a row tonight."

Charlotte, Stephanie, and Margaret smiled at each other.

"If you remember," Mike went on, watching the women smirk, "Us guys beat them four times yesterday."

"Yeah, and you didn't hear us whining," Stephanie added.

"Ray, would you like some cheese to go with that whine?" Margaret laughed. Ray shot her a look.

"What's bothering you, Ray?" FJ asked. "We've been beaten worse by the women, and I haven't seen you act like this."

"You're thinking about Sara, aren't you?" Stephanie asked.

Ray nodded his head.

"I know. We all have."

"While the cards are being shuffled, how about I fix us another blender of Brandy Alexanders?" Charlotte commented, rising from the table.

"Ray, would that make you happier?" Margaret asked.

"It couldn't hurt," Ray replied, smiling.

Chapter 8

The western shoreline of Tybee Island lacks the beautiful sandy beaches like the eastern coastline. Instead, the western shoreline is a sea of waist high weeds and grasses stretching as far as the eye can see. This massive expanse of green is broken by a maze of twisty turny waterways with names like Lazaretto Creek, Tybee Creek, Chimney Creek, Oyster Creek, Half Moon Creek, Bull River, and Wilmington River, just to name a few. Numerous ditches worm their way through the marsh, making navigation a nightmare for all but the seasoned local fisherman. To make matters worse, at low tide which occurs twice a day, 2 a.m. and 1 p.m., most of the smaller ditches and creeks are nothing more than mud holes.

"Where're we going Bubba?" Frank asked, squeezed in between Pete and Bubba in the cab of the Nissan.

"I told you yesterday, we're getting a boat," he replied. "Just off Highway 80, on Old Highway 80, is *Tybee Island Bait and Tackle*. It's on Lazaretto Creek, which is a straight shot to the Savannah River and the ocean beyond. A lot of fishermen get their deep-sea supplies there, but they also rent boats, skidoos, canoes, and kayaks."

The Nissan came to a sudden stop beside the *Bait and Tackle*, scattering gravel and raising a small cloud of dust. Climbing out the cab, Frank strolled over to the Lazaretto Creek Marina boardwalk running along the creek. It turns out, the *Bait and Tackle* wasn't the only establishment on this stretch of the creek. Beside the *Bait and Tackle* was *Captain Mike's Dolphin Tours*. A weathered sign painted on the front of the building stated Capt. Mike's has been offering the best in dolphin tours, sunset cruises, and deep sea fishing for the last twenty-five years. *CoCo's Sunset Grille*, next to Capt. Mike's, offered burgers, fresh shrimp, and free Wi-Fi. And beside the Grille sat the *North Island Surf and Kayak Shop*.

Frank turned his attention to the small marina. *Not much of a marina,* he thought. Moored to the concrete boardwalk was a small assortment of fishing crafts, skidoos, kayaks, canoes and three large shrimp boats, each with double trawling nets.

"Which one's ours?" he asked as Bubba and Frank walked up.

"I don't know," Bubba replied. "You guys stay here while I go and take care of the paperwork."

When Bubba disappeared inside the building, Frank leaned over to Pete.

"What's your gut telling you about this whole deal?"

"It's telling me we've made a big mistake coming down here with Bubba."

"Do you always trust your gut?"

"Most of the time."

"My gut's telling me the same thing. So, what are we going to do about it? Run for the hills?"

"Nothing."

"Nothing? What do you mean, nothing?"

"Bubba was right when he said we're in it as deep as he. If one of us gets caught, we'll all hang."

"Do they still hang people nowadays?"

"I don't know, dumbass. I'm just saying, when we stand before a judge, we'll get the same sentencing."

"But we had nothing to do with killing the girl."

"Shut your frickin mouth," Pete said, looking around, making sure no one was near. "It doesn't matter to the law if we killed her or not. If we get caught, we're all screwed."

"Then we can't get caught."

"We need to find this damn bomb, get our money and get the hell out of Dodge."

A flock of a hundred or more seagulls flew in from the river and landed on the concrete boardwalk on the opposite bank. A woman and man, parked near the boardwalk, silently got out of their car and slowly made their way toward the birds. The man held his cell phone ready to take a photo. Suddenly, the woman began running toward the birds and through the birds, waving her arms. The birds exploded in a mass, rising into the air, flying around and over the woman.

"Got it," the man said, showing the woman the photo on his phone.

"That is awesome," she said. "I want a copy so I can hang it in my office at work."

For a few minutes, Pete and Frank stood there watching the birds circling overhead; each man lost in his thoughts.

"You think you could kill someone?" Frank suddenly asked.

"Hell, I don't know. Maybe, if my life was in danger or I was about to get caught. Frank, I'm not going to prison, no matter what. I'm not going to end up being somebody's shower bitch. As far as killing someone, I hope I never have to find out."

"Me too."

***

As they made their way into AJ's restaurant, FJ asked, "What's that supposed to be?"

Before him laid a long slender tube with a pointy nose and fins attached to one end. "Looks like a big-ass dart."

"Looks like a torpedo to me," Ray replied.

"I think it's some kind of rocket," Mike chimed in.

"That's a hydrogen bomb," an old man stated, standing beside the entrance to the restaurant. "Or at least, what a hydrogen bomb should look like."

"Really?" Stephanie asked.

"This your first time here?" the old man asked.

"Nope. We eat here every year we come down, and I don't ever remember seeing that here," Mike commented.

"It's been here since the restaurant opened back in 2003. You've walked by it every time you've come here."

"Really? I've never noticed."

"You ever heard the story about the bomb?"

"Nope."

"Most people haven't, even the locals. Those who have, think it's a fairy tale made up to draw in tourist. The truth is – the government did lose a hydrogen bomb somewhere around here, back in 1958, and nobody's found it."

"You're saying there's a hydrogen bomb still out there, somewhere? Ready to blow us to frickin Hell and back?" FJ asked.

"If you believe the story," the old man said with a laugh. "So, you say you've been here before. What's your favorite thing on the menu?"

"I always get the flounder," Mike answered.

"I like the fried oysters and conch," FJ said. "With lots of beer."

"You can't beat the shrimp and grits," Ray added.

"Grits suck," Mike piped in.

"Don't forget the beer," FJ added.

"With the big overhead fans going full tilt, I love eating on the dock overlooking the river and the marsh," Margaret said. "It's so beautiful when the sun sets."

"That's why they call it *AJ's Dockside Restaurant*," the old man laughed. "Have you noticed you don't get very many mosquito bites while you're eating on the outside deck?"

"I have."

"It's because of the fans. Mosquitos don't like moving air. Good to know . . . When you folks leave here today, be sure to stop by the gift shop and buy one of the 'Tybee Island Bomb Squad' t-shirts."

"I think I will," Mike replied, looking at Stephanie for her approval. "My name's Mike Roach by the way. What's yours?"

"I'm AJ," the old man said with a smile, holding the door open for them.

Chapter 9

"You think that's our boat?" Frank asked, looking at a shiny red and black fishing boat.

"That would be sweet," Pete replied. "My uncle has one. It's a Seafarer, model 226. That one's brand new. It's got an enclosed Cuddy Cabin which helps keep the rain off and a single badass outboard diesel engine. She can haul-ass through the water. You talk about a chick magnet. There's no telling how much that baby rents for. It's probably not ours."

"I'll keep my fingers crossed."

Bubba showed up with papers in hand, along with three rod and reels and a bucket of bait.

"Is that our boat?" Frank asked, pointing at the new Seafarer.

"Hell no," Bubba exclaimed. "You think I can afford that? No, ours is on the other side of the shrimp boats. Its number is XL906."

Walking to the end of the boardwalk, Frank stopped; his jaw almost hitting the ground.

"You're kidding," he gasped. "That rusted piece of shit? No, wait, that's our boat alright. There's the number, plain as day, XL906."

Before them floated an ancient fifty-foot steel trawler, well, mostly steel. From the few patches of un-rusted metal, you could see the boat had been navel grey one time in its life. The front third of the boat was a small structure containing the crew quarters, head and galley. Stairs led from either side of the quarters up to a narrow deck circling the wheelhouse, with most of the windows of the wheelhouse cracked or missing. A single crane tower rose from the rear of the boat for loading and unloading cargo. The deck was covered in trash, bird poop, joints of rusty pipes, broken glass, cans of industrial grease used to lubricate the gears on the crane and some overturned empty barrels for fuel and oil. A thin film of oil coated the surface of the water where the inboard diesel engine hid.

"Is that thing seaworthy?" Frank asked.

"Sure, except in a big storm. I had to sign a release saying we wouldn't take her out on days threatening rain."

"It's a death trap," Pete whispered.

"So, what's up with the rod and reels?" Frank asked, trying to take his mind off the rust-bucket.

"We're on a fishing trip, right? That's what I told them when I called about the boat. So, how would it look, if we didn't have rod and reels?"

"Good point."

"Let's go aboard and check her out," Bubba exclaimed. "Maybe we can start her up and take her for a spin."

After a dozen cranks, she finally started, blowing a dark, smelly cloud from the exhaust.

"Well, it started, sort of," Pete laughed. "You know how to drive this thing?"

"Sure," Bubba commented. "Once we're out in open water, I'll show you guys the controls and the gauges to keep an eye on."

"What do you mean – gauges to keep an eye on?"

"There are a few gauges when in red means, she's going to blow."

Frank and Pete stared at each other.

"Pete you go to the bow and cast off the line. Frank take care of the stern."

Heading north along the creek, they passed under the Highway 80 Bridge and entered the Savannah River. Turning east, going downstream, they made their way to the ocean.

"We need to stay close to shore," Bubba cautioned. "If you get too far out a wave could swamp you."

"How far offshore can we go?" Pete asked.

"A couple of hundred yards would be the limit. Anymore

won't be safe."

As they passed the turtle gazebo, Pete noticed Bubba staring at the shore. It must have been somewhere around here, where it happened, he thought. The spot where the girl was murdered. The spot where their lives were turned upside down.

"What happens if we meet one of those massive cargo ships?" Pete asked, trying to get the girl out of his mind.

"As far as I'm concerned, they get the right-of-way."

For the rest of the afternoon, Bubba showed Frank and Pete how to control the trawler, even letting them take turns at the wheel. For an hour, they tried out the reels. They were supposed to be fishing; they might as well fish.

***

Established in 1982, MacElwee's Seafood House is one of the oldest restaurants on the island. That evening the place was packed, forcing the six to wait on the deck, in the heat and humidity.

"I'm getting beer battered shrimp and a cold beer," Ray said, his mouth watering, his forehead sweating.

"Charlotte and I are going to split two dozen steamed oysters," FJ stated. "And a lot of beer."

"And a lot of beer," Charlotte confirmed, shaking her head no.

"Me, I'm getting a burger with fries," Mike said, watching the traffic on Highway 80 as it made the ninety-degree bend at the ocean.

"You're kidding, right?" Ray asked. "You come all the way to the ocean, and you're not eating fresh seafood?"

"I've had enough fresh seafood for a few days. I want a cow with American Cheese, tomato, pickles, onions and ketchup, and lots of beer."

"Amen on the beer," FJ exclaimed.

"I hate to break up this riveting conversation, but isn't that Deputy Brown over there, parking his patrol car?" Stephanie asked, pointing.

"Yeah, it is," Ray replied. "Oh shit. He's seen us . . . Here he comes."

"Ray, play nice," Margaret whispered.

"I always play nice."

"Bullshit."

"Margaret said a bad word," FJ squealed. "Margaret said a bad word."

"Shut up Frederic," Margaret said, giving him the eye. "People are watching you."

"They're always watching me, Margaret. I'm a 'little person,' remember? But I'm used to it."

"Sheriff," Brown said, nodding his head as he walked up.

"Deputy," Ray replied, nodding his head, playing nice.

"You have a few minutes?"

"Sure, I guess." Deputy Brown noticed the others staring at him. "In private, please. Let's walk down to the corner."

The rest watched as they walked off.

"Damnit, I wanted to hear what he had to say," FJ commented.

"We all did," Mike came back.

"Well, if they call our name for a table, we're not waiting for Ray," FJ stated flatly. "Let him get his own damn table."

At the corner, a gentle breeze was flowing in from the ocean across the street, and it felt a lot cooler here.

"Sheriff, I want to apologize for the way the Chief acted the other day."

"You don't have to apologize for him."

"No I don't, but you don't understand the pressure he's going through."

"Like what?"

"The family of the deceased is demanding an end to all this. The town council wants the murderer caught, and to them, it's taking too long. This is the peak of our tourist season, and the merchants are worried this murder will drive away business. I haven't noticed any decrease in tourist. I think the council and merchants are full of it. Anyway, everyone's blaming the Chief. This is the first murder on Tybee in years, and the Chief is catching hell from the mayor and the newspaper. There's a growing number of people saying the Chief is incompetent and should resign."

"Hell, it's only been a couple of days," Ray stated. "This isn't *CSI Miami*. Those fancy tools they have on those shows aren't real. It takes a lot of leg work, interviews, paper shuffling and luck to come up with the right answers."

"Well, he's also catching hell because it was you who found the body, not him. Everyone knows he walked right past the crime scene. That's why he was blunt with you and told you to stay away from the case."

"Okay, the Chief isn't the asshole I made him out to be. Now, can you tell me something about the case?"

"The girl died from suffocation. Sand coated the inside of her mouth and lined her lungs. But the killer wanted to make sure. There were huge dark postmortem fingerprints around her neck. She also had several broken ribs."

"Was she . . ."

"No. Thank God. The rape kit came up negative."

"That's good at least. I bet her parents are relieved. So, what was the motive? Why kill a sixteen-year-old girl on vacation?"

"Your guess is as good as any. Maybe she saw or heard something."

"Something worth dying for?"

"I know. It doesn't make any sense."

"Maybe she saw someone unloading a boat load of drugs."

"We thought about that, but that shit doesn't happen around here. You need to go down to the Keys for that."

They stood there a few minutes in silence watching traffic whiz by. Finally, Ray realized the conversation was over.

"Well, thanks, Deputy. If you come up with anything new, please let me know."

"I'll try Sheriff, but it would have to be off the record."

Ray nodded. When He got back to the restaurant, the others had already gone in.

Chapter 10

"We need to run into Savannah this morning," Bubba said, waking Frank from a deep sleep on the sofa. "There's something we need to pick up."

"What's that?" Frank asked, rubbing the sleep out of his eyes.

"A submersible Geiger counter and a remote metal detector."

"You know how to use those things?"

"Sort of. You let the Geiger counter run along the bottom, and if it senses anything radioactive, it lets out a ping. The metal detector hangs off the side of the boat. It's like a big-ass fish finder, with a screen and everything, but it looks for metal."

"Bubba, where're you coming up with all this money?" Pete asked from the kitchen. "You rented this condo, brought expensive weapons, rented a boat, and now, a Geiger counter. Like Frank and me, you don't have a pot to piss in, and I bet those things don't come cheap. So how are you paying?"

"Who said I was paying?"

"Bubba, what did you do?"

"You're right. We don't have the funds to carry this off. So, I called a friend."

"A friend? Good God, how many people know?"

"Hold on. Both of you know Wally Wilkins."

"The guy who used to put on those dog fighting matches in Atlanta?"

"That's him. He -"

"I thought he got busted." Frank interrupted.

"Damnit. Shut up, Frank. Wally did get busted, that's the whole point. While he was in the pen, he met some interesting people. People who know people. I told him enough to get him interested, and now he's our backer and wants ten percent of whatever we get."

"And what happens if we don't find anything?"

"You better pray to God we do."

"Shit, Bubba, we've got the cops looking for us, and now Wally Wilkins wants our balls if we can't deliver."

"He'll do more than take our balls if we don't come through."

***

The line stretched all the way to the corner from *Mrs. Wilkes Dining Room* at 107 West Jones Street. The restaurant, located in the historic district of Savannah, sat square in the middle of a block of priceless buildings and homes with spiral staircases rising to the front doors located on the second level. Trees, covered in Spanish moss, formed a dense canopy over the cobblestone inlaid streets and sidewalks.

With his eyes closed, FJ imagined people in fancy clothes, the men in top hats and the women wearing hooped dresses, surrounded by their servants, coming and going to fancy parties and teas. If he had been around during those times, he would have probably been an entertainer because of his size and talents. He could hear the clip-clop of horse-drawn carriages of times past, carrying people home from a long day at the office down by the river, or from a grand tea party at one of the many gardens located around the city. Suddenly, he opened his eyes.

He really could hear clip-clops. Looking up and down the street, he noticed an antique horse-drawn carriage carrying four tourists on a guided tour of historical Savannah. The horse looked hot, tired and old. Right behind and up under its tail was a square box to catch droppings.

The doors to Mrs. Wilkes opened at 11 o'clock, and the "Tybee Island Six" thought getting there by 9:30 would give them time enough to get in, in the first group; they were wrong. But there was good news. Mike had done a head count, and they would definitely get in, in the next group. Mrs. Wilkes' dining rooms were located in the lower level of the boarding house and consisted of over a dozen large tables that could sit ten people each; tables that would be shared by friends and strangers alike. When a table emptied, the staff would hurriedly remove the dirty bowls, clean the table, set clean plates and silverware and reload fresh bowls and platters with steaming foods.

A man at the front door would then ask for the next group. If the group were less than ten people, the door man would ask for a party with the correct number to complete the ten. They would then be led to their table already crowded with platters of fried chicken, meatloaf, pot roast, cornbread dressing, mashed taters, sweet potato soufflé, black-eyed peas, green beans, sweet creamed corn, mac and cheese, stewed tomatoes, okra gumbo, corn muffins, and biscuits, and the list goes on and on.

Bowls were passed, family style, around the table and when a bowl emptied, it was promptly refilled. As far as drinks, sweet tea was in order, and a full glass would be waiting for you at your place at the table. If you want water, coffee or unsweet tea, you have to ask for it. When you finished your meal, you were asked to take your plate to the kitchen, something the house had been doing since the 1800s when it was a true boarding house. Also, what most people didn't know, Mrs. Wilkes takes only cash or checks. No credit cards.

"I told you we should have left earlier," FJ complained.

"Oh, shut up," Stephanie whispered. "You did no such thing. You know we always have to wait at Mrs. Wilkes. So, quit your bellyaching. Go get a drink of water from the cooler at the front door."

Making his way through the forest of people lining the sidewalk, FJ finally made it to the front of the restaurant and found the orange Igloo cooler with its stack of cone shaped paper cups. The water was cold and refreshing, which helped FJ's mood.

"Excuse me, Mr. Dinklage," a soft female voice whispered. "Could we trouble you for an autograph?"

Turning, FJ was rewarded with two beautiful college-age

women. The blond who was talking had to bend over to be heard, giving FJ a full view of her cleavage. He could see she wasn't wearing a bra.

"My pleasure ladies," he replied taking her pad and pen. In bold script, he wrote – Peter Dinklage.

"Oh my," the other girl exclaimed, bouncing up and down with excitement. FJ couldn't help it, but his eyes hypnotically bounced up and down with her boobs.

"Are you here working on a movie?" she asked.

"I'm sure you'll understand when I tell you, I really can't talk about it."

"Oh, we understand all right. How about a photo of the three of us?" she asked, showing FJ her cell phone.

"Photo? Oh, I'm sorry, I don't do photos. My agent, the bastard, would say I'd have to charge you for a picture."

"We'll pay for it."

Thoughts of how they could pay flooded FJ's mind. He envisioned the three of them, a jar of whip cream, and a waterbed; the thought made him lightheaded.

"No my dear. I'm sorry, but the price would be outrageous. You will have to excuse me now, but I see my entourage is going inside. I hope you have a wonderful day."

"You too," the blond replied, touching his shoulder.

As FJ entered the dining room, he heard the blond telling her friend, "Oh my God, I touched him. Can you believe it? I touched him." FJ smiled. He loved making people happy, especially young women.

Once inside, Stephanie bent over so only FJ would hear. "You did it again. Didn't you?"

"I can't help it," he smiled back. "It made their day. They'll get on Facebook and tell all their friends how they met Peter Dinklage. What's the harm in that?"

"If the real Peter Dinklage ever heard of what you're doing, he'd kick your ass . . . By the way, you do know Facebook's outdated. Everyone's on Twitter and Instagram."

"Whatever."

The meal was well worth the wait. Bowl after steaming bowl was passed around. The fried chicken disappeared first, followed by the mashed potatoes, but these were promptly refilled several times. After an appropriate period, when everyone's eyes were about to pop out of their heads from being so full, waiters brought around a platter with tiny bowls of banana pudding or peach cobbler. Every person got their choice of one of the delicious treats. An hour later, stepping back out into the heat, the six had to excuse themselves through the crowd.

"Did you save anything for us?" someone asked, causing those around him to start laughing.

"Barely," Ray replied, joining in the laughter.

"Is it as good as advertised?" asked another.

"No. It was better."

Climbing back in the van, Charlotte moaned.

"You okay?" Ray asked, taking his seat beside her.

"I'm stuffed," she replied.

"We all are," Margaret laughed.

"When we get back to the condo," Charlotte continued, as she fastened her seatbelt, "I think I'll take a stroll on the beach to walk off some of this food."

"Don't take too long. As soon as you get back from your stroll, we'll make some Brandy Alexanders and start a game," Stephanie said, digging in her purse for a mint.

"I'll be back before you get the cards shuffled."

Chapter 11

Ray stood, leaning on the rail of the upper story balcony, watching Charlotte walking across the turtle-bridge on her walk. He noticed Charlotte stopped at the spot she had talked with Sara. From his vantage point, he had the prefect 180-degree view of both the river and the ocean. On the other side of the river, which at this point was over two miles wide, was Hilton Head, South Carolina, with its famous golf course. Off in the distance, he could see the walk-bridge where Sara's body was found.

"What are you doing?" FJ asked, handing Ray one of the two beers he was carrying.

"Watching Charlotte and thinking," Ray replied. "I think we got it all wrong."

"What's that?"

"Everyone thinks Sara Sinclair saw or heard something over there on the beach, where she was killed. But that's not the way it happened."

"Why do you say that? You a mystic or something?"

"The footprints. They're right there under our noses, in plain sight. Why should we ignore them? The footprints start at the turtle-bridge gazebo, run along the dune, then to the beach and then back to the dunes. She was trying to outrun someone. Someone who, somehow, tripped her and killed her."

"That makes sense, but the Chief firmly believes the footprints belong to someone who was playing with their kid, playing tag or some such nonsense."

"He's an idiot, and he's wrong."

"Okay, we know he's an idiot and let's say he's wrong. Where does that leave us?"

"Asking questions."

"What questions?"

"What or who did she see? Where was she when she saw him? Let's tackle the 'where' first."

"Okay. Let me start . . . She was standing on the gazebo at the end of the bridge. About where Charlotte is," FJ said, pointing. Ray took it from there.

"If she was standing on the gazebo in the shade, was the killer there as well? Don't think so. He could easily kill her there, and there would be no footprints in the sand . . . If she had been standing under the gazebo and the killer was on the dunes, she would have run this way, not toward him . . . If she was under the gazebo and the killer was on this side of the pond, from the length of the bridge, she could easily outrun him along the dunes. So, that rules out the gazebo."

"What's next," FJ inquired.

"She's on this side of the pond, not on the turtle-bridge . . . If she was on this side and the killer was standing on the dunes, she would run to one of the condos for help . . . If the killer were on this side as well, he would have killed her here, again leaving no footprints . . . If the killer was on the bridge, again, she could run to one of the condos."

"That leaves, she was on the bridge."

"Yes . . . If she was standing on the bridge and the killer was standing on the dunes, she would run this way to her condo . . . If both of them were on the bridge, he would kill her there, and there wouldn't have been a chase . . . That leaves only one scenario, and I think the likely one. She was standing somewhere on the bridge when she saw something or heard something on this side of the pond. She knows she has no chance to get to her condo or any condo, so she turns toward the beach. The killer sees her and realizes she has seen something she shouldn't have. So, he takes off after her. She has a small head start, but the sand slows her down. He trips her. He kills her."

"That's so creepy," FJ exclaimed. Ray nodded his head.

"So, now the question of 'who,'" Ray said, draining his beer.

"You think you have the answer to the 65-million-dollar question?" FJ asked, draining his beer.

"Could be. Let's think it through. Sara was standing on the bridge, and her killer was on this side of the pond; that leaves very few possibilities."

"Really?"

"Facing the river, as we are right now, let's take each condo in turn."

"Okay. What about the condo to our right?"

"No good. There's a family from Virginia staying there, father, mother, two small kids. They don't fit the bill of being cold blooded killers."

"How do you know that?"

"I saw them yesterday. The parents had a little red wagon full of beach toys and a beach umbrella and were heading toward the walk-bridge to the beach by the townhouses. Which, by the way, is the closest way for them to get to the beach. The father was pulling the wagon and carrying one child, while the mother carried the other. Each had funny looking hats on to protect them from the sun."

"How do you know they were from Virginia?"

"I looked at their license plate."

"Okay, not the family from Virginia. How about the blue condo?"

"Our condo?" Ray laughed. "I think I can pass over us. There's no one here that would be a threat to Sara unless you've been exposing yourself again."

"That's not funny Ray. I may be a little kinky, but I'm not a damn pervert, especially with a minor."

"I know," Ray smiled. "I'm sorry. I think we can move on to the next condo."

"Well, the lot to our left is vacant, so that leaves the condo on the corner, with the three men."

"Back up. It could also be someone parked in front of the empty lot. But I doubt it. It was late, almost dark. Most people are back in their condos suffering from the sunburns they got that day. Or, they're out eating . . . So, the only possibility is the condo on the corner. If Sara was standing on the bridge, I doubt if she could have heard anything coming from the corner condo. Too far away. So she must have seen something; something that scared her. Something that made her run. Something that made one of the men chase her and kill her."

"Well, don't stand there . . . Do you want a drum roll? What did she see?"

"I have no frickin idea."

"Oh, God. What a letdown. If you don't have the answer to what she saw, how about who killed her?"

"I do have an idea on that."

"Well, what are you waiting for? Judgement day? Who killed her?"

"The large African-American guy."

"So now you're a racist?"

"Don't be stupid. Deputy Brown said the marks on her neck were made by huge hands. The only one over there that fits that description is that black man."

"So, Charlotte is right," FJ whispered.

"I think she is," Ray replied.

A pelican floated in the air currents over their heads, distracting them for a moment.

"Look at their condo," Ray continued. "Notice anything odd about it?"

"Other than their beat-up truck, no."

"More than that. Look closely. All their window blinds are down. And it's been like that every day since we've been here. Even if you don't get out, who travels all the way to the ocean and not want to look at it. Some of us don't walk on the beach like you or Charlotte, but we do like the view. We love seeing the palm trees, the dunes, the beach, the sparkling water, and the large ships. We love the gentle breezes. We love the salty smell of the ocean."

"So, you going to walk over there and knock on the door and ask to speak with that guy? 'Sir, you didn't by chance kill a girl last night, did you?'"

Ray stared at FJ.

"Just kidding . . . Are you going to Chief Rogers with your new theory?" FJ asked.

"No."

"And why not?"

"We have no proof, just speculation. You can't get a search warrant on speculation. You need something, something solid, if only a tidbit," Ray replied, looking at his beer bottle.

"Where are you going?" FJ asked.

"Back inside. My beer's gone, and I'm starting to sweat. Besides, Charlotte said we needed to have the cards shuffled by the time she got back."

"I'm right behind you."

Chapter 12

Charlotte crossed the dunes and found herself staring at the river. A few skidoos raced by, buzzing the shoreline. Kids played in the surf or made sandcastles while their parents kept a close eye on them. A family was flying a kite. A man was fishing. Two young people, probably honeymooners by the way they touched each other, were playing fetch with a Golden Retriever. One parent was taking a photo of a sand angel his kid just made. In a minute, he would post it on *Instagram*. A few white gulls circled overhead looking for discarded garbage. One brave bird wandered in and out between the sunbathers, looking for tasty tidbits. A massive cargo ship with an Italian name was making its way out to sea. Frightened by Charlotte, a land crab with his claws raised in defense, scurried back into his hole. *Just another day in Paradise.*

Charlotte thought about crossing the beach to the water's edge and walking in the cool surf. But she hadn't been on this section of beach since IT happened.

No, that's not the way I want to go.

Turning, she walked toward the ocean along the base of the dunes. She wanted to see where Sara had died. She needed to see where Sara had died. She needed closure. Ahead she noticed a few sticks with police tape strung on them.

That must be the place.

When she arrived at the circle of sticks, she noticed a note attached to the tape – Turtle Nest. Do Not Disturb.

These sticks weren't here the other day. Has to be new. How cute.

I wonder when they're going to hatch. I'd love to be here when that happens; watching hundreds of them, sand covered, climbing over each other trying to get to the safety of the water. Was Sara trying to get to safety that day?

Continuing, she came to the walk-bridge to the townhouses, almost missing the sand angel, or what was left of it. *I can see how the Chief missed it in the dark.*

Charlotte stood there a minute saying a silent prayer. This is where Sara's future was stolen; the place where her life and dreams were crushed. No more birthday cards and candlelit cakes. Her hands would never decorate another Christmas tree or wrap a present. Gone were selfies with friends; summer vacations with mom, dad, and little brother. Her dog would forget her. No more favorite foods, sunrises, sunsets, movies, music or clothing crazes. No more boyfriends. She'll never go to prom or have a wedding. There'll be no one to fall in love with. No Prince Charming. No happy ever after. No children. No grandchildren. She never had the opportunity to say goodbye; to say the final – I love you.

Only a cold and lonely casket awaited her. A casket covered with beautiful flowers that would wilt and die. A casket surrounded by family and friends tearfully saying goodbye. Her future now – an earth covered grave; a tombstone engraved – Loving Daughter, Now and forever. Tears flooded Charlotte's eyes and freely flowed down her cheeks. It wasn't right. How could a loving God let this happen? Why would an omnipresent God let this happen?

Charlotte thought about climbing the dune and seeing THE place, but it wasn't worth it. She didn't need to see the spot where Sara's body had been covered in sand. It was here she died. Charlotte had seen enough. Sara's smile on the bridge would haunt her forever.

I pray to God they catch the bastard while we're here. I want to live long enough to look into his eyes and give him a piece of my mind. I desperately want to vent my anger on the scumbag.

Charlotte wandered on; her mind lost in a fog. Suddenly she found herself at the man-sized boulders forming the breakers between the coastline and the river. She'd walked long enough and was getting tired and sweaty. It was time to head back. Time to take a shower and hope it would wash away some of the sadness.

***

"Damnit, Wally, I'm not goofing off," Bubba said, with his cell phone pressed to his ear. Bubba stood in the shade of the gazebo, watching the condos, making sure no one was in hearing distance or spying. "Yes, I know who's funding us, and we won't let you down. We're all business here . . . Damnit, we will find the bomb, and I expect you to find a buyer . . . We'll give you twenty percent. Hell. Twenty-five percent . . . You don't think I'm serious. I'll tell you how serious I am. I killed a girl who saw too much . . . That's right. I killed a girl . . . Hold on a second." Turning slowly to a faint sound, he saw one of the women from the blue condo stepping up on the gazebo deck. "I'll get back to you Wally. Something just came up."

"What did you hear?" Bubba demanded, startling Charlotte.

"Nothing, I heard nothing," she replied, trying to step around him.

"I think you did," he said, stepping in front of her, blocking her path.

"Please. I didn't hear anything."

"I don't believe a damn word you're saying."

"No. I didn't hear a thing. I don't know what you're talking about. Please let me pass."

Charlotte looked in the direction of the condos. There was an older couple walking down Captain's View about to turn onto Sea Breeze Lane. She opened her mouth to scream, but before she could, Bubba's right fist crashed into the side of her face. There was the sickening sound of bones crushing and snapping. Darkness became Charlotte's closest friend, and she went down like a slain ox and didn't move. Bubba looked toward the dunes and back to the condos. No one was out, only an old couple walking away from them. He prayed no one was looking out a window. Sweat broke out on his forehead. His heart was pounding. Looking down at the woman, it didn't look like she was breathing.

God Damnit, I did it again. I couldn't help it. I can't be blamed for this. It's all her fault. The bitch shouldn't have snuck up on me. She shouldn't have been eavesdropping. She would have ruined everything. Jesus, now what do I do with this body?

Chapter 13

Ray stood looking out the sliding door in the dining room. Besides their backyard, he had a clear view of the turtle-bridge and the dunes beyond.

"What's he doing?" Margaret asked coming down the stairs from her nap.

"He's waiting for Charlotte," Stephanie replied.

"How long has she been gone?"

"Almost three hours."

"That's not like her," Mike added, sitting at the dining table.

"Ray, what are you thinking," Margaret asked, walking up beside him.

"I don't know Margaret. I don't know . . . I know this, Charlotte's been gone too long, and I don't like it."

"Why don't you do something?"

"I've been thinking about doing just that. I think I'll take a walk on the beach and see if I run into her."

"I'll walk down Captain's View to the townhouses on Van Horne," FJ said, "and cross over their walk-bridge that goes to the ocean. I'll meet up with you somewhere on the beach."

"Sounds good," Ray said, sliding the door open.

Late afternoon and most of the beachgoers had already packed up and headed back to their condos to cool off, but the few diehards that remained were romping in the waves or hanging out on the beach smoking and drinking beer. Charlotte wasn't among them. Ray fought his way through the sand along the base of the dunes, stopping now and then to catch his breath; stopping now and then to check for any signs of violence. *Charlotte, where are you?*

Ray paused at the turtle nest and the river walk-bridge, the spot where Sara had been killed. Blowing wind and sand had about destroyed the sand angel. Still no Charlotte. It was then Ray heard someone calling his name from the breakers. Excited, he turned to the call. It was only FJ. Disappointed, Ray waved him over. No way was he walking across the soul sucking sand.

"Well?" Ray asked.

FJ, breathing hard, bent over at the waist with his hands on his knees and shook his head,

"Nothing."

"Okay. It's time to head over to the police station."

Ray's gut was killing him from nervousness. This wasn't good. Tybee Island was small, compact and as safe a place as you would want to visit, at least it was until now.

Back in the condo, everyone agreed. It was time to go to the police station.

"Mike, give me the keys to the van," Ray said, standing by the front door with his hand outstretched. "There's no need in everyone going."

"The hell you say. I'm not letting you drive my van. Ever. I rode with you once to Mount Saint Joseph, and ever since, I thank God every day we made it there alive. I'm driving."

"Mike, there's no reason we all need -"

"We're going too," Margaret stated firmly, as she and Stephanie joined them at the front door.

"Well, it looks like it's going to be a full house," Ray said, shaking his head. "How about you FJ? You coming?"

"You need to ask?" he replied, slipping past Ray out into the heat.

Passing the townhouse dumpster on Van Horne, four cats could be seen munching on IFCP provided food. A little farther down, a bucket truck was parked off the road, with a man raised high, trimming palm branches.

"I've wondered how they kept them looking so good," Mike said passing them with a wave.

"Can you imagine people asking you what you do for a living,"

FJ laughed. "Oh, I work for the City. I trim palm tree branches."

Mike pulled the van into one of the handicap parking spaces by the front door. Reaching in the glovebox, Ray removed Margaret's handicap sticker and hung it from the rearview mirror. In force, the five stormed the police station. As they made their way to the front desk, FJ noticed Grace sitting at her desk, and he made a detour.

"Why haven't you called," she whispered.

"I'm sorry, but we've been really busy. I promise before the week is out, I will call."

"You better . . . What brings all of you in?"

FJ told her what had gone on for the last couple of hours.

"That's horrible. Do you think she could have gone out with someone?"

"Charlotte? No. We don't know anyone down here. Besides, she would have told us if she had anything planned. No, something's happened to her."

"I haven't heard of anything around here. Have you tried the hospital? She could have been hit by a car if she was walking on Captain's View or Van Horne . . . Oh, you're being summoned."

FJ looked behind him and saw Ray waving for him to come over. "Okay. Thanks, Grace. I'll give you a call soon."

"Looking forward to it."

FJ crossed the lobby and noticed it was Deputy Brown the group was talking to.

"FJ, Deputy Brown wants to know what, if anything, you saw when you were searching for Charlotte."

"Nothing. The same old thing. People are hanging out on their balconies at the townhouses, drinking and smoking. People are swimming and sunbathing. Kids are playing tag. Dogs are pooping in the sand. The usual stuff."

"Why don't you all head back to your condo, and I'll call Chief Rogers," Brown suggested. "He's off shift, but I know he'll come back in for this."

"Thanks, Deputy," Margaret said, taking Deputy Brown by the arm.

"It's okay," the Deputy replied. "I'm sure everything's going to be fine."

"You should check the local hospitals," FJ threw in.

"That's a good idea FJ," Ray responded. "I should have thought of that."

"That's not a good idea, Ray. Not a good idea at all," Margaret exclaimed. "That means something has happened to her."

"Margaret, it has to be done."

"He's right Margaret. I'll call around after I've talked with the Chief," Deputy Brown promised, patting her hand still resting on his arm.

***

"What in the hell did you do now?" Pete yelled, looking at the unconscious woman lying on the couch. "Good God, look at the side of her face! What did you hit her with? A 2x4?"

The left side of the woman's face was split along her cheek bone, and the surrounding flesh was slowly swelling. Pete gently pressed the area around the split and found the skin tightening from the swelling, but mushy beneath. Probably broken bones. Nothing he could do about that, but at least, he could put a Band-Aid on the wound.

Your eye will be swelled closed by morning, Pete thought, as he stood.

"Good Lord, Bubba. Her cheek's shattered."

"I hit her with my fist, Pete. I swear. I hit her with my fist, that's all. It wasn't that hard."

"You could have killed her."

"I thought I did. She lay there on the deck of the gazebo, and I didn't think she was breathing."

"Why did you bring her here?" Pete asked.

"Bubba, Pete, two patrol cars just pulled up in front of the blue condo," Frank interrupted.

"That's good, Frank. Keep watching and let us know if anyone comes our way . . . Bubba, why did you bring her here?"

"What was I supposed to do with her? She overheard me telling Wally I killed the girl. You think I should have left her, so she could tell everybody when she woke up? I don't think so, dumbass . . . I know what I should have done."

"What's that?"

"I should have made sure I killed her and buried her like I did the girl."

"Is it that easy killing someone?" Pete asked, sarcastically.

"It's not as hard as I thought it would be," Bubba replied, staring at the woman.

"Oh my God," Pete exclaimed, walking around the living room in circles. "Oh, my Sweet Jesus. Why were you even talking out loud about killing someone? You didn't think someone could be listening?"

"I was looking, and I didn't see anyone. Besides, Wally didn't believe we meant business about finding the bomb, so I told him we did. You should have heard him change his words after I told him about the girl."

"So, what are we going to do with her?" Frank asked from the window.

"We sure as shit can't keep her here," Pete answered.

"So when did you become the boss-man?" Bubba asked.

"When our last one lost his frickin mind, that's when."

"Don't push me, Pete."

Ignoring Bubba, Pete walked into the kitchen and in a few minutes, came back with ice cubes rolled up in a dishcloth. Sitting beside the woman, he gentle pressed the cool rag against her cheek.

"It'll help with the swelling, but won't do a damn thing for the broken bones . . . Bubba are you sure no one saw you?"

"I didn't see anyone."

That doesn't mean you weren't seen, shithead.

Pete rolled his eyes. "How'd you get her here without being seen?"

Bubba's eyes lit up.

"The gazebo sits on the bank on the other side of the pond. Right? (Pete nodded.) If you walk in the grass, which leaves no footprints, toward the edge of the subdivision, you come to a thick undeveloped patch of woods and underbrush. (Pete nodded again.) The edge of the woods run right to the back of our condo. So, I gathered the woman up under my arm, and when the coast was clear, I ran like hell to the woods. It was easy from there. I just stayed in the woods out of sight and made it to the rear of the condo. Then I brought her in through the backdoor."

"So, what are we going to do with the woman?" Frank asked from the window.

"That is the question," Pete confessed.

"We're going to have to kill her," Bubba answered, flatly.

"We're not killing anyone today," Pete insisted.

"Then what are you going to do with me?" the woman asked.

Chapter 14

Ray opened the door and stepped out of the way for the Chief and Deputy to enter. The Chief paused in the entry and extended his hand.

"Sheriff Harris, I need to apologize for the way I acted the other day. I've been under a lot of pressure, and I kinda lost my cool."

"Apology accepted," Ray said, taking the Chief's hand. "We all lose our cool, sometimes. Come on in to the living room. Everyone's waiting."

The Chief nodded to everyone as he stepped into the room.

"I hear you have someone missing," he stated, sympathetically. "Deputy Brown says it's the lady who talked with Sara Sinclair the day she died."

"It was Charlotte, Charlotte Knott," Ray conferred.

"I made calls to all the local hospitals," Deputy Brown added. "No one from the island has been admitted today."

"That's good," Margaret sighed.

No, it's not Margaret. Ray thought. *If she had been admitted, we'd know where she was. We'd know if she was alive or dead.*

"So, what now?" Mike asked.

"Do any of you have a picture of Mrs. Knott? I'd like to pass it around the neighborhood, the local hangouts, and stores."

Everyone looked at each other and shook their heads.

"We don't normally carry a family photo of ourselves," FJ stated.

"You guys are family?" Chief Rogers asked.

"No," Mike answered. "That's Frederic's way of being funny.

Overlook him. We all do."

"We may have a picture," Stephanie said, "if it will work."

"What's that?"

"Her driver's license, if she brought it."

"That might help," Deputy Brown said. "If we enlarge it, it just might."

Stephanie hurried off to Charlotte's room and soon returned with her purse. Taking the purse to the dining room table, she started emptying its contents. It wasn't long before Stephanie handed Charlotte's license to the Chief.

"This will work," he said, handing the license to Deputy Brown. "Good idea."

"Thanks," Stephanie said, glad she could help.

"I'll take this to headquarters and have Grace enlarge it," Deputy Brown said, placing the license in his shirt pocket.

"I can take it to Grace if you want?" FJ said, holding out his hand.

"That's okay," Deputy Brown said. "We'll show it around. Maybe somebody saw her walking on the beach or on a street."

"So, what do we do in the meantime?" Mike asked.

"Not much I'm afraid. I'll have copies of the license made before this evening and tomorrow we'll start passing it around."

"Why not do it now?" Ray asked.

"Most of the officers will be going off duty by now."

"I can enlarge it," Brown suggested.

"And we can help showing it to people," Margaret added.

"Sure. I see no reason why you couldn't."

"It will give us something to do. Waiting is such a bitch," Stephanie said flatly.

The Chief shook his head. "I have a man already on the beach, one on the river and one on the ocean, searching. They'll work all night if they have too."

"Half of us could hand out copies of her driver's license, and the rest could help search," Stephanie added.

"That's up to you, but don't go hassling anybody," the Chief warned. "I'd hate to have to lock you up for disturbing the peace."

All sat there in silence.

"Tell the Chief what you and I talked about earlier," FJ said, looking at Ray.

"What's that?" Chief Rogers asked.

"It has nothing to do with Charlotte, but about Sara Sinclair."

"You think they're both related?"

"I don't know what to think."

"Then tell me about it. God knows I need help on that case as well."

Ray spent the next few minutes relating to the Chief what he and FJ discussed while on the upper deck, and how it strengthened Charlotte's idea the large black man must be involved. Chief Rogers listened intently, nodding his head now and then.

"You made some good observations Sheriff," Rogers admitted. "But, you know as well as I, we can't get a warrant on observations. We need hard evidence."

"I know. That's what I told FJ."

"There's nothing to keep us from paying them a visit and asking if they've seen Charlotte," the Chief added. "But I won't bring up Sara." Everyone stood. "No. No. No. Not everyone can go," Rogers laughed. "Just me, Deputy Brown and the Sheriff, if he wears his badge."

***

Charlotte tried to sit up, but her head started spinning. She touched the side of her face. It felt swollen, and her left eye was blurry.

"My head is splitting open," she complained, lying back down.

"I can imagine," Pete said softy. "Your left eye will be swollen shut by morning, I'm afraid. Bubba, get five aspirins out of the bathroom for . . ."

"Charlotte Knott," Charlotte replied, with her hand covering her eyes blocking the overhead light.

"For Charlotte Knott," Peter continued, friendly.

"Let Frank get it for her," Bubba spat.

"Frank's busy keeping a lookout."

"Alright," Bubba spat, giving Pete the "who made you the boss" look.

"There's a box of Band-Aids there as well. Bring a couple."

When Bubba disappeared down the hall, Pete whispered, "Charlotte, tell me now before he gets back, what you heard."

"Nothing," she lied.

"It's okay Charlotte. I have to know. It'll help me determine what we're going to do with you."

"I know what your friend wants to do. He wants to kill me. What do you want to do?"

Pete stared at the hallway where Bubba disappeared.

"You're not going to die if I can help it."

"Then why do you want to know? What difference does it make? Why don't you just let me go?"

"I can't do that. Not right now. The only thing the cops can charge us with is kidnapping. That is unless you think you heard something."

"Damnit. I didn't hear a thing. What is it you think I heard?"

"Okay, we'll play it your way, for now."

"Here's your frickin aspirins and the Band-Aids," Bubba said, walking back into the room. "She say anything?"

"Nothing. She said she didn't hear you say anything," Pete answered, applying the Band-Aids.

"And you believe her?"

"Not for a damn minute."

Charlotte lay there burning holes through Bubba with her eye, wishing her eye was a laser, a real laser burning real holes. Her laser eye lingered in the area of his crotch, praying he would suddenly bend over grabbing himself in pain. Her prayer wasn't answered, and why not God? Here was the man that murdered Sara. Here was the monster that killed an innocent sixteen-year-old child. Here was the beast that stubbed out her life. Even if her eye wasn't a laser, she still would like to hold his head in the sand, slowly sucking the life out of him.

"Somebody's coming," Frank exclaimed from the front window.

"Who?" Pete asked.

"The Chief and Deputy Brown. The old man from the condo is with them. Bubba, I can see he has a badge pinned to his shirt. Shit, I think he's a cop."

Pete looked down at Charlotte like he was asking a question.

"He's the Sheriff of the town we live in, back in Kentucky."

"Bubba, take Charlotte back to one of the bedrooms. Charlotte, don't say a word if you know what's good for you, what's good for your friend."

"I don't think I can walk."

"Bubba carry her back."

Bubba reached under Charlotte with both arms and easily picked her up. Carrying her to the nearest bedroom, he flopped her down on the unmade bed. Reaching behind him, he pulled a gun from his belt and pointed it at her. "Not a sound. Not a frickin sound. You understand?"

Charlotte nodded her head.

Back in the living room, Pete called to Frank standing in the front hall, "Get back in here and sit on the couch. Act natural. You understand? And for God's sake, don't say anything."

"Sure Pete. I know how to act . . . Aren't you going to open the door?" Frank asked as Pete sat down beside him.

"I'm not going to the door until they ring the doorbell or knock. If I opened it before they got here, they would think I was watching for them," Pete replied, turning on the TV. The doorbell rang, making Frank jump.

"Just be cool," Pete said, rising and going to the door.

Opening the door wide enough for the three lawmen to get a good look inside, Pete asked, "Hi guys, what can I do for you?" Before the Chief could answer, Pete added, "Hey, you're our neighbor. I didn't know you were a cop."

"I haven't been wearing the badge."

"I'm Chief Rogers. I was here the other day," the Chief continued. "This is Deputy Brown and Sheriff Harris. We were wondering if you've seen a woman from the blue condo earlier today."

"Which one? I've seen three women over there."

"The smaller one."

"Yeah, I saw her earlier today, or maybe yesterday. I don't remember. Why? Has something happened to her?"

"What do you mean?"

"I heard from Bubba about your visit the other day, about the young girl. Now someone else has gone missing. That's all I meant."

"She seems to be missing, and we're asking everyone on the street if they've seen her."

"I understand. Cool. Sorry Chief, but like I said, I saw her either earlier today or yesterday taking a walk. I really can't remember when. Does this have something to do with the other murder?"

"Why do you say that?"

"I don't know. It just seems funny to me. Not funny Ha-Ha, but funny weird."

"I understand. If you guys are out and about, keep your eyes and ears open. If you see or hear anything out of the ordinary, call the station."

"You'd be the first person we'll call, for sure."

The three turned to leave, and Pete slowly started closing the door. Suddenly, the Chief stopped and looked over his shoulder.

"Yes, Chief," Pete said, standing in the partially closed door.

"You guys are going to be in big trouble."

"What do you mean?" Pete asked, placing his unseen hand on the gun hidden behind his back.

"Something doesn't smell right."

"Chief?"

"I can tell standing out here, you've got garbage piling up in there. It smells like old pizza crust, sour milk or cottage cheese, rotten potato peelings, and rancid meat. I've had the owners of these condos file complaints before. The renters weren't cleaning up after themselves. There are two dumpsters per condo; use them. The trash is picked up twice a week. Take your trash out."

"Yes sir, Chief," Pete smiled. "We'll clean up here before we check out. I swear."

"Make sure you do."

When the three were back at the blue condo, Ray asked, "Well Chief, what do you think?"

"I don't know. He seemed nervous sure enough, but it could be he's not used to three officers of the law showing up on his doorstep. We'll have to keep an eye on them."

"Well, what do you think?" Frank asked as Pete walked back into the living room.

"I don't know. He seemed suspicious like he knew something. We'll have to keep an eye on them."

"Hey, Pete, look at this," Bubba said from the hallway. Looking in his direction, Pete watched as Charlotte slowly walked into the living room, holding on to the wall for support.

"It's good seeing you up," Pete said, looking to make sure no one was looking through the decorated glass in the front door.

"We heard the police talking," Bubba said.

"So?"

"So, what are we going to do with her?"

Charlotte's good eye darted to Pete. What he said in the next few minutes would determine her fate. This could be her last day on earth. Pete walked over and sat down in the recliner, placing his head in his hands. For a few minutes, the room was deadly silent.

"So, what are we going to do with her?" Bubba said, breaking the silence.

Yes, what are you going to do with me?

"Okay, here's what we're going to do . . . Bubba, there's a hardware store where Highway 80 ends at the southern tip of the island."

"T S Chu Department Store?" Frank asked.

"That's the one."

"I remember," Frank continued, "because I thought 'T S Chu' was funny."

"Bubba, I want you to go there and pick up a sturdy chain, about fifteen feet long, two hefty locks and a tall, sturdy plastic bucket with a lid. Frank, you run over to the IGA and get a case of bottled water, snacks, duck-tape, three large flashlights and a six-pack of toilet-paper."

"What's all that shit for?" Bubba asked.

Frank started laughing. "Pete said, 'toilet-paper' and Bubba said, 'shit.' That's funny."

"We're taking Charlotte on a boat ride," Pete continued.

"The hell we are," Bubba exclaimed.

"We need her now in case the police get too close. We may need a hostage."

Oh, thank God, Charlotte thought.

"So, I'll ask again. Pete, what's all the shit for?"

"We'll chain Charlotte in the bow of the boat. That's what the chain and locks are for. We'll be able to keep an eye on her."

"And the bucket?"

"She'll need something to crap in. That's why it needs a lid."

"And that's why I'm getting the toilet-paper," Frank laughed again.

"That's the reason, Frank. That's the reason."

Chapter 15

Two o'clock in the morning and nothing stirred, no one was out. All was quiet and still. Even the breeze was holding its breath. The moon, knowing something was up, hid its face in a bank of dark overhead clouds. The lights in the blue condo went to bed at 1 a.m., and now all the lights, in all the buildings around the street, were sleeping. Earlier, Bubba backed the Nissan up under the carport next to the back door, and Pete made sure there would be nothing to trip over in the dark when they left the building.

"Nice and slow," he told Charlotte and the others, as he slowly closed the backdoor. "Not a sound if you know what's good for you. Bubba, you'll drive. I'll ride shotgun, with Charlotte in between. Frank, you're in the bed of the truck with the supplies."

Charlotte's left eye, completely swollen shut, ached, as well as her cheek and jaw. Her head pounded and her neck screamed every time she turned her head to the left. Pete continuously fed her aspirin, which eased the pain, barely. The wound along her cheek needed stiches, but that wasn't going to happen. Several times already, Pete had changed the Band-Aids. In the beginning, there had been a lot of blood, but with each changing the blood was flowing less and less.

Charlotte knew Bubba wanted her dead, but thank God, Pete convinced him they needed a hostage. She would live a while longer, and during that time, she would plan her escape, or so she hoped.

The stoplight at South Campbell and Highway 80 was red, and Bubba sat there a long time, staring at *Bowie's Seafood* sign offering fresh shrimp daily. At two o'clock in the morning, there was no traffic.

"You can turn right on red," Pete reminded him, getting impatient.

"Oh, yeah, I know," Bubba replied, snapping out of it.

Pressing the gas pedal the truck jumped forward, only to have Bubba slam on the brakes. At that moment, from out of nowhere, a frickin police cruiser was crossing the intersection right in front of them.

"Shit," Bubba whispered, smiling. Bubba raised both his hands as if to say, sorry. The police officer shook his head and mouthed "dumbass," before continuing.

"Oh Bubba," Pete sighed. "You almost gave me a heart attack. You'll be the death of us all."

"Piss on you, Pete," Bubba exclaimed. "You want to drive?"

"No. Just be careful, okay? You think we'll be able to get aboard the boat this early in the morning?"

"In the contract, it says we have access to the boat any time we want. Its low tide right now, so we'll have to wait a few hours before we can take her out."

***

The Nissan suddenly stopped at the Marina, throwing gravel and raising a dust cloud. Both Charlotte and Pete had to grab the dashboard to keep from slamming into it.

"Why do you always do that?" Pete asked.

"I like raising dust clouds," Bubba laughed.

Nothing stirred. The only source of light came from a sonar light attached to a pole. Bugs were circling the light, like Indians circling a wagon train. All the buildings were dark. Earlier, Pete wondered if there would be security cameras. So he had driven down to the dock as if he was checking on the boat. He saw none, but that didn't mean there weren't any.

Once on deck, Frank carried all the supplies below, while Pete and Bubba scanned the surrounding darkness. All seemed clear.

"Charlotte, this way," Pete said pointing to an open hatch in the bow of the boat. "There's a raised platform down there. It will keep you out of the water."

"Out of the water!" she exclaimed.

"The boat leaks, but the sump pumps take care of it. You'll be okay."

Pausing for a moment, Pete placed his hand on a tuba-shaped thing sticking out of the deck.

"Bubba told me what this is and what it's for. This is a Dorade Vent, and this horn-shaped thing is the ventilation cowl. There's one at each end of the boat. They allow air to move through the belly of the boat. It will help the smell down there when the boat is moving."

"The smell?"

As soon as Charlotte's head disappeared below the main deck, her nose and sinus overflowed with the smell of diesel fuel, oil, rust, and rot. The raised metal platform did keep the water at bay, just barely. From the glare of the flashlights, Charlotte could easily see the sides of the boat were rusted and flaking off. Rusty iron pipes overhead looked like they were about to disintegrate, and a few had sprung pin-sized leaks. Any exposed wood showed signs of rot and mold. Water could be heard dripping somewhere. Charlotte thought she heard a squeak.

"This is it," Pete apologized. "Tomorrow, I'll have Frank run into Walmart."

"What for?" Bubba snapped.

"I didn't think it through yesterday. Charlotte's going to be our guest until we finish what we came here for. She needs medical treatment, but that's not going to happen. So there's no reason we can't make her stay with us as easy as we can. In the morning, Frank will run into Walmart and get Charlotte a cot, pillow and a couple of blankets. We'll be eating a lot of takeout's, probably Burger King and KFC. So, he might as well get her a toothbrush and toothpaste as well."

"You paying for this?" Bubba asked.

"No. You are," Pete replied. "You've got a money man, use him . . . Charlotte, I'm afraid you'll have to sleep on the metal platform tonight. It will be easier tomorrow. Frank place the bucket over there and place the toilet paper on top."

Taking the chain and one lock, Pete attached one end of the chain to a solid metal support beam. He then wrapped the other end of the chain around Charlotte's ankle and attached the other lock.

"You should be able to reach the bucket from here. Frank will empty it every day."

"I'll do what?"

"Everyday . . . There will always be one of us on the boat, so don't get any idea of screaming for help." After a moment, he continued. "Frank you might as well get cots, blankets, and pillows for all of us. We'll go ahead and move out of the condo and stay on board from now on."

"What? No TV?" Frank whined.

"Pete, who's running this outfit? You or me?" Bubba asked, getting angry.

"You are," Pete replied, seeing the look on Bubba's face. "So, what do you suggest?"

Bubba stood there looking at the filthy water. "I think we should move in here. We won't have to worry about anyone spying on us."

"Good point," Pete agreed. "Charlotte, we'll leave you now, but we'll be around. Frank, leave your flashlight with her."

"What? Why do I have to leave my light with her?"

"Shit, Frank. We'll get you a new one, a better one, tomorrow . . . Charlotte, there's a porthole on either side of the bow. That should let in enough light during the day to see by. Don't go shining your light through them, or I'll take it away and leave you in the dark."

Charlotte panned her light up the ladder, watching as the three left. The hatch cover banged when it closed. Banged like the closing of a tomb. Alone, she panned her surroundings. Alone, she was frightened. It was hopeless. No one would ever find her. At this moment, she was a speck; a speck in the vast darkness of the world.

Chapter 16

Ray walked in from the patio carrying his empty coffee mug.

"The guys next door are moving out," he said, getting a refill.

"What'd you say?" FJ asked.

"I said, the guys next door are moving out. They've already filled both their dumpsters and one from the neighbors with trash and garbage, and they've finished loading their truck. They'll be leaving any minute."

"Kinda strange don't you think?"

"What do you mean?"

"These condos are rented from Saturday or Sunday to the following Saturday or Sunday. Seven days, no exceptions. You remember two years ago when we had to leave early because Charlotte's mom had a heart attack? We didn't get a refund of any kind. So, why are they leaving today?"

"You think I know the answer to that?"

"Maybe you and the Chief scared them with your surprise visit. Maybe they're thinking someone is getting too close to the truth. Maybe they're going home because one of their moms had a heart attack. Maybe they're taking Charlotte with them."

"That's too many maybes."

"Maybe, we should follow them."

"Maybe we should . . . Mike?" Ray called out.

"You don't have to yell. I'm right here in the living room. What's up?"

"We need to take a road trip."

"Where?"

"Just get your keys. I'll tell Margaret and Stephanie we're

going out for a while."

"They'll want to know where?"

"We need to run over to the IGA."

"For what?"

"Hell, I don't know. I'll think of something."

The three men walked out into the heat and climbed in the van. They sat there with the air running, waiting, watching. The Sinclair's left yesterday afternoon, and the cleaners were there today preparing the condo for the next set of occupants. The family from Virginia were loading up their little red wagon for another day on the beach. The newlyweds were walking their dog. *Life goes on,* Ray thought to himself.

"What did you tell the girls?" Mike asked, breaking Ray's train of thought.

"I told them we were running to IGA for Preparation H."

"You said what?"

"Get off my back. It was the first thing that came into my head."

"You having problems with your hemorrhoids?" FJ laughed.

"Hell no. I told them you were . . . Mike, they're pulling out of their drive."

"I see them. When they pass us, I'll let them get to the corner before I pull out."

Mike kept his distance so as not to give themselves away. This was exciting. Just like in the movies. *Follow that car!* At the stoplight at South Campbell, the Nissan took a right onto Highway 80. Mike did as well.

"Looks like they're going to Savannah," he said.

"If they're just going to Savannah, why did they pack all their stuff?" Ray asked.

"Maybe they're going home," FJ answered.

"Tell me again why we're following them?" Mike asked.

"I feel they had something to do with Charlotte being missing."

"We feel," FJ corrected.

"We feel they had something to do with Charlotte being

missing."

"I agree with your theory on Sara Sinclair, but what proof do you have that they had anything to do with Charlotte?"

"Just a gut feeling. Did you notice how many were in the cab of the truck?"

"No. Not really," Mike replied.

"Two. Where's the third guy? If they were leaving, going home, wouldn't all of them be going? They're up to something."

"We'll follow them for a while, but I'm not leaving the state."

The bridge over Lazaretto Creek loomed ahead.

"They're slowing down," Mike said, "They're getting ready to turn off."

"Stay on Highway 80, but slow down going over the bridge. We can turn around at the foot of the bridge, at the boat ramp," Ray said, straining to see out the window.

"That's the boat rental place down there," FJ stated, sitting on his knees to see. "I wonder what's going on . . . Yep, they stopped in front of that old rust bucket, and they're getting out. I can see the third guy on the deck."

"Maybe they're going fishing," Mike said, making a U-turn at the boat ramp.

"They loaded up all their crap just to go fishing? I don't think so."

"Now what?" Mike asked.

"I don't have a clue," Ray confessed. "They're not going back to the condo, that's for sure. I wish I could take a look inside that boat."

"Ain't going to happen," FJ stated flatly, staring at Ray.

"You know, with the guys out of the house, the police could check the place out; check for fingerprints, strands of hair, thrown away clothes, blood if they hurt her, and anything that could belong to her."

"Check for a body," FJ added.

"Don't go there FJ," Mike spat.

"Let's head back to our condo, but stop by the police station on the way," Ray said.

***

"Where's your IGA shopping bag?" Margaret asked as they walked in.

"IGA shopping bag?" Ray asked.

"Yeah. For FJ's hemorrhoids," Stephanie added.

"I don't have hemorrhoids," FJ shrieked from the living room.

"We didn't think so," Stephanie chimed in. "Where did you go?"

"It was Ray's idea," FJ screamed from the living room.

"Ray, it was your idea," Mike added. "You might as well tell them. They'll bug the pee out of us if we don't."

"It was FJ's idea too," Ray threw in.

"I have no frickin idea what you're talking about," FJ said, acting innocent as he walked in from the living room.

"Will one of you tell us where you went?" Margaret demanded.

"We followed the guys next door."

"Why?"

"They packed up all their stuff and left."

"And you decided to follow them, without taking us?" Margaret spat.

"You would have thought it stupid."

"Correct. But we would have gone."

"So, why did you follow them?" Stephanie asked.

"My gut tells me; they know where Charlotte is."

***

"About time you guys got back," Frank said, standing beside the gangplank.

"It took longer to clean up the condo and pack our gear in the truck than we thought it would," Pete said, coming aboard carrying a trash bag. "Quit whining. All you had to do was sit on your ass and babysit. How's she doing?"

"Fine. She ate the sausage biscuits, but wouldn't touch the biscuits and gravy . . . What's in the bag?"

"As we were cleaning up the condo, we made sure to get anything that could point to her; the dishtowel I used with the ice-cubes; the blanket from the bed she was lying on when the cops paid their visit; the bloody Band-Aids. We ran a load of dishes to get rid of any fingerprints. We wiped down everything she touched. We vacuumed the couch for hairs, and the vacuum bag is in the trash-bag."

"Wow. How did you know to do those things?"

"I've watched a lot of *Forensic Files* on TV."

"I'll see if I can get us up and running and we'll cast off," Bubba said, walking to the wheelhouse. "I'm excited to get going."

"I'll check in on Charlotte," Pete commented, walking toward the hatch.

"What do you want me to do?" Frank asked.

"Get the fishing gear ready," Pete asked. "We're supposed to be fishing after all."

The groaning of the hatch cover being opened startled Charlotte. She hoped it wasn't Frank coming, again, to see if he needed to empty the 'P-O-S' (Pot of shit), as he called it. Pete had been telling the truth when he said the portholes would light the cargo hold of the boat,but just barely. To see any details, she still needed the flashlight. For hours, Charlotte tested the strength of the locks and chain. Too new, too strong. The beam, to which the chain was attached, even though rusty, was too thick to bend or break. She doubted a sledgehammer would have any effect on it.

"Hey down there," Pete called from above, as his boots appeared on the ladder. "You doing okay?"

"What do you think?" Charlotte replied, sarcastically.

"I know Charlotte, and I'm sorry."

"Why can't you let me go?" she pleaded. "I won't tell anyone."

"Now, now, Charlotte. I believe you would tell. I saw how you looked at Bubba."

"He killed her. How could anyone do that to such a sweet girl?"

"So, you did hear his conversation . . . Don't look like you just let the cat out of the bag. It's okay, Charlotte. You probably won't believe this, but no one was supposed to get hurt."

"So, why?"

"Bubba loses it sometimes."

"That's not acceptable, and you know it. Pete, you're a good man, but Bubba's going to drag you down to his level."

Ignoring Charlotte, Pete pulled a bottle of water from a package and approached her. "Hold your flashlight close to your face and let me look at your eye."

The eye was completely shut, swollen and puffy, black and blue. Her cheek was swollen to the size of a golf ball. The wound oozed. Pete shook his head.

"What a mess . . . Hold your head back and let me clean it."

Pete slowly poured the clean water from the bottle, letting it flow down her eye and cheek. He did this until the bottle was empty.

"That's the best I can do for you. I'm sorry."

"You can let me go."

"Here's a new bottle of aspirin for you," Peter said, ignoring her again.

The trawler's engine fired up, filling the cargo hold with vibration and noise.

"Where are we going?" Charlotte yelled.

"How much of Bubba's conversation did you hear?" Pete yelled back.

Charlotte thought a moment, and while she did, the engine died. "He said something about looking for a bomb . . . Oh, my God. You guys aren't looking for the bomb the government lost?"

"You know the story?"

"We heard about it at AJ's. You don't believe it exists?"

"Bubba does."

"What makes you think you can find it, while others have been looking for it for fifty years?"

"Hell, I don't know. It was a good idea when Bubba first suggested it."

"You killed a girl searching for a fairy tale!"

"Damnit, I didn't kill her."

"No, but you didn't do anything about it."

"Like what?"

"You could have gone to the police."

"In the beginning, but not now. It's been too long. Frank and I will face the same punishment if we're caught?"

"Pete, there's still time."

Pete threw the empty water bottle in the oily water beside the platform and sadly shook his head. "No there isn't Charlotte. The bed's been made, and the three of us have to lay in it now . . . I'll check in on you later. I'll bring you a bologna sandwich, chips and a coke for lunch."

"Pete?" Charlotte pleaded, but it was too late. Pete had already started back up the ladder.

Chapter 17

Ray walked into the dining room and found everyone sitting around the dining room table.

"Dealing cards?" he asked.

"We're not in the mood," Stephanie replied.

"Me either . . . So, what are you doing?"

"Going over our predicament," Margaret replied.

"How so?"

"We were supposed to go to Sundae Café tonight. Mike thinks we need to cancel."

"I agree."

"Everyone agreed . . . Ray, why don't we know anything? Where is she? It seems like it's taking forever."

"I know how everyone's feeling. I feel the same. Margaret, I've been in the business long enough to know, it just takes time."

"Which we don't have," FJ added.

"What do you mean?" Ray asked.

"We've got to be out of here Saturday, by ten o'clock. That's tomorrow. The way things are going, we ain't going to find Charlotte by then."

"If we can't stay here, then we need to find somewhere else to stay."

"Easier said than done," Stephanie stated. "Every place is going to be booked."

"Maybe not," Ray stated. "We can call the people we're renting this place from and see if it's open next week."

"You know how much this place cost?" Margaret asked.

"No idea."

"Well, it's 3,000 dollars a week," Stephanie added. "That's 500 dollars per person. Not bad for a week if you split it up among six people, but Mike and I are stretched as it is. I'm not sure we could afford another week."

"Maybe we can find a vacancy at one of the hotels along the beach. All we need is two rooms."

"Two rooms?"

"Margaret and Stephanie can room together, and the guys can share another."

"I bet they're all booked too," FJ said.

"It's worth a try," Ray insisted. "What do we have to lose?"

An hour went by with Stephanie on her cell phone, and a phone book open before her on the table. It turns out, their condo was booked for the rest of the season, as were all the other condos she called. The first three hotels called were booked, but *My Beach House Rentals*, at the bend of Highway 80 and the beach, had a last-minute cancellation. A group of eight college kids from Indiana phoned saying they weren't coming and gave no reason why, and they couldn't understand why they lost their deposit. There was now a small condo available with two bedrooms, unbelievable. Stephanie put the house on her credit card, and they could take possession tomorrow.

***

Retired Marine Sergeant-Major Preston Mullins and his son-in-law, Parker Davis, had spent the last five years trolling Wassaw Sound, located five miles south of Tybee Island, searching for the lost bomb. The murky brown water of the Sound connects the mouth of the Wilmington River to the Atlantic Ocean, and it was here the bomb should be found. Happily, Preston took a drag off a huge expensive stogie. He enjoyed coming here every year looking for a fairy tale. Everything was going according to plan. Their small refurbished Chesapeake Bay Oyster Boat arrived yesterday, loaded with the latest sonar, infrared cameras, two rear-mounted cranes, and an assortment of tow-behind Geiger counters. This was going to be the year he found it. This year was going to be different; he had that feeling.

With the onslaught of Hurricane Miles and it's higher than average surge, Preston hoped the bomb would finally be uncovered, allowing them to get a good ping off the Geiger counters. Even if the Geiger counters failed to register a ping, they planned on taking mud samples from the bottom of the Sound. These would later be sent to Vanderbilt University and tested for radioactive materials.

If they were lucky, the bomb would be found lying in shallow water somewhere along the coast. But if it weren't in shallow water, the cranes aboard would be able to retrieve the bomb from the Sound's deepest point, which wasn't more than forty feet deep.

Once found, Preston wasn't sure the government would even want to remove it. At the time, the Air Force said the bomb was incapable of a nuclear explosion because it lacks the plutonium capsule needed to trigger an atomic blast, something a later report retracted. The government's worst fear – the 400 pounds of conventional explosives resting inside the rusting metal exterior of the weapon, made the bomb unstable. Any attempt to move the bomb could cause the explosives to detonate, spewing plutonium for hundreds of miles. Theoretically, a slight touch could set the weapon off.

If it did explode, according to the government, the blast would be small, but would destroy Tybee Island, killing all 3,000 residents, not counting tourists. It would be the end of the shrimping business for hundreds of years to come. The Savannah River would be affected. The river is the shipping channel for the Port of Savannah, the nation's tenth-busiest port for oceangoing container ships. An explosion would create a radioactive hotspot, making the river unusable. No one mentioned – depending on the wind's direction, anyone coming in contact with the plutonium fallout could end up with burns, blisters, blindness, and cancer. There would be an ungodly amount of miscarriages, and the children born could be horribly disfigured. If the wind were blowing west by northwest, the fallout would affect Savannah's 146,000 residents.

The final government report stated the best thing to do was to leave the bomb alone. Surely, it was entombed in five feet of mud, in five to forty feet of water. The bomb was buried, as was any future discussions on the matter. It wasn't worth the time, effort, or money. But not for Sergeant-Major Mullins. Not since 9/11. Not since all the bad guys in the world lusted for a dirty bomb, and it was lying out here somewhere, ripe for the picking.

"What are those guys doing over there?" Parker asked his father-in-law, pointing. Mullins raised a pair of binoculars and scanned the other side of the Sound near the mouth of the Wilmington River. It took a moment to find the boat and another to focus.

"Looks like a bunch of fishermen," he replied. "I can see one man with a rod and reel standing on the bow."

"Why such a big boat just to go fishing?"

"Maybe that's all they could afford. From what I can see, it's not much of a boat. Interesting. Let's go over and say, 'Hi.'"

***

The trawler rocked gently in the ocean waves flowing into the Sound on the rising tide. For Frank it made him sleepy; for Charlotte, it increased the pounding in her head. Her left eye was still swollen, and blood oozed from her wound. Her ankle stung from the heavy chain rubbing it raw. Several times she tried to pull her foot free but to no avail. The rusted steel hull of the boat made the interior a breath sucking convection oven. Charlotte knew now how Shadrach, Meshach, and Abednego must have felt when Nebuchadnezzar threw them into the fiery furnace. The only relief was sitting beneath the vent while the boat was moving. Her clothes were uncomfortably sweat soaked, and she badly needed a shower and shampoo.

"There's a boat coming toward us," Pete yelled from the main deck.

"Coast Guard?" Bubba yelled back from the wheelhouse.

"No," Pete replied, holding a pair of binoculars to his eyes. "It's a small boat. I can see a man spying on us with his own set of binoculars."

Bubba picked up his AK-47 leaning beside the open hatch. He pulled back and released the charging handle, making sure a round was chambered. The fire selector, a large lever located on the right side of the rifle, acts as a dustcover and prevents the charging handle from being pulled fully to the rear when it is on safe. It is operated by the shooter's right forefingers and has three settings: safe (up), full auto (center), and semi-auto (down). Bubba placed it on full auto. Attached to the AK-47 was its standard 30-round curved magazine, and beside the doorway, in a metal box, were ten more magazines. Satisfied, Bubba placed the automatic back beside the open hatch. Bubba was not an expert with a gun, but in his mind, if you throw enough bullets at something, one of them would surely score a hit.

Parker, standing in the bow of the oyster boat, threw Frank a mooring line, which Frank attached to the rail. Sergeant-Major Preston came forward with a smile on his face. "Nice day to be out ..."

"Fishing," Peter said, joining them at the rail.

"Nice day to be out fishing," Preston finished.

"What are you guys up too?" Pete asked, looking at all the equipment on their deck.

"We're looking for the bomb." Pete looked at Frank and then toward Bubba. He could tell by the look on Bubba's face; he had heard every word.

"Bomb?" Pete asked. "You're kidding. Right?"

"Not at all. You haven't heard about the lost bomb?" Pete shook his head.

For the next thirty minutes, Preston retold the amazing story of how the government lost a hydrogen bomb. "And that's why we're here," he finished.

"Here to do what?"

"Why, find it of course."

"And what are you going to do when you find it?"

"That's up to the government, as long as they do something. We wouldn't want the bomb to end up in the hands of terrorists.

Would we?" Pete shook his head, looking at Bubba. "No, I guess we wouldn't," he replied.

Charlotte had seen the small craft pull up alongside the trawler but couldn't hear the conversation. She had to get their attention. Someone had to know she was here. But how? Looking around, she noticed a piece of one-inch pipe about three feet long. Taking it in her hand, she walked to the porthole and started banging on the rusty trawler's wall.

"Do you hear something?" Parker asked his father-in-law.

Pete had heard it, as well as Frank and Bubba. "Frank, go down in the hold and find out what's making that noise," Pete commanded. "And stop it."

"We've been having a problem with a pulley belt on the engine," Pete continued. "It probably broke, and it's slapping the bottom of the boat. You know how these old tubs are."

"I'm well aware of these things," Preston smiled. "I was a Marine for thirty years, and I worked on worse boats than this. You need some help?"

"No. I'm sure we can handle this. But, thanks anyway."

The banging continued, coming from near the waterline, coming from near a porthole.

"Look there," Parker exclaimed, pointing. "There's a woman screaming at us through that porthole. Something's wrong."

Thirty rounds from Bubba's AK-47 ripped the air. Thirty rounds ripped the oyster boat's decking, shattered the glass windows of the oyster boat's bridge, and the bodies of Marine Sergeant-Major Preston Mullins and his son-in-law, Parker Davis. They were torn apart.

"Oh my God," Frank exclaimed running up to the rail. "Oh my God . . . What are we going to do, Pete? What are we going to do?"

Pete couldn't believe it. His eyes darted over their surroundings. At any moment, a shrimper could be pulling out of one of the rivers into the Sound. The Coast Guard was always passing by, staring hard. Hell, real fishermen could pop out of any of the creeks and ditches. He stood there in amazement, thinking. Nodding to himself, Pete tested the oyster boat's mooring line making sure it was securely tied to the trawler. Pete turned and looked up at Bubba with eyes full of hate. "Take us out in the ocean as far as we can. Find a deep spot. We need to sink their boat . . . I'm going to have a word with Charlotte."

Chapter 18

From her vantage point, Charlotte couldn't see the carnage aboard the oyster boat. But she heard the gunfire, and she knew what was happening. Pete would now be coming.

The groan of the hatch cover made her jump. It always did, but this time an ass-chewing was coming. She sat on her cot, the pipe still in her hand.

"Are you out of your frickin mind?" Pete chastised her, taking the pipe. "Two men just died."

"And you killed them," Charlotte spat.

Pete shook his head. "I didn't kill them."

"Then Bubba and Frank killed them."

Pete shook his head again. "They didn't kill them."

"Then who in the hell did?"

"You killed them, Charlotte. You killed them . . . If you had kept your hands to yourself and your damn mouth shut, they would be alive right now. We would have talked about finding the bomb, had a good laugh and they would have been on their merry way. Later over beers, they would have made jokes about three idiots in a rusted tub, fishing. Now, I have to do something with their lifeless bodies. Any suggestions, Charlotte? What would you do with their bodies? You want me to bring them down here with you? Think about what could happen the next time you try something stupid."

"Pete," Frank yelled from the hatch opening. "Bubba says we're there."

"Think about it," Pete said over his shoulder as he climbed out of the hold.

On deck, Pete scanned the surrounding water three hundred and sixty degrees. Nothing could be seen in any direction; nothing as far as the horizon. "How far offshore are we?"

"About a hundred yards."

"How deep's the water?"

"The depth gauge says a hundred and twenty feet," Bubba replied.

"How old and reliable is the gauge?"

"Brand new. It better be. It's the only thing keeping us from running aground at low tide."

"Then hold up here Bubba . . . Frank, you come with me."

Climbing onto the oyster boat, Pete grabbed the Sergeant-Major's legs. "Frank, you take the other man's legs."

"You're kidding, right?" Frank asked, looking at the blood covered deck and the torn remains of Parker. Pete continued like he hadn't heard.

"We'll put them in the hold of the oyster boat, and seal it somehow. We don't want them floating to the surface when their bodies begin to bloat."

"Bloat?" Frank said, making a face.

The job was taxing in the noonday heat, but both bodies now lay in the shallow hold of the oyster boat. Pete found a rusty piece of half-inch diameter rebar and lodged it in the cabin door.

"That will keep them in. I hope," Pete said, as he and Frank climbed back aboard the trawler.

Finding an old plastic bucket, Peter lowered it into the salty water tied on the end of a rope. As best he could, he washed the blood from his hands and arms. It reminded him of a story his Southern Baptists parents told him when he was a little boy.

"Pontius Pilate washed his hands," his stern father preached, "blaming Jesus and the Jews for Jesus' blood covered back, and his ultimate fate." Today, Pete was washing his hands, blaming Bubba for the blood covered deck and the two lifeless bodies.

Cutting the mooring line, Pete pushed the smaller boat away from the trawler with a grappling pole; poles used to pull fishing lines from the water.

"Are we going to let them float away?" Frank questioned.

"No. We can't let anyone find them."

"Then what are we going to do?"

"Bubba, show us how to use the rifles you brought," Pete said, throwing the pole to the side.

Stationing themselves along the rail, Pete scanned the horizon, seeing nothing. "Aim low, just below the water line. We put enough holes in her, and she'll sink. If she doesn't, we'll circle to the other side and do the same thing there."

It took six clips per side, three hundred and sixty rounds for the oyster boat to finally start sinking. Pete held his breath, praying no one would appear on the horizon, or pop out of the marsh. It took an hour for the small boat to fill and disappear beneath the surface, and another hour to be completely submerged.

"God, that took forever," Pete said, turning away from the surge of bubbles breaking the surface.

"That's three," Pete said, handing Bubba back the AK-47. "Three innocent people."

"It's not my fault."

"How in the hell do you figure that?"

"If she hadn't been banging on the wall, they'd still be alive."

"Really? And how about Sara?"

"That was Sara's fault."

"Bullshit," Pete spat, turning away.

Bubba had had enough of Pete and his holier than thou attitude. Pete needed to be taught a lesson; needed to be taught who the real boss was. As Pete walked away, Bubba slammed the butt of his AK-47 between Pete's shoulders, causing Pete to fall forward to the filthy deck. With a curse, Pete was up and coming at Bubba.

"Don't do it, Pete," Bubba commanded.

"Go to Hell," Pete yelled. He had had enough of everything. He wanted to get away, away from Bubba, away from Frank, away from Charlotte, away from this damn ocean, away from death. Within Bubba's reach, Pete took a blow to the jaw and fell back to the deck, spitting blood from a split lip. Wiping his lip with the back of his hand, Pete looked at the blood, stood, and came at Bubba again.

"I told you not to," Bubba pleaded, striking Pete again.

Pete went to the deck and sat there a moment. Spitting more blood, he sprang at Bubba, but Bubba was ready. With a wide swipe, Bubba caught Pete on his left shoulder, knocking him to the deck a fourth time.

"Stay down Pete," Frank pleaded. "He's just going to kill you."

Taking a breath, Pete rose and came in low, wrapping his arms around Bubba's waist, his head buried in Bubba's side, pushing. It was like trying to push over a house. Reaching under Pete's waist with both arms, Bubba easily picked him up. Pete was now hanging upside down, at Bubba's mercy. Twisting sideways, Bubba flung Pete to the wooden deck. Pete moaned and slowly got up, turning again to Bubba. It was then that Frank jumped between them.

"Get out of the way Frank," Pete said, spitting out a mouthful of blood.

"Look over on the horizon, along the coastline," Frank pointed. "Something's coming from Tybee."

Forgetting their differences, for now, the three walked over to the rail, looking toward Tybee.

"What do you think it is?" Bubba asked.

"Holy shit. It's the Coast Guard," Pete answered.

"You think they saw us?" Frank asked.

"I don't think so," Pete answered. "Too far away. But it does look like they're coming our way."

"What are we going to do, Pete," Frank asked, about to jump out of his skin. "We can't take on the Coast Guard."

"Calm down. We can't stay here, that's for sure. There are still bubbles rising from the boat."

"So, what are we going to do? Make a run for it?" Bubba asked, heading toward the wheelhouse.

"And go where. We can't outrun them," Pete assured him. "And we sure as shit, can't get in a gun battle with them."

"I'll be damn if I'm going to turn myself in," Bubba spat.

"No. It's too late for that. Too late for all of us," Pete said, sadly. "Bubba set a course straight for them."

"Are you out of your frickin mind?"

"I just might be."

Chapter 19

The trawler intercepted the Coast Guard Cutter along the coastline, about a mile north of the sink site. When the Cutter was within a quarter mile of the trawler, Bubba cut the engine letting her drift and joined Pete and Frank standing on the lower deck.

"Bubba, let me do all the talking," Pete commanded.

"Why? You think I'm going to say something stupid?"

"Yes," Pete replied, walking to the rail.

"Boy, I'd like to have her," Frank said, referring to the Cutter.

The coastal patrol boat was of the Marine Protector class. Eighty-seven feet of bright white and red stripes, the boat could fly through the water at twenty-five knots, or, for the land lovers, twenty-nine miles per hour. Each boat in the fleet is named after a marine predator. This one was the Barracuda. Pete noticed a boat launching ramp at the stern, used for unloading and loading the boat's inflatable rescue craft. A more deadly sight – Mounted on the port and starboard pintles were fifty caliber machine guns. Pete knew, the primary mission of the coast Guard in this area is combating drug smuggling, illegal immigration, marine fisheries enforcement and search and rescue support. Since the September 11, 2001 attacks, many have a Homeland Security mission in the form of ports, waterways and coastal security.

When the Cutter came within a hundred yards of the trawler, Pete sent Frank to sit with Charlotte in the hold. He was to remind her of the talk they had earlier.

"I don't care what you have to do, but keep her silent and away from the portholes."

"Will do, Pete."

The Cutter cut its engines and coasted to within a foot of the rusty trawler.

"Good day, gentlemen," an officer said standing beside the rail.

Peter nodded, noticing there were men and women manning both machine guns, and the machine guns were pointed in their direction.

"What brings you guys out here in that?" the officer asked, referring to the trawler. "Aren't you afraid she might rust out beneath your feet?"

"It's all we could afford," Pete replied, laughing. The officer laughed.

"So, really, what are you boys doing out here?" the officer asked sternly.

"We're looking for the bomb."

"Say again?" the officer asked, not sure he had heard correctly.

"We're looking for the bomb."

"That's what I thought you said. You really believe that old story?"

"Why not?"

"If the story's true, how do you think you're going to find it when others have failed?"

"Luck. Pure and simple. Look, I know it's been missing for over fifty years, and a lot of people have been looking for it. So, why not us? If we don't find it, at least we would have had a great vacation."

"If you were to find the bomb, what are your plans?"

"If, when, we find it, you'll be the first one we call. We're not in this for our own rewards. We think it's a real threat and we don't want it falling into the hands of some nutcase."

"If you boys do find it, which I doubt, don't touch it. Call us immediately."

"What happens if we touch it?"

"It could detonate." Pete looked toward Bubba. "We wouldn't want that." Turning back to the officer, "When we find it, we'll call you on the trawler's shortwave radio."

"That would be the wise thing to do . . . You know you're not the only ones out here this week looking for the bomb?"

"I didn't know that."

"Yeah. There's a retired Marine and his son-in-law searching. He's been coming here a few years now, looking for it. He'll be in a converted white oyster boat. If you see him, you guys should talk. He could give you guys some pointers."

"Thanks. We'll keep our eyes open for him."

"Where're you boys moored?"

"Over at the Lazaretto Creek Marina. (The officer nodded.) We were heading there when we saw you. We've been searching all day, and it's starting to get late. We're worn out, need a shower and food. We're going to run down to *Quarter's Grill* on First Street for burgers and beer."

"That's a great place to eat . . . You boys be careful. I wouldn't take your trawler out in heavy seas."

"Thanks for the advice."

Pete and Bubba returned to the wheelhouse and watched as the Cutter pulled away.

"I wonder if the bubbles have stopped," Bubba whispered.

"I sure as shit hope so. If they maintain their current course, it could take them straight to the spot."

"No 'could' about it. They're going straight at it," Bubba exclaimed, starting the engine.

"Hold on," Pete said calmly. "Just hold on."

The Cutter continued on its course, coming ever closer to the wreck.

"Jesus, Pete, they're going to find her. We've got to do something."

"Hold on for one more minute, Bubba, one more minute."

"They're slowing down . . . Does it look like they're slowing down to you, Pete? It looks like they're slowing down."

Suddenly, the Cutter turned to starboard, heading into the Sound, making its way toward the Wilmington River. Bubba and Pete let out the breaths they were holding.

"If we find the bomb, do you think it'll blow up if we touch it?" Bubba asked, several minutes later.

"If?"

"When we find it."

"I hope not."

Bubba went back into the wheelhouse leaving Pete staring at the site where the oyster boat lay.

How long will it take before they're declared missing? How long will it be before they are found? Will they ever be found, or will they be like the elusive bomb, forever lost?

Chapter 20

Moving day.

"We should be going home . . . all of us," Stephanie said zipping up Charlotte's travel bag. "All six of us. Where in the world is she? Is she hurting? Is she alone? I bet she's frightened. I'd be frightened. Why is it taking so long to find her?"

"I know how you feel," Margaret stated, coming out from Charlotte's bathroom. "I asked Ray the same thing. He said, 'No news is good news.'"

"Bull crap," Stephanie came back. "The longer we wait, the longer she ain't coming back."

"Stephanie don't talk like that. She'll be back. I don't know why she's missing, but she'll be back."

"You two done up there?" Ray yelled up the stairwell from the entry hall.

"Keep your pants on Raymond," Margaret yelled back. "We're coming."

She called him Raymond more as a joke because he hated being called Raymond.

FJ stood watching Mike load the suitcases in the back of the van. It was 8:30 in the morning and the temperature was rising. A new family was moving into the Sinclair's condo; a family and a cat in a carrier. The newlyweds were walking their dog, who, straining on his leash, really wanted to say hello to the cat. The siblings wanted to say hello to the dog. The cat wanted nothing to do with the dog.

"This has been one hell of a week," FJ sighed. "Mike, what do you think happened to Charlotte?"

Mike paused, wiping the gathering sweat from his forehead. "I hate thinking about it."

"Me too. But that's all I've been doing lately. Thinking. The worst part is not being able to do anything. Sitting on your ass sucks."

"I know that feeling. After we get moved, Ray's going to head over to the police station and see if they have any new leads."

"What's your feeling on Ray's idea about the three boys?"

"I think he's on to something, but the Chief won't see it through. According to Ray, the Chief's hands are tied. Ray feels sorry for him, somewhat."

"You know the guys are camping out on their boat."

"I know. We've seen them every afternoon when we cross over the bridge going toward Savannah. So, what's your point?"

"Maybe we need to watch them closer and check out their boat when they're away."

"Okay, that sounds good, but -"

"But what?"

"How do you know they leave their boat?"

"They have to eat sometimes, and we've seen their truck gone once or twice."

"They could have left someone behind."

"We don't know that. And why leave someone aboard if you're going out to eat? Wouldn't they all want to go?"

"Probably."

"Probably, my ass. We need to stake them out and take a quick look while they're gone."

"And how would we do that?"

"I haven't thought that far ahead."

"You guys ready to go?" Ray asked as he and the girls came around the corner of the garage.

"Sure," Mike answered closing the rear-end door.

"You got the AC on?" Stephanie asked, knowing the answer.

"I will in a minute," Mike replied, hurriedly climbing in behind the wheel.

The *My Beach House Rentals* were just that, a two-story house, a house with six condos, three per level. This particular house was located on Highway 80 at the bend along the ocean. The rear of the condos looked east, facing the ocean. Step off your patio, and you were standing on the beach. The front entrances faced west, looking along Highway 80, with MacElwee's Seafood House in easy walking distance. Each condo had a good-sized living room, kitchenette, laundry room, two bedrooms, and each bedroom had their own bathroom. Not bad for the money. After lugging their bags up to their bedrooms, the five flopped down in the living room, all lost in thought, all thinking the same thing.

"That's done. What now?" Stephanie asked, breaking the silence, bringing to light what everyone was thinking.

"We wait," Ray answered.

"We could wait at home," FJ said, staring at a seascape of a large white bird with a long beak. Every condo had one. FJ felt everyone's eyes on him, staring holes in him as if he had just said the mother of all curse words.

"What?" he said, with both hands raised. "You know what I mean. We might as well be on the moon for what we're doing now. Wait. Wait. Wait. Well, I'm tired of all this damn waiting. I want to do something."

"Like what?" Mike asked.

"I want to check out them boys and their damn boat."

"You think Charlotte's on their boat?" Margaret asked.

"She could be," FJ replied. "Don't look at me like that Ray. You know she could. You think so yourself, but you don't have the balls to say it."

"Calm down Frederick," Stephanie said softly. "We're all on edge right now."

"No. FJ's right," Ray admitted. "I think she is on the boat, but we can't just go rushing in. It could get her killed." Margaret gave Ray a hard look. Ray continued. "Margaret, if they killed Sara, they won't hesitate killing Charlotte. Look, everyone has the right to privacy, even those boys. It would take hard evidence for Chief Rogers to get a search warrant. It would take hard evidence for him to even set foot on that boat."

"But it wouldn't us," Mike said, staring hard at Ray.

"Do you have a plan?" Ray asked.

"I think I do," Mike replied. "It's crazy, but it just might work. Realistically, it just might get us killed."

"So, let's hear it."

Chapter 21

Her escort led Lisa Clark along a brightly lit corridor of grey painted concrete block walls, white ceiling tiles, and a shiny white linoleum floor. There were no pictures or potted plants spaced along any of the walls. The hallway felt sterile and cold, nothing warm, friendly or inviting. Stopping before a smoke glass door, Lisa couldn't believe she was standing here. Painted on the glass in black letters – Michael Carson. And below his name, in a smaller print – Assistant Director of Cyber Security.

The FBI is the lead federal agency for investigating cyber-attacks by criminals, overseas adversaries, and terrorists, homegrown and foreign. The threat is incredibly serious and growing. Cyber intrusions are becoming more commonplace, more dangerous, and more sophisticated. Our nation's critical infrastructure, including both private and public sector networks, are targeted by adversaries. American companies are targeted for trade secrets and other sensitive corporate data, and universities for their cutting-edge research and development. Because of its importance, the Assistant Director of Cyber Security is second in line to the Director of the FBI.

Lisa Clark did her graduate work at the University of Michigan – Ann Arbor. This prestigious school, with its 32.2 percent acceptance rate, was the only school Lisa wanted to attend, and with her 4.00 GPA, had no problem getting in. Graduating at the top of her class with a Ph.D. in Logistics Systems Analysis, Lisa was recruited by the FBI three days after she had received her diploma.

Lisa's escort knocked on the glass door and was rewarded with a click, like an electric lock being released. Her escort held the door open for her but did not enter.

"Go on in. Mrs. Haragan, the Assistant Director's Admin, will be giving you a briefing and will take you to your office. Welcome aboard, Miss Clark."

Lisa wanted to tell her she could call her by her first name, but her escort had already turned and walked away.

"Come on in," a friendly voice welcomed. "Take a seat."

Lisa gave the room the once over as she walked in. It felt a little warmer. The walls were a pale pink, but the ceiling tiles and floor were still white. Mrs. Haragan, a middle-aged woman with short hair and no makeup, sat behind a simple wooden desk. There were no papers or folders to be seen, no family photos, flowers or knick-knacks, only a black cordless phone with dozens of buttons. Lisa took the only seat before the desk. The odd thing about the room – there was one picture hanging on a wall, nothing else. It was a large picture of the twin towers, burning and smoking before the collapse.

"I see you're staring at the photo. We hung it there to remind us of that day, and with the knowledge that if we had our ducks in a row back then, it could have been avoided. It was only later, we learned of the money transfers, secret meetings, phone conversations, and text messages. If we had the data, 2,000 people would not have died. 2,000 families wouldn't be missing a loved one."

"I know. It's so sad," Lisa commented.

"What do you know of Cyber Security, Miss Clark?"

"You eavesdrop on phone conversations and text messages looking for terrorists."

"Okay. Wrong. Just for the record, we don't eavesdrop on anyone or anything. There are laws against those things unless you have a warrant. In the United States, there are over three billion phones calls a day, ten billion around the world. In the United States alone, there are over twenty-three billion text messages per day or almost sixteen million per minute. No, Miss Clark, we don't eavesdrop on cyber messages. We don't have the manpower.

"Off the record. We don't eavesdrop, but we do have

computer programs that do. There are algorithms that look for key words: a terrorist's names, any one on a no fly list, any form of the word murder, killed, bomb, or weapons, etc. The number of search words are endless, and new words are added daily."

From a hidden drawer, Mrs. Haragan placed a sheet of paper in front of Lisa, along with a pen. "Read this, please. Read it twice. If you have any questions about anything written here, ask. Your signature will confirm your agreement to the terms and conditions. This form is a confidentiality contract. If you ever disclose anything you do or hear while working here, you will find yourself locked away in a dark and smelly cell, with the key thrown away. If you want to be a member of our team, you must sign the form. Do you understand?"

"Yes."

"Good. There's a sentence about halfway down the form which states I warned you and that you understand. There's a box before the sentence. Please place an 'X' inside the box and your initials beside it. Very good. Now, read the entire form and if you agree with everything, sign your full name at the bottom, as well as date it."

Lisa handed the form back to Mrs. Haragan, who looked it over and signed beside Lisa's.

"Welcome to Homeland Security, Miss Clark. Are you ready to get started?"

"I'm chewing at the bit."

"Then let's get started."

Mrs. Haragan led Lisa down a maze of grey corridors before stopping beside a black metal door. "Each office has a key-code and iris scanner. Your key-code is 91101."

Mrs. Haragan entered her key-code and then leaned over, placing her eye near an oval opening. Pressing a button, a blue ray scanned her eye. A click followed it.

"We'll set up your eye scan later this afternoon," she said, holding the door open for Lisa. "This is your group. Get to know them well. There will be four of you: a linguist, a computer hacker, a geologist, and you, the master of logistics. Your test scores indicate a supreme ability for detailed coordination of complex operations."

This room was different from Mrs. Haragan's office. It consisted of four black metal desks with mesh swivel chairs, forming a square in the middle of the room. As a team, the four would be facing each other. On each desk was a laptop, phone, a stack of paper, a cup full of pens. Hanging around the room was an array of large screen monitors, filing cabinets and several paper shredders.

Three people rose from their chairs and came forward to introduce themselves. The first was a tall, skinny kid in his mid-twenties, with short curly black hair and a shaggy beard, dressed in a white t-shirt, faded jeans, and red suspenders.

I bet he's wearing sandals. Lisa looked. He was. *Not much of a dress code,* she thought.

"I'm Matt; I'm the computer hacker."

"Miss Clark, we don't like to use the word 'hacker' around here," Mrs. Haragan stated, staring at Matt. "The word hacker indicates something unlawful. What Matt does is within the law."

"Most of the time," Matt laughed, causing Mrs. Haragan to frown.

A middle-aged woman, blond haired, dark glasses, slim, average height, introduced herself next. "I'm Glenda. Like in the Wizard of Oz. I'm the geologist."

Next was the linguist. He had to be in his eighties, with thin, balding white hair, wearing a Kentucky Wildcat's sweatshirt with jeans. He wasn't wearing sandals. "Good to meet you. I'm Harry. I'm your linguist."

"What do you mean, 'your linguist.'?"

The other three looked at themselves and then to Mrs. Haragan.

"What he meant, Miss Clark, is they work for you. You are the team coordinator."

"Should we call you, Boss?" Matt asked, smiling.

"Lisa. Lisa will be fine."

"Okay, Miss Clark," Mrs. Haragan said, "Here's a thumb drive. It contains your first assignment. If you don't already know, Matt will show you how to upload the encrypted contents. Good day to you all. And Miss Clark, kick some terrorist's ass today."

As Mrs. Haragan closed the door behind her, Matt pointed to a poster hanging on the back of the door. It was black with big white letters. *Did you kick a terrorist's ass today?*

"Well, let's get started," Lisa said. "It's time to kick a terrorist's ass . . . Which desk is mine?"

Chapter 22

After un-encrypting, there were three files on the thumb drive, two Word Documents, and an MP3.

"Let's open the smaller word document first," Matt said, clicking on a file. Inside the document were two phone numbers. Nothing else.

"Okay, that was a blowout. Now the other word document."

The attached MP3 file is a conversation between two individuals. The keywords that capture the conversation were bomb/kill or any form or combination of those words. The other word document contains the phone numbers of the two individuals.

"Are you ready to listen to the MP3?" Matt asked. All three nodded. Clicking on the MP3 file opened an MP3 player. As each person spoke, his or her words would be displayed along the bottom of the player, along with waving lines showing the pitch pattern of each person and all surrounding noise. If need be, the noise could be filtered out, leaving only the conversation. The four analysts were glued to the screen.

Speaker 1:"Hello."

Speaker 2:"Bubba, you asshole. You're jerking my chain, right? You boys are screwing with   me big time. My gut tells me you're down there partying, screwing around,   goofing off, and on my dime."

Speaker 1:"Damnit, Wally, I'm not goofing off."

Speaker 2:"I've already given you a hell of a lot of money, and I haven't gotten anything in return.

Speaker 1:"Yes, I know who's funding us and we won't let you down. We're all business here."

Speaker 2:"So, where's the hydrogen bomb? People have been looking for it for years. What makes you think you can find it?"

Speaker 1: "Damnit, we will find the bomb, and I expect you to find a buyer."

Speaker 2:"I'll get you a buyer. You don't worry about that. But I will want more in return."

Speaker 1:"We'll give you twenty percent. Hell. Twenty-five percent."

Speaker 2: "You're all talk. You're just blowing smoke out your ass."

Speaker 1:"You don't think I'm serious."

Speaker 2: "Hell no. This is just a game to you."

Speaker 1:"I'll tell you how serious I am. I killed a girl who saw too much."

(Shocked, the analysts looked at each other.)

Speaker 2:"You did what?"

Speaker 1:"That's right. I killed a girl."

Speaker 2:"Holy shit. Bubba, you may have just pissed in the soup."

Speaker 1:"Hold on a second."

[Background Noise]

Speaker 1:"I'll get back to you Wally. Something just came up."

[End of transmission]

"That was interesting," Lisa said, leaning back in her chair. "So, what do we know?"

"Well," Glenda started. "Two men, one named Wally and the other Bubba. Who would name their kid 'Bubba'? It looks like Bubba is a murderer, and Wally is the front man."

"I agree," Lisa added. "It also doesn't look like Wally had anything to do with the murder. We need to determine who these men are, where these men are, who was murdered, and what's up with a bomb."

"I'll take the phone numbers and run them through the system," Matt said, pulling the thumb drive and taking it to his computer. "Probably won't do any good," he said sitting down. "Most of the times these guys use 'disposable burner phones.' Since prepaid burner phones can be bought with cash and without a contract, they're much harder to track. So it's easy for people to use them for certain 'illegal' activities and then simply dump the phone. Unless you're an idiot, you would never use your personal phone."

Lisa looked over at Harry. "What does their speech tell you?"

"Southern boys. There are eight regional American English dialects across the lower forty-eight states. There's the East North East dialect, which is pretty much the New England states. There's the Mid-Atlantic dialect, covering the cities and areas around New York, Philadelphia, and Baltimore. The Southern dialect stretches from Texas and the southern half of Missouri to the East Coast, from the Chesapeake Bay down to Florida. The Midland dialect starts in Ohio, then runs directly west to the northern half of Missouri. All the northern parts of the states that border the Great

Lakes are in the Inland Northern dialect. The western states that border Canada are in the North Central dialect. All the other states out west are in the Western dialect."

"God, I had no idea," Lisa confessed.

"It's more complicated than that. There are no hard boundaries between regions. Dialect regions merge. Any region may also contain speakers of 'General American,' a perceived mainstream accent widely spoken throughout the United States. Furthermore, you have to take into account speakers of ethnic, cultural, or other not-strictly-regional varieties, such as African American Vernacular English, Chicano English, Cajun English, etc. All regional American English dialects, unless specifically stated otherwise, are rhetoric, with the father–bother merger, Mary–marry–merry merger."

"So, boil all that down. What can you tell us about our guys?"

"Like I said, Southern. I would also add, this Wally is of Hispanic descent, and Bubba is African American. From his tone and word choice, Wally thinks himself important, in control, a mastermind. Bubba is defiantly subordinate but thinks higher of himself."

"You guys won't believe this, but Bubba is also an idiot," Matt interrupted. "I checked the phone numbers in the Word Document. The first number must belong to Wally because it is a burner. So we probably can't trace him. The other number belongs to Bubba. Would you believe, he used his own personal cell phone? I even found his contract with AT&T. Bubba's real name is Joe Ray Henry. Three first names. Who would give their kid three first names? You can't trust a man with three first names. I also did a trace on Bubba's phone's current location, and it's somewhere on Tybee Island, Georgia. On the north end of the island."

"I've never heard of Tybee Island," Lisa confessed.

"It's about twenty miles east of Savanah, along Highway 80," Glenda said speaking off the top of her head, from behind her computer monitor. "Highway 80 is also Butler Avenue, the main drag on Tybee Island."

"Matt, you said 'somewhere on Tybee Island.' Why can't you narrow down the location of Bubba's cell phone?"

"Phones on land lines are stationary, easy to locate. Cell phones, on the other hand, work off cell towers which can only show the cell phone's location within five miles or so of the tower. If you have three close by towers, you can triangulate and tie down a call within a hundred feet. No such luck on Tybee. The biggest problem – cell phones can travel."

"Okay. We have a general location on Joe Ray Henry, a.k.a. Bubba. But why Tybee Island and what's the deal with this bomb; more importantly, what's the deal with the murder of this girl?"

"I think I can answer the last part," Glenda chimed in. "I just checked the police reports on Tybee Island. There was a young girl, one Sara Sinclair, who was murdered there a couple of days ago. As of today, there's no suspect. Her death occurred on the northern end of the island."

"Where Bubba's phone is currently," Lisa commented. "So, if Bubba is telling the truth. He did kill her. But why? Is there a connection? Were they there together? Was it an accident, and he's afraid to come forward? Did she see or hear something she shouldn't have? And what's up with this bomb?"

"I just Googled that," Harry said, "I figured who would lose a hydrogen bomb around Tybee Island."

"Don't tell me; you got a hit?" Lisa asked.

"According to *Wikipedia*, the United States of America did indeed lose a hydrogen bomb around there."

"No shit," Lisa exclaimed.

"Back in 1958, it says here. And it's never been found. That's what Bubba's looking for. As with a lot of the 'untruthful' things on *Wikipedia*, I'll start digging around and see if I can come up with some of our classified documents and see if there's anything to the story. It could take a while."

"Go for it. We need to know what we're up against," Lisa said, nodding her head.

"Why would this Bubba be looking for a lost bomb; a bomb that's been missing for over fifty years?" Glenda asked.

"I'm afraid that's an easy question to answer," Lisa said. "Bubba wants to make a dirty bomb, or at least, sell it to someone who does . . . I need to take this to Assistant Director Carson."

"Good luck," Matt laughed.

"What do you mean by that?"

The other three looked at each other and started laughing.

"What's so funny?" Lisa asked.

"Assistant Director Carson doesn't exist," Matt answered.

"No way. I was in his office earlier."

"Really. Did you meet him?"

"No. I met with his Admin, Mrs. Haragan."

"In his office?"

"No. In hers."

"Did you see a door to an interoffice, his office?"

"No," Lisa answered slowly. "No, I didn't."

"Because it doesn't exist. You were in the Assistant Director's office."

"So, you're telling me Mrs. Haragan is the Assistant Director?"

"Bingo."

"So, why all the mystery?"

"For protection. If you want to protect the Assistant Director of Cyber Security, make him or her invisible, nonexistent . . . She did give you a clue."

"How so?"

"When she signed the confidentiality form, did you notice what she wrote?"

"No."

"You should have. I noticed."

"I did too," Glenda added.

"As did I," Harry chimed in.

"What did she write?" Lisa asked, getting a little perturbed.

"Michael Carson," Harry answered.

"So I need to talk with the Assistant Director's admin," Lisa laughed, rising from her chair. Walking to the door, Lisa stopped.

"Could one of you show me to his or her office? I'll never find it on my own."

Stopping in front of the Assistant Director's office, Matt pointed out something Lisa had missed earlier.

"You see this button built into the doorframe?"

"I do now. It's so small and the same color as the frame."

"It's a LED light. If it's red, it means she's in a meeting, don't knock, go away; come back again some other day. (He laughed.) I'm a poet, and I didn't even know it. Oops, I did it again."

Lisa laughed.

"If it's black, as it is now, you may knock. If she doesn't open the door in a minute or two, it means she's not here, or she doesn't want to be disturbed."

Lisa knocked. A moment passed, then Lisa heard a click as the door unlocked itself.

"That click means, she pressed a button on the lip of her desk unlocking the door. You can go on in," Matt said with a smile.

"How does she know who knocked?"

Matt pointed to the ceiling and to another button, white this time, to match the ceiling tile.

"Camera . . . You want me to wait to take you back?"

"No thanks. I think I have it now. A left, two rights, another two lefts, and a right and you're at our office."

"Nice," Matt said, turning to leave.

The Assistant Director, Mrs. Haragan, smiled as Lisa approached her desk.

"Have a seat, Miss Clark," she said.

"Assistant Director," Lisa said nodding.

"Assistant Director? I'm sorry Miss Clark, but the Assistant Director's not here. Only me. Can I help you with something?"

"Oh, I'm sorry," Lisa replied, catching her mistake. "My group has come up with some disturbing information, and I wanted to pass it on to the Assistant Director."

"Go on, please. I'll pass it on to him."

"We have discovered a plot to make a dirty bomb. And worse, a murder."

"How do you know someone wants to make a dirty bomb?"

Lisa told the Admin the story of the government's lost bomb.

"How do you know they're making a dirty bomb?"

"I'm not sure they are. On the phone call, they mentioned

wanting to find a buyer. Most of the components of the weapon are probably useless, but the plutonium detonator isn't. The most bang for the buck would be a dirty bomb. But you haven't asked about the murder."

"I'm sorry Miss Clark. The murder of a person is horrible, but you're talking about only one person. A dirty bomb would be the death of thousands of people. More deaths than the twin towers. We must set our priorities."

"But we know the person responsible for both. Arrest him, and both cases are closed."

"How do you know he's the murderer?"

"He admits it on the phone call."

"Kinda stupid, don't you think . . . Has he found the bomb?"

"Not as of the phone call."

"What's the odds of him finding it?

"Slim to none. Mostly none."

"Then we shouldn't worry about it."

"I also said slim."

"If we arrest him now, we'll never get his buyer. No, we need to wait. Keep an eye on him but wait. If he finds the bomb, we'll let him set up the buy. At the moment of transfer, we arrest all parties."

"If he doesn't find it?"

"If he doesn't find it, we'll arrest him for the murder."

"How long do we wait?"

"I don't know Miss Clark. That's your job. Take a day or two. Work things out, and then, you tell me."

Unhappy, Lisa nodded, and silently rose to leave.

"Miss Clark, the murder of someone is unforgivable, but more so, are the deaths of thousands. Look at that photograph of the twin towers real close, and you'll see a jumper, someone who couldn't stand the heat and flames. Can you imagine what he looked like when he hit the pavement? Do you think he had an open casket? I went through this once, and I swore, never again."

"It was a sixteen-year-old girl," Lisa whispered. "I'm sure her parents would like closure."

"I'm sure they would, and they will, but it will have to wait a day or two. If they make a dirty bomb and someone sets it off, she won't be the only sixteen-year-old girl that dies. Numerous children will die, but not only them, but their parents, grandparents, aunts, uncles, brothers, sisters, and cousins will also die. Whole generations will die. No, Miss Clark, we will wait, but that doesn't mean we're going to sit on our asses and do nothing."

"What then?"

"I'll send you the name, phone number and email address of one of our agents in Savannah. His name is David Mulder. He'll be your lead in Savannah. Give him a call and bring him up to date. Keep monitoring the cell phones. Miss Clark, I want the buyer."

"And the police in Tybee? Should we inform them?"

Mrs. Haragan thought for a moment. "No. Not now. When we have to move, we'll bring them in."

"Why wait?"

"Because I don't want them getting in the way of our investigation. What they don't know, won't hurt them."

"I respectfully disagree. What they don't know, could kill them."

***

Charlotte was roasting and starting to smell overcooked. Her filthy sweaty hair clung to her head, face, and neck. Her clothes smelled sour. The chain around her ankle was rubbing the skin raw. The swelling on her cheek was starting to go down, and her left eye was slowly opening, blurry and blood red, but opening. The smell of oil and diesel in the boat's hold was overpowering and sickening. Mosquitos, flies, and gnats were buzzing her face. How did Charles Dickens' put it? *It was the worst of times.* Charlotte craved a long hot shower and shampoo. Mostly, she craved fresh air. To help, Pete had left the hatch open. But it didn't help. She knew if she ever got out, this smell would be with her the rest of her life.

"Charlotte?" Pete asked from up on the deck.

"I'm still here," she replied.

"I just wanted to let you know I'm coming down. I didn't want to interrupt you if you were going to the bathroom."

"I wish I had a bathroom."

"Okay, smartass. I meant, I didn't want to catch you taking a shit."

"Come on down."

As Pete climbed down the steps, Charlotte could see he had a bag of something and a six-pack of bottled water.

"Burgers again?" she asked, sadly.

"If that's what we're eating," he replied. "You can eat the same. It could be worse."

"Pete, I'm dying here. The vent isn't bringing in enough fresh air, and the smell is unbearable."

"So, what do you think I can do about it?"

"Let me come out on deck."

"Hell no. You'll be waving at every boat or ship that passes. You think I'm an idiot?"

"You're not an idiot. You're the only person here that cares what happens to me. Bubba would kill me in a heartbeat, and Frank has no idea what's going on."

"Charlotte, if push comes to shove, if it means you or me, I will kill you. Make no mistake about that. I'm not going to prison. Right now, you're a hostage. And Charlotte, that's the only thing keeping you alive."

Charlotte could see in his eyes and the way he said it; he didn't mean it. He wasn't a bad man. He had just gotten himself mixed up in something and was in over his head.

"What if I give you my word?"

"Your word?"

"Pete, I'm dying here."

"Eat your lunch," he said, climbing back up the ladder.

The bag contained two cheeseburgers through the garden, a small bag of Ruffles, a roll of paper towels and two rolls of toilet paper. Charlotte heard and felt the engine start up and movement of the boat. They were heading out again. Charlotte sat there eating in the dark, but tasting nothing, enjoying nothing. When she finished, she threw the trash in the murky water at her feet and laid down on the cot. It was hopeless. She wished they would find the damn bomb and be done with it. Time dragged, and with nothing to do, Charlotte fell asleep.

***

"Charlotte?"

"What Pete?" Charlotte said, sleepily.

"Did I wake you?"

"That's okay. What do you want?"

"I'm coming down . . . I talked with Bubba and Frank."

"About what?"

"You coming up on deck?"

"And?" Charlotte asked, her heart pounding.

"I can attach the chain to the top step of the ladder. That will give you enough room to move around on deck near the bow. It will also allow you to come back down here at night."

"Oh Pete, that would be wonderful." "I'm not through . . . While you're on deck, Frank will be your shadow. He will constantly be near you, watching you. If he, we, tell you to get back below deck, you will haul ass. You understand that?"

"Yes. Haul ass."

"Also, you have to ask to come up on deck. That way, we can make sure no one is near."

"Yes, Pete. I understand. Thank you. Thank you."

"I'm not finished . . . We're required to moor every night at the marina. So, when we're passing the City or coming down the river, you have to be in the hold. You will stay there until the next day when we're out at sea again. Any questions?"

"None."

Pete pulled a key out his pocket and tried it in the lock. Nothing happened.

"Wrong key," he laughed. Taking the other key, he removed

the lock. "Sit still while I chain it to the top step."

Once chained, Pete went up on deck. After a minute probably spent looking for boats, Pete yelled below. "Come on up."

Charlotte felt she had died and gone to Heaven. The breeze coming off the bow covered her in a cool spray, soaking her hair, face, and clothes. Smiling for the first time in days, she sucked in a deep breath of the salty air. Frank stood at the rail smiling.

"Feel better?" he asked.

"Oh God, yes. You have no idea."

Pete walked around the side of the cabin and came back carrying a green plastic lawn chair. Kicking trash away, he placed the chair by the hatch. "You can sit on this while on deck."

"Where's my chair?" Frank asked.

"Get your own damn chair," Pete shot back.

Chapter 23

Stephanie stood looking out the front window, watching the palm branches swaying in the gentle sea breeze, watching the hustle and bustle on Highway 80. This condo, located at the ninety-degree bend on Highway 80, allowed Stephanie a full view of the road, both west toward Savannah twenty miles away and south to the pier a mile and a half away.

Bicycles built for one or two were coming and going to the beach. Golf carts built for four, six and eight passed on their way to restaurants farther down the island, to the Tybee Pier, to the IGA or the numerous gift shops around the island.

From her vantage point, Stephanie could see the huge thirty-foot metal Great White Shark hanging on the exterior wall of the *Waves Beach Wear Surf & Gifts* shop. Couples, arm in arm, were out for a stroll. People with pooper scoopers were walking their dogs. Tybee Island is pet friendly, but only if you take care of their poop. Parents, making their way to or from their condos and the beach, were yelling at their sunburned kids, trying to keep them together or out of the street. Gulls, pelicans, crows, starlings and sparrows darted here and there, reminding Stephanie of Alfred Hitchcock's movie *The Birds*. A solitary tabby cat, pretending to be a fierce predator on the African Savanna, crouched in the shade of a palm, eyeing the birds.

An early crowd, those fierce predators of Urban America,were already gathering on the front deck at MacElwee's, waiting for the chance to grab the first table. The top of the Tybee Island lighthouse could be seen far off to her right. On their first trip down, the group had paid a visit to the lighthouse. Built in the early 1800s, the black and white tower stood over one hundred and fifty feet. For a small maintenance fee, you were allowed to climb to the top via an internal metal staircase.

From there, a beautiful panoramic view of the beach, from the Savannah River down to the pier, awaited. FJ bitched and complained all the way to the top about the steps not being made for little people.

"They're back," Stephanie said over her shoulder.

"About time," Margaret whispered, rising from the sofa, going toward the kitchen.

An hour ago, Mike, FJ and Ray took the van over to the police station. Mike and Ray wanted to see if there were any breaks in Charlotte's case. FJ was worried about Charlotte as well, but he also wanted to see officer Grace.

"How'd it go?" Stephanie asked as soon as the three entered the room.

"I almost ran over a damn yellow cat," Mike answered, going to the fridge.

"Officer Grace is still a goddess," FJ sighed flopping down on the sofa.

"Nothing new I'm afraid," Ray stated flatly, taking a bottle of water offered by Mike.

"What are we going to do now?" Stephanie asked.

"I just ordered pizza from *Lighthouse Pizza*," Margaret said, walking back in from the kitchen. "They'll be here in forty-five minutes to an hour."

"That's good," Stephanie stated. "But what I meant was what are we going to do about Charlotte? We can't just sit here, doing nothing."

"You're right. I think it's time we try out Mike's stupid plan," Ray commented, taking a sip of water.

"Stupid?" Mike exclaimed.

***

Mike, with FJ, walked through the automatic doors at *T S Chu*

Department Store.

"Are you sure you need a knife?" Mike asked.

"If Charlotte is on their boat, they would have her tied up."

"And one of the knives in the kitchen wouldn't work?"

"They're so dull; they couldn't cut through a marshmallow."

"You mean 'cut through soft butter'?"

"No, 'Cut through soft butter' is so cliché . . . I wonder where they keep their knives?"

"Let's find somebody to ask," Mike replied, looking around.

"Oh my God," FJ exclaimed, pointing and staring at a girl behind a counter.

The teenager, dressed in black, with black spiked hair, wide black eyeliner, black lips, and bare arms completely covered in black tattoos, stood behind a cash register filing her black fingernails.

"Pardon me Miss, but could you tell me where the knives are located?" Mike asked.

"Kitchen or hunting?" she replied, staring at FJ.

"Kitchen or hunting?" Mike asked FJ.

"Hunting," FJ replied, staring back at the girl.

"The back of the store," she said, not taking her eyes off FJ.

"Thanks," FJ said as they walked away, not taking his eyes off the girl.

"That was kind of awkward, don't you think?" Mike asked when they were out of hearing range.

"I get that all the time," FJ replied.

"I was talking about you."

They found the back of the store easy enough, but it took a few minutes to find the case containing knives. A portly baldheaded man, with his back to them, was arranging boxes of shotgun shells on a shelf behind the case. He had to stretch to place the boxes on the shelf, so much so, his butt crack was climbing out of his pants.

Should have been a plumber, FJ thought.

"Excuse me," Mike said, getting the man's attention.

"What can I do for you and your son?" the man asked turning to them. "Oh my," he exclaimed, noticing FJ's beard. "I'm sorry Sir. But -"

"It's okay," FJ assured him. "Happens all the time. But I'll be damned if I'm his kid."

"What can I do for you gentlemen?"

"I'm looking for a knife," FJ replied, peering in the case.

"Okay. What type of knife do you want? A folding pocketknife or one with a fixed blade?" the man asked bending over, unlocking the case.

"Fixed blade," FJ replied.

"Length of the blade?"

"Four to six inches would be fine."

"That's a good place to start. Here are a few examples. You have here a Drop Point knife. This is a Trailing Point. There's the Straight Back, Spear Point, Straight Edge, and finally my favorite, the Clip Point. Do any of these interest you?"

"I like the Drop Point. It looks like it has a good balance."

"Good choice. Here, see how it feels in your hand."

FJ took the knife and balanced it across his pointer finger.

"Why are you doing that?" the man asked.

"That's the sweet spot. It lets me know if the knife is blade heavy or grip heavy."

Taking the knife, he flipped it, catching it blade first. Flipping it again, he caught it grip first. He did this several times, speeding up with each flip.

"That's pretty impressive," the portly man commented.

"I used to be a knife thrower in my other life."

The man made a face of disbelief. "No, he's telling the truth," Mike assured him. "Well, FJ, what do you think?"

"It does have good balance. Thin. Not too much weight," FJ said, satisfied. "I'll take it."

"Great. Do you want a belt sheath to go with it?" the man behind the counter asked.

"Sure . . . do I need to pay up front or here?"

"It doesn't matter. You can pay here if you want."

As Mike and FJ neared the exit, the Gothic girl at the front counter stopped them with a wave of her hand.

"Excuse me. But I just realized who you were Mr. Dinklage.

Could I have your autograph?"

FJ smiled, nodded his head and turned toward her. Mike rolled his eyes. Reaching down, Mike took FJ by the collar and shoved him through the automatic door.

***

Once today, Charlotte was forced to duck below deck because of an oncoming boat. It turned out, it was only a shrimper coming out of Blue River into the Sound. It was making its way home, home to a warm supper, home to a loving family. Tears built up in Charlotte's eyes as she watched it through the dirty porthole. *Will I ever get home?* Her mood changed. One moment sadness, the next anger. *I don't care what it takes; I will get home.*

"You can come up," Pete said from the hatch opening.

"You feeling better?" He asked when Charlotte had joined him on the deck.

"A little better, yes, thank you," Charlotte replied. "My eye is almost open but still blurry. My head and cheek still hurt like hell."

Pete noticed the swelling on her cheek was going down, but the wound still oozed. It was going to leave a nasty scar if she didn't have it looked at soon. The left side of her face, from the eye to the jaw, was black and blue, mostly black. The white of the eye was still blood red.

Damn you Bubba, he thought.

"It's getting late. So, we're calling it quits for today, and we'll be heading back to the marina. Once we get close to the City, you will have to go below for the night. I'll have Frank run into Savannah and get us KFC for supper. Would you like something besides water to drink? Maybe a beer?"

"Water will be fine. As far as beer, I only like the first cold sip out of a bottle. After that, it doesn't taste good to me. Funny, huh?" Pete smiled and nodded his head.

"Pete," Bubba yelled from the walkway above them. "A ship's coming in from the ocean. She'd better get below."

Pete nodded and pointed to the open hatch. "Go with her

Frank. Charlotte, not a sound."

As the boat got closer, Peter could see it was shiny white with red stripes.

"It's the Coast Guard," he yelled up to Bubba, who was standing in the wheelhouse door. "You might as well shut her down and wait."

"How do you know she's coming to see us?"

"Just a gut feeling."

Fifteen minutes later the utter pulled up beside the drifting trawler.

"How you boys doing?" the same captain from the other day asked.

"Fine. We're calling it quits for today."

"You had any luck finding the bomb?"

"Not yet, but we're not giving up, at least until Friday."

"What happens on Friday?"

"Our rental runs out." The captain laughed, scanning the horizon. "You haven't seen the oyster boat lately, have you?"

"Not lately. She stopped by the other day, and we talked for a while. I haven't seen them since. Why?"

"It appears she's gone missing."

"You need help looking for her?"

"No, that's okay. She probably got tangled up in the salt marsh. It wouldn't be the first time. It is strange, however."

"How so?"

"He has a short wave and a cell phone. Why hasn't he called for help if he's stuck?"

"Maybe his short wave is broke, and he has no cell phone coverage."

"Could be. But both things going out at the same time? I doubt it. Besides, you see that short pole over there sticking out of the sawgrass? That's a cell phone tower. They don't have to be tall around here, only a couple of feet above the grass. They're all along the coast and the major rivers. It allows the shrimpers to call home, letting the family know when they're coming in."

"Good to know."

"We'll keep an eye out for them. If you do see them, have them phone home."

"Just like E.T.," Pete laughed, getting the joke.

As the cutter entered Blue River, Pete hollered down the hatch opening. "You can come on up now."

"You think they know something?" Frank asked, placing his hands on the rail, making sure he didn't place them in bird crap.

"How could they?" Pete asked in return. "As much as we're out in the Sound, we would have seen them searching for the boat over there. No, they're still looking inland."

"And when they get tired of looking inland?"

"We'd best be gone."

Charlotte took her seat, leaned back and closed her eyes. The sun was starting to sink in the sea of grass, and the temperature had fallen a few degrees. She sat there thinking about Sara and her beautiful smile. She sat there thinking about the two men in the oyster boat. Was she really responsible for their deaths, as Pete said? It's true; if she had kept silent, they would be alive today. If she had kept silent, they wouldn't be lying dead on the bottom of the ocean. The thought made her angry.

No Damnit. If Bubba hadn't killed Sara, the two men would be alive today. If Bubba and Pete hadn't taken me hostage, they'd be alive today. If the three of them hadn't taken me hostage, I'd had no reason to try and escape, and they'd be alive today. No, I didn't kill them.

"You think we'll be moored before it gets dark?" she asked through closed eyes.

"We should make it fine," Pete answered. "Frank, I'm going up to have a word with Bubba. Keep an eye on her."

"Will do, Pete."

Charlotte sat there, letting the breeze blow through her hair, trying to forget about Sara, trying to forget about the two men entombed in their boat. How long does it take a boat to rot and fall apart? Someday, would pieces of the boat float to the surface? And, what are the odds of someone discovering them? What are the odds of someone, someday, finding her lifeless body?

Bubba will never let me go alive, no matter how much Pete's against killing me. I must do something, something very soon. If Pete was telling the truth, their rental runs out Friday. That's only six days from now.

"You guys need to clean up this pigsty," she commented, making conversation to take her mind off of death.

"Why?" Frank asked.

"I don't know why. It would give you something to do. It would help the smell. It would keep us from getting some infectious disease. Frank, at night I think I hear rats in the dark."

Frank snickered.

"Frank, why are you here? You're not like Pete or Bubba. You're a good man."

"Miss Charlotte, I'm sorry you're here, and I'm sorry Bubba did that to you. But Pete and Bubba are my friends. My only friends. Miss Charlotte, I don't know if you've noticed, but I'm a little slow. Kids used to laugh at me; made fun of me; called me an idiot and worse. Pete and Bubba never laughed or called me names. And no one laughs at me when they're around . . . I'm glad Pete told me to watch out for you. I'll never harm you Miss Charlotte, and if you need anything, you just let me know."

"Thank you, Frank. I believe you when you say you'll never hurt me. I really do. I'll never make fun of you. You and I could be friends. (Frank smiled.) Frank, you just said if I need anything, I should ask you."

"Yes, Ma'am, I did. Is there something you want?"

"Yes. You can help me escape."

"Anything but that, Miss Charlotte," Frank laughed. "Anything but that."

"Frank, you know you're never going to find the bomb."

"Why do you say that?"

"Because it doesn't exist."

"You don't know that," he spat, turning his back to her. "You leave all that to Bubba and Pete. You . . . You just sit there and keep your mouth shut."

Well, that went well. Not. I guess that conversation's over, Charlotte thought, looking around.

The deck was cluttered with trash from some bygone day; bird poop, empty overturned rusty fuel barrels, half empty cans of grease used to lubricate pulleys and gears, broken beer bottles and crushed beer cans, rolls of rusting bailing wire, a dead rat or two, tattered tarps, old ripped and torn fishing nets, rings of rotting ropes, and a few piles of things Charlotte couldn't identify. Charlotte looked out to sea and the surrounding coastline. The white caps were now sprinkled with orange and red from the setting sun. *What a beautiful setting,* she thought. *Beautiful, if I wasn't a prisoner.* Suddenly her good eye opened wide. Looking down at her ankle and the chain entrapping it, she noticed a half empty can of grease used to lubricate gears lying beneath her chair.

Chapter 24

Early morning and the five slowly made their way over the Lazaretto Creek Bridge, peering down at the rusty trawler still moored at dock side.

"What do you see?" Mike asked trying to see while driving.

"Keep your eyes on the road," Stephanie replied. "Lord knows, we don't need to have an accident."

"The big black man is standing beside the wheelhouse door, either looking at his watch or updating his Facebook account," Margaret said, "The truck is gone."

"I bet one of the guys is in the hold with Charlotte," FJ said, kneeling on his knees to see, "and the other is getting breakfast."

"I bet you're right," Mike agreed. "Because, here comes their truck. Looks like one person in the cab. He should be passing us any second."

The Nissan passed at the crown of the bridge.

"Who was it?" Stephanie asked from the backseat.

"Pete, I think," Ray replied. "Mike, turn into the boat-ramp road at the foot of the bridge and let's head to the opposite side of the river. We should be able to watch them without being seen."

The side road ended at a concrete walkway with a handrail, running parallel to the riverbank. Mike parked the van in a grove of palm trees hoping they were out of sight of anyone aboard the trawler. Several early morning fishermen were gathered at the railing with their lines already cast in the murky water. Gulls were circling overhead waiting for anything playing on the surface. A dolphin broke the surface of the creek down by the *Grille*.

***

Bubba stared at the clock on his cell phone. 7:53 a.m. "Come on," he hissed. Impatient, he scanned the surrounding area. Nothing but a couple of fishermen on the other bank, but they've been coming here every day since they rented the boat. No worries. A van just pulled into the palm grove, out of sight, or so they thought. "Probably a couple of teenagers getting it on," he laughed, looking at his watch again. 7:56 a.m. "God this is taking forever." The sound of gravel being crushed turned his attention to the parking lot. It was Pete.

"About time," he said as Pete came aboard.

"The line was long at Burger King. You make the call already?"

"It's not eight o'clock."

"Are you sure?"

Bubba looked at his watch, 8:01 a.m. "Shit," he exclaimed. Dialing the number, he waited.

Bubba wiped the sweat growing on his forehead with the back of his free hand.

"Well?" Pete asked.

Bubba stepped out on the walkway, raising his hand for Pete to be quiet. "Only a minute," he said to Wally on the other end of the line. "Pete distracted me."

Pete pitched him a finger, threw him a bag of sausage biscuits and went below.

"No problem. You got the buyer?" Bubba asked. Pause. Bubba pitched a finger into the air.

"We'll find it today or tomorrow. We've searched the whole damn coastline. Now we're going into the marsh. Miles uncovered a lot of coastline and marsh, and it just takes time." Pause. "That was the name of the hurricane that came through Tybee a few weeks ago." Pause. "Oh, we'll find it alright, don't worry."

Pause. Bubba double pitched a finger into the air. "Wally, I swear to God, we'll find it. Have you got a buyer?" Pause. "That's great, Wally. We'll find it, today or maybe tomorrow."

Pause. "Wally, I can taste it. It's out there waiting for us."

Bubba looked at his cell phone. The line was dead. Bubba pitched a finger at his phone. "You better hope so," he said, mocking Wally, who had just hung up on him.

"How'd it go?" Pete asked, startling Bubba.

"Good, really good. Wally may have a buyer, but we have to find the bomb . . . Today or tomorrow."

"Today or tomorrow? Jesus, Bubba, people have been looking for the damn thing for over fifty years. You going to go out there and say, 'Hey, Mr. Bomb, would you let me find you?'"

"Don't turn on me too, Pete. We'll find it."

Pete shook his head and left the wheelhouse. Bubba pitched him a finger.

"We'll find it," Bubba said to himself, as he started the engine. "We'll find it."

***

"They weren't here very long," FJ said, as the trawler pulled away from the dock.

"Did you notice how the black man was acting while he was on the phone?" Margaret asked.

"He didn't seem too happy," Ray answered. "You notice how many times he gave somebody the bird?"

"Maybe he was talking to his mother," FJ commented.

"Talking to his mother?" Stephanie exclaimed. "You would give your mother a finger?"

"Sure. She abandoned me, you know . . . What do we do now?"

"We'll come back this afternoon, and do some fishing," Ray answered.

"Fishing?" Mike asked.

"It was your plan."

"I never said anything about fishing."

Chapter 25

"Hot off the presses," Matt exclaimed, looking at his monitor.

"Hot off the presses?" Lisa asked.

"Since we've added additional search phrases and locations, I just got a hit off the words – Tybee and bomb."

"Then play it, by all means," Harry said, as he and Glenda joined them.

Speaker 1: "You're late."

"That's Wally," Harry commented.

"Shssss," Lisa whispered.

Speaker 2: "Only a minute. Pete distracted me."

Speaker 1: "Don't let it happen again."

Speaker 2: "No problem. You got the buyer?"

Speaker 1: "You found the bomb?"

Speaker 2: "We'll find it today or tomorrow. We've searched the whole damn coastline. Now we're going into the marsh. Miles uncovered a lot of coastline and marsh, and it just takes time."

Speaker 1: "Miles?"

Speaker 2: "That was the name of the hurricane that came through Tybee a few weeks ago."

Speaker 1: "That still doesn't mean you're going to find the bomb."

Speaker 2: "Oh, we'll find it alright, don't worry."

Speaker 1: "You're the one who'd better worry if you don't find it."

Speaker 2: "Wally, I swear to God, we'll find it. Have you got a buyer?"

Speaker 1: "I'm waiting on a call. Should hear from him today around noon, our time. He'll come through with the money, if you come through with the bomb. As soon as I'm done with the buyer, I'll give you a call. Bubba, you better come through with the bomb."

Speaker 2: "That's great, Wally. We'll find it, today or maybe tomorrow."

Speaker 1: "Today would be better."

Speaker 2: "Wally, I can taste it. It's out there waiting for us."

Speaker 1: "You better hope so."

[End of Transmission]

"Well?" Lisa asked.

"Did you catch, 'you better hope so' at the end of the conversation?" Glenda asked.

"I did. Bubba's ass is grass if he doesn't come through," Lisa answered. "Harry, did you hear anything new?"

"Same two of course," Harry answered. "Both Southern.

I listened to the earlier tape over and over again. I'm convinced Wally isn't from the Deep South, more like the Atlanta area."

"Harry's right about Wally," Matt said. "He's using a burner phone, so I can't tell you his street number, but I can tie down the city, and it is Atlanta. Bubba is still on Tybee Island."

"To bring everyone up to date," Harry started, "I did some checking from our end . . . About the bomb. I was able to uncover a few classified documents. The bomb was indeed lost near Tybee Island, and the government did cover up the fact the trigger was attached to the bomb. So if these men do find the bomb, it could end up in the hands of some really bad people."

"All that's well and good, but where does that leave us?" Glenda asked.

"Matt, if you know when somebody's going to call, could you listen for it?" Lisa asked.

"If I knew the number?"

"What if you only knew the city?"

"I doubt it. Why?"

"Wally said he was getting a call from the buyer at noon."

"He also said the buyer wasn't in their time zone," Harry added.

"You want me to listen to all the phone calls incoming to Atlanta, at noon today."

"Yes. Piece of cake, right?"

Matt, leaned back in his chair with his wrists pressed against his forehead, thinking.

"Well?" Lisa asked after a few minutes.

"It might be done . . . If,"

"If what?"

"You had three hundred agents monitoring three hundred different incoming channels at the same time."

"You're asking for a lot," Lisa said, walking back to her desk.

"So are you, Boss. But, given time, I could come up with an algorithm that might help."

"How much time would it take?"

"Wally said he was getting the call at noon, Atlanta time. I can have the code ready by eleven, eleven thirty, Atlanta time. But, can you get three hundred agents?"

"We're talking about a dirty bomb, America's worst nightmare. I think the Assistant Director can loan me three hundred agents from, say, eleven thirty to twelve fifteen. I'll go and talk to her face to face. It's always better that way."

Lisa paused at the door. "By the way, we have a small team from Savannah already on Tybee. They're fishing where Bubba's boat is moored."

"Fishing," Matt exclaimed. "Must be nice. Why couldn't I have gotten that job?"

***

Charlotte sat sipping her coffee, watching the horizon, watching Frank, and stealing glances at the grease can beneath her chair. How could she get her hands on the can without Frank seeing her? And if she did, what would she then do with it? She couldn't hide it. She wouldn't have much time either. Her plan: Apply grease to her ankle and foot, enough to slip her foot out.

Okay, you're free, now what? She thought.

Jump overboard and swim away, hoping Pete would let her escape. *How likely is that?* Not very. *When should I do it?* Somehow Frank must be distracted, and they must be close to shore. Charlotte could swim, but she wasn't a long-distance swimmer. *Where would I swim?* Anywhere but here. *This is crazy as hell.* The only apparent means of escape was within arm's length. She couldn't pass it by.

"How are you doing today?" Pete asked coming around the Crew's quarters.

"The same as always," Charlotte replied.

"Frank, why don't you take a break? I'll keep an eye on Charlotte."

"Thanks, Pete. My bladder is screaming at me."

"Why didn't you holler?"

"I didn't want to bother you or Bubba." Pete shook his head.

"Frank, Frank, what are we going to do with you? Go take

your piss."

"I won't be gone long."

"You know he doesn't belong here," Charlotte said when Frank was out of sight.

"We're his friends," Pete replied.

"What has that got to do with anything? Pete, he still doesn't belong here. He doesn't understand how serious all this is. When you're caught, and you will be, he'll be going to prison with you and Bubba. You want that?"

"We won't be caught."

"Everyone gets caught."

"Not this time."

"And what happens to me?"

Pete stared at her for a long time. "We'll see."

"That's not what I want to hear."

"I know what you want to hear, and damnit Charlotte, we'll see."

You're giving in to Bubba, Charlotte thought. *You know damn well he wants me dead. Now I know, if I want to live, it's going to be up to me.*

"You married?" Pete asked, changing the subject and breaking the intense silence.

"Widowed."

"Sorry about that."

"Why? Did Bubba have something to do with it?"

Pete shook his head and turned to leave.

"Bitch," he whispered to himself.

"But we have two boys," Charlotte shot in, causing Pete to stop and turn around. "One lives in Louisville and has two kids. The other son lives in Owensboro, and also has two kids."

"I've heard of Louisville and Lexington. They play pretty good college basketball there. But I've never heard of Owensboro."

"Owensboro, Kentucky, it's on the Ohio River, about one hundred miles southwest of Louisville . . . I bet they're worried about me right now. Wondering if I'm dead."

"Knock it off Charlotte."

It was Charlotte that broke the silence this time.

"I bet my friends are worried."

"Your friends? Oh, you mean the ones staying in the blue condo with you. How do you know them? Relatives or something?"

"No, they're not relatives, just friends, close friends. We've known each other for years. We all go to church together. All except FJ."

"FJ?"

"The little person. (Pete nodded his head.) He never goes to church, except when he's down here with us. You should hear the men picking on each other."

"What do you mean?"

"Of course, FJ is little. So, there's a lot of 'little jokes.' Mike is missing two fingers on his left hand, so there are 'handicap jokes.' Ray is the oldest, so there are a lot of 'old man jokes.' Ray is also hard of hearing, so the other two mouth their words when talking to him. Drives Ray crazy."

"That sounds mean to me."

"It would be if they weren't close friends. Hell, they love each other like brothers, and you better bet, no one else can make fun of any one of them if they're around. And you better not be making fun of a stranger, no matter how physically challenged. They'd be all over you."

"Sounds like a bunch of good guys."

"They're the best. And there's Margaret and Stephanie. You can't find any better friends than them. They'd do anything, for anyone, if need be. They were with me when my mother died. We were all with Margaret when her father died. All of us are close. That's why they're worried."

"Within our group, we have twelve kids, twenty grandkids, and three great-grandkids. Mike and Stephanie's son, just last week, remarried. They're Catholic, and the bride wants five kids."

"Charlotte."

"What?"

"Stop it."

"Stop what, Pete?"

"Stop trying to get in my head. Stop trying to make me feel guilty by telling me about your families. It won't work. Yes, you're in a shitty situation and I'm sorry about that, but there's nothing I can do about it now."

"Hi guys," Frank said, joining them.

"Feeling better?" Charlotte asked.

"Yes, Miss Charlotte. Better."

"Pete," Bubba called from upstairs. "I need your help. I'm ready to drop the metal detector in."

"On my way," Pete hollered back. "Keep a close eye on her Frank."

"As always."

***

Lisa and her team, with earphones on, were scanning three hundred channels of phone conversations. When a call came into Atlanta, Matt's algorithm would pick up and listen for keywords. If all factors fell into place, the call was directed to an agent. Three hundred other agents were also listening. Listening is not a good word. It was more like waiting or ease dropping in real time. Lisa looked at her watch, 11:58 Atlanta time. *I hope he's punctual.*

Noon came and went, 12:03. Suddenly, a button on Lisa's phone lit up.

"Hello," Lisa said. "Great."

Lisa pressed an auxiliary button and listened. Everyone's face was glued to her. "Oops," Lisa said, pressing the speaker button.

Speaker 1: ". . . in the middle of something."

Speaker 2: "That's fine. Well?"

Speaker 1: "I have someone interested in your . . . Item. Very interested."

Speaker 2: "How interested?"

161

Speaker 1: "Interested to the tune of fifteen million."

Speaker 2: "For me?"

Speaker 1: "That's your cut, yours and your friends. Take it or leave it."

Speaker 2: "It's a deal. How do we make delivery?"

Speaker 1:"You have the item already?"

Speaker 2: "No. But my guys say, today or tomorrow."

Speaker 1: "I have a contact in Savannah. He delivers certain items to me from America a couple of times a year. I don't see how this item would make a difference. I'll send him a text and get back with you. Make sure you have the item. I don't like getting screwed if you know what I mean."

[Line dropped.]

Lisa looked in Matt's direction.

"Before you ask," Matt stated. "No, I can't trap his text message without knowing a time."

"Okay then. Back to the present, what do you guys make of the phone call?"

"Looks like we have a buyer?" Glenda said.

"To the tune of fifteen million," Matt added.

"That's not a lot of money for a hydrogen bomb. I wouldn't take less than a hundred million," Lisa stated. "I bet Wally won't tell Bubba and Pete this . . . Harry, what can you tell us about the caller?"

"Well, we all know Wally's voice by now. The other guy is European, Irish by his accent."

"Why not Scottish?"

"When you listen to the two, Irish and Scottish, you could mistake the accents as being the same. They have similarities, but these accents greatly differ from each other. Let me tell you; it's taken me years of practice to tell the difference. If you listen closely, you'll be able to notice the differences between the two. The pronunciation of the words, especially the vowels and some consonants, and the intonation of the way the accents are spoken differ from each other."

"If you say so," Lisa said.

"The man was Irish. I'd start with that."

"I ran his number, and it's a burn phone."

"Can you tell where he's calling from? What city?"

"No. I can't even tell you which country. The call was routed through a dozen servers, in several countries, before reaching Atlanta," Matt commented. "It could have originated anywhere."

"Okay. If we can't catch him there, maybe we can get his people here, and they can point us in his direction. He says he has a contact in Savannah, and if this contact is sending him 'things,' it would be through the Port of Savannah. All we need to do is discover which ship is bound for Ireland."

"What if there is more than one ship bound for Ireland?" Glenda asked.

"Why are you making it difficult for us?" Lisa smiled. "I'll get our agents in Savannah to start asking about ships that fly the Irish flag or are bound for Ireland. We can start there. We also need to lock down Bubba's location. I want to move on them the second they try to make the exchange."

Chapter 26

From the Wilmington River, the rust-bucket took a hard turn to port entering the smaller Skidaway River. Bubba manned the wheel; Pete manned the metal detector.

"You know these waters aren't very deep," Pete said, watching the depth gauge bounce up and down like a yoyo. "If we're here at low tide, we'll find ourselves belly up in mud."

"Yeah, but as the tide comes back, we'll unstick. Happens all the time around here. You see expensive boats resting in the mud at all the private docks, and the owners don't get upset. It's a way of life in these parts, and they're used to it."

"Savannah is only five or six miles west of here, across the marsh grass," Pete said, cupping his eyes, trying to make out any buildings in the far distance.

"I know. I bet no one ever searched this section of the marsh," Bubba replied. "I feel good about this, Pete. This is going to be a special day."

By late afternoon, it had become a long and uneventful day. The beating sun roasted Pete and Bubba in the wheelhouse, and Frank and Charlotte weren't doing much better. Charlotte moved her chair around into the shade of the crew's quarters, but stayed within easy reach of the grease can, praying she would get the chance to use it. Frank removed his shirt hoping that would help; it didn't.

Bubba made several passes up and down the river, but not that first damn ping off the metal detector. It was getting late in the day and time was running out according to Wally. Only one more day to find the bomb, he had said.

"Where to now?" Pete asked.

"We'll try that ditch over there," Bubba said, pointing. "It's wide enough to back the boat into."

"As long as we don't get stuck."

"I'll keep an eye on the depth. You keep an ear on the detector."

As soon as the trawler backed into the narrow ditch, the metal detector went crazy.

"Oh my God," Pete exclaimed, as Bubba shutdown the engine.

"What's that noise?" Frank asked, looking up toward the wheelhouse. To Charlotte, it was now or never.

"That has to be the metal detector," Charlotte answered. "I bet they found it. You should go check."

"I was told to stay with you."

"Look around you, Frank. Where am I going? Really? And how would I get there? I'm chained you know. Aren't you dying to know what they found?"

"Damn straight," Frank exclaimed, heading off for the stairs.

Charlotte grabbed the grease can and sat down. She knew she didn't have long. Pete will send Frank back down the moment he saw him.

***

"That's it," Bubba said joyfully, staring at the screen. "It has to be."

"I'm not sure," Pete said. "Looks like three separate things."

"It must have broken up on impact. But that doesn't matter; it's still worth a fortune. That's it alright. God, we're going to be rich."

"You going to call Wally and let him know?" Frank asked, standing behind them.

"Damn straight I am," Bubba replied, reaching for his cell phone.

"Frank, what are you doing up here?" Pete exclaimed.

A splash from the bow stopped Frank from answering. Turning, the three ran out onto the upper catwalk.

"There," Frank yelled, pointing to a spot several yards ahead of the boat. "It's Miss Charlotte."

Charlotte's arms sliced through the muddy water. Twenty yards separated the boat from the marsh line, the sea of grass, and freedom, and Charlotte was halfway there.

"Damnit Frank," Pete hissed. "You let her get away. You go get her."

"In that?" Frank shrieked, pointing at the muddy water.

"In that."

When Frank entered the water, Charlotte had just disappeared into the sawgrass. She instantly was hit by a swarm of flying bugs. She found the going harder than she thought it would be. Sawgrass gets its name from its long, narrow, grass-like leaves having sharp, often serrated, saw-tooth-like margins. The blades tore at Charlotte's hands, arms, face, and clothes, painfully slowing her down. The plant tops stood a good three feet out of the water, and with Charlotte sinking almost up to her waist in the water and mud, the grass was completely over Charlotte's head. She plowed through spider webs, getting them in her hair and mouth. She fought her way through the dense forest of grass, completely lost. She had no idea where she was going, or if she was going in the correct direction. She just wanted to get away. For all she knew, she could be running in a circle. It didn't take long before her lungs were near bursting from the effort, and her legs aching from fighting their way through the knee-to-waist-deep soupy sucky mud. She had to stop if only for a moment, to catch her breath. Something small and gray slithered off to her left, causing her skin to crawl. *Snakes. God how I hate snakes.*

The sound of grass being crushed by something heavy, came from behind her. There was no time to rest.

Has to be one of the men coming after me, she thought.

Then the sound of grass being crushed came somewhere slightly ahead of her, off to the right.

Two of them. They're trying to trap me in the middle.

As hard as she could, she tried to force her legs to move, but it was no use. Charlotte's legs were getting weaker just standing there, and her breathing was becoming more labored. She'd had enough.

Pete would chew her out, no doubt, but she'd be out of this leafy sea of Hell.

I give up.

Something hissed off to her right, something large like a giant snake. Was it a python? Charlotte once saw a report on *Fox and Friends*, and they said that Burmese pythons were native to Southeast Asia, but had established a breeding population in South Florida. Although Burmese pythons were first sighted in Everglades National Park in the 1980s, they were not officially recognized as a reproducing population until 2000. The simple reason snakes from Asia were now making babies in Florida – private collectors had released them when they became too large and unmanageable, or they escaped from zoos and pet shops when tornados or hurricanes passed through. Had they made it all the way up here? Stealing a glance out of the corner of her eye, she saw something slide through the grass and disappear. Only for a moment did she see it. It looked like a huge muscular flat tail covered with bony plates. Turning back to the first sound, her legs found new strength. Pushing blades of grass out of the way with bloody hands, she plowed through the muck. She heard grass parting behind her which helped increased her speed.

Pushing aside a green wall of saw-toothed blades, she came face to face with Frank, almost running him over.

"Run," she gasped, as she passed him. "Run, or you're dead."

"What the hell are you talking about," Frank asked standing there, watching as Charlotte disappeared in the weeds.

"Alligator," he heard coming from the spot where Charlotte had disappeared.

"Oh, shit," he hissed.

Charlotte broke from the grassy plain into the river, right in front of the boat. Safety was floating thirty yards away. At that moment, it was the most beautiful thing she had ever seen. Pete and Bubba were standing on the main deck waving at her.

"Come on Charlotte," Pete yelled, laughing. "You're wasting our time with all this foolishness."

"Get your ass over here, bitch," Bubba screamed. It was when

Charlotte was halfway to the boat; Frank popped out of the weeds. "Good job Frank," Pete yelled.

Taking the grappling-pole, Pete lowered one end into the water.

"Take hold," he said to Charlotte as she neared. "I'll pull you up and grab your arm."

"Holy shit," Bubba exclaimed, pointing

Pete took his eyes off Charlotte and looked in Frank's direction. Frank was less than halfway to the boat, swimming hard, and coming out of the sawgrass was a monster. Pete remembered reading a newspaper article about a record-breaking alligator captured on Lake Seminole in southern Georgia. It measured thirteen feet, ten inches and weighed six-hundred twenty pounds. It was the largest gator ever caught in the state. This monster made that one look like a minnow. It had to be over fifteen feet in length and probably weighed over a thousand pounds, with a head eighteen inches wide and three feet long. With its eighty teeth, it could easily crush a turtle shell, but something small as that would probably be swallowed whole. If need be, it will use its sharp teeth to seize and hold its prey, while shaking it into smaller pieces. If its prey was very large, like a deer or a human, the gator would bite and then spin on the long axis of its body, tearing off easy to swallow pieces.

"Damnit Frank, swim faster," Pete screamed, through cupped hands. "Come on Frank; you can do it. Don't look back, just swim."

Pete pulled Charlotte from the water, and she collapsed onto the deck. She was covered in blood and mud. She sat there silently crying. Turning back to Frank, Pete lowered the pole again into the water.

"Come on Frank. You're halfway home," he yelled. "You're going to make it, Buddy. Just, come on." Pete could see Frank's arms were slowing down. He was getting tired. The monster lazily swam toward Frank; its tail swinging left then right. "Damnit, Frank. Move your ass."

Shots rang out, making Pete and Charlotte jump. Dozens

of points of water splashed and played around the alligator, and it slowly sank into the murky brown water.

"I got it," Bubba exclaimed, holding a smoking AK-47. "Filled that son-of-a-bitch full of holes."

"You think so? What if you're wrong? God Damnit Frank, get a move on," Pete screamed.

Pete could see the determination in Frank's face. The boy wasn't giving up.

"That's the way," Pete screamed.

Suddenly, Frank's body jerked backward and slid beneath the murky water without a sound, without a scream. One moment Frank was there, the next, gone. Pete, Bubba, and Charlotte stood there shell-shocked. The water started churning, throwing up mud and bottom vegetation, turning the water brown and red, bloody red.

For the longest time, the three stood there staring at the surface of the water, which was calm now, with only an occasional bubble popping to the surface.

"Maybe it turned him loose somewhere upstream, maybe downstream," Bubba said, searching the shoreline.

Pete turned to Charlotte with his eyes full of hate. "No Bubba, it didn't turn him loose. It drown him and will probably stash him somewhere under a log, saving him for later. That's what they do. It will guard him like a trophy and eat him at its leisure. But the gator wouldn't be the only one that benefits; other small marine creatures will feed on Frank. Bit by bit, Frank's flesh will be picked and torn apart. Soon, there would be nothing left but a skeleton."

"I'm so sorry," Charlotte cried.

"What?" Pete hissed. "No, it's not my fault Pete. Or, if it weren't for this or that, he'd still be alive. Charlotte, I'll overlook the other three deaths, but Frank's blood is on your head."

"Pete, you know, as well as I, if you -"

"Shut up Charlotte. Shut the fuck up." Pete pulled a folding knife from his pocket, opened it, and walked toward Charlotte. Charlotte slowly backed away, with both hands raised in defeat.

"Please, Pete," she pleaded. "Don't."

"Shut up Charlotte and take off your tank top."

"What?"

"I said, take off your damn tank-top. Look at your legs."

Charlotte stole a glance at her right leg; attached to it were a dozen worm-like things. Her left leg had just as many.

"Oh my God, what are they?"

"Leeches."

"Oh shit," Charlotte whispered.

Pete went on, "The swamp is full of them. There's probably that many beneath your tank top. So, take it off so I can get to them."

"What are you going to do with that knife?"

"I'm going to use it to scrape off the leeches. It won't hurt."

It turned out; there were only eight leeches attached to her back and stomach. Where each leech had attached itself, was a tiny circular hole oozing blood.

Pete walked over to the bow of the boat to be alone. He stood there scanning the river, while Bubba kept his eye on Charlotte.

What am I going to tell his folks? He didn't deserve to die like that. Who does? What am I going to do with Charlotte? I can't keep an eye on her and help Bubba at the same time. She'll just slip the chain off again. Pete spun back to Charlotte. *Maybe, just maybe, she won't.*

Pete shook his head and returned. "Come with me, Charlotte."

"You going to kill her now?" Bubba asked. "Damn late, if you ask me. If you had killed her the other day, Frank would still be alive. I told you to be rid of her, but no, you didn't have the balls to do it."

"Shut up, Bubba."

"I kicked your ass the other day. Don't think I still won't."

"Bubba, we still need her."

"Why?"

"Because our situation is falling apart. The way this is going, we're sure as shit going to be needing a hostage . . . Come with me, Charlotte."

On wobbly legs, Charlotte followed Pete around the crew

quarters. Bubba followed close behind wondering what Pete was up to. Reaching down, Pete picked the grease covered end of the chain.

"Smart, Charlotte," he said, noticing the grease can lying nearby. "Pretty smart. I should have thought of it. If I had, then Frank would still be alive. You see, it's just as much my fault as yours that he's dead. Well, it won't happen again." Removing the lock, Pete placed the chain around Charlotte's neck. Pulling it tight, he replaced the lock.

"You won't slip out of this," he said, stepping back, looking at his handiwork. Picking up the can of grease Charlotte used to free herself, he handed it to her. "Here you go, Charlotte. Knock yourself out . . . Okay Charlotte, back in the hold."

"Pete, please," Charlotte pleaded. She looked a sight. Mud and blood from the sawgrass cuts covered her body and was starting to dry and cake on her.

"You're not allowed to come out unless Bubba or I am with you."

Once Charlotte's head disappeared, Pete closed the hatch.

"Bubba, let's take a look at this bomb."

Chapter 27

Pete and Bubba surrounded the small green digital screen displaying three smaller, brighter, fuzzier green objects.

"There she is," Bubba said, excited. "Right there for all these years and we found her. Not the government. Not some rich bastard on his expensive boat. You and me, Pete. You and me."

To Pete, it seemed the death of Frank was nowhere in Bubba's thoughts, it was like it happened years ago.

"Don't forget about Frank," Pete said softly. Bubba nodded his head. "Yeah, you, me, and Frank." Pete walked over to one of the broken windows, looking at the spot Frank disappeared.

"What is it?" Bubba asked.

"I want out," Pete said, not taking his eyes off the water.

"What do you mean by that? We've found it. Think of all the money we're getting. Hell, we'll even be able to split Frank's cut." Suddenly, Pete turned, his eyes full of hate.

"Frank hasn't been dead fifteen minutes, and you're already talking about splitting his share. Is that all that matters to you? The God damn money?"

"No, Pete. Frank was a friend, but he's gone. Pete, I need your help. I can't do this myself."

"I'll help you get the bomb onboard, but after that, I'm washing my hands of you."

"What's your plan?"

"Once we get to the Port of Savannah, I'll take Charlotte and leave."

"Why do you want to take her? We'd be better off with her dead."

"I may need a hostage."

"How about me? You don't think I may need a hostage?"

"You'll have Wally and his guys, and the buyer's guys. They'll get you out of the country."

"I'll go someplace the U.S.A. can't extradite me," Bubba said, smiling.

"You can go to Hell for all I care." Bubba's eyes blazed up, and his hands tightened on the AK-47. Pete noticed.

"You can't do this by yourself. You just said that, remember? Let's see if we can get a better focus of your bomb on the monitor."

After turning a few buttons, the screen showed three objects in excellent detail. Three objects. Three fifty-five-gallon drums lying on their sides.

"Shit," Bubba said turning away.

"Shit," Pete whispered, walking to the window again, staring at the spot where Frank lost his life for three fifty-five-gallon drums.

"Some shrimper probably dumped them in the ditch when they were empty," Pete whispered to himself. "Didn't want to take them back to port and fill out all the paperwork necessary for the disposal of oil drums. Son-of-a-bitch."

Pete felt something touch his foot. Looking down he saw a rat sitting on its hind legs, staring up at him. Pete took his anger out on the rat by kicking at it, but it sprang out of the way before Pete could make contact.

"We're done Bubba. I'm tired, and I can't do it anymore."

"The hell you can't. We've got one more day. If we don't find that bomb, we're dead. Wally will make sure we disappear just like Frank. One more day Pete, that's all I'm asking you for."

"One more day," Pete added. "We need to head on over to the marina. It's getting dark."

***

Margaret and Stephanie were pissed because Ray's new plan didn't include them. The three men were going to scope out the boat, leaving them behind. Ray preached it was the best thing for all of them. If they didn't return by morning, the women were to call the police.

"Bullshit," Margaret said, making FJ laugh, laugh until Margaret gave him a hard look. "Why don't Mike or FJ stay behind and call the cops," she argued.

"Because FJ can move faster than you or Stephanie. No offense Steph. (Stephanie nodded.) And Mike wouldn't let anyone else drive the van."

"Bullshit," Margaret said, giving FJ a look before he had a chance to start laughing.

"Why don't you just call the cops and let them check out the boat?" Stephanie asked.

"They can't set foot on the boat without a search warrant, and no judge is going to give them one. Margaret, Stephanie, what we're about to do is illegal. Hell, we could all end up in jail."

"Or dead," Stephanie added.

"I like the jail part better," FJ commented

"Okay Ray, go over this plan again, one more time," Margaret said.

"We'll wait on the opposite side of the river on the concrete walkway the fishermen use. When we see the boat coming in, I'll pretend to be fishing. Mike and FJ will wait until one of the three men leave for food. They will then drive back over to the marina. Mike will stay in the van with the engine running, while FJ goes aboard the boat."

"Why FJ?"

"He's the smallest, and he can move better and faster than Mike or me."

"And because I'm more handsome."

"What if the men come out of their quarters?" Stephanie said, ignoring FJ.

"That's why I'm there," Ray continued. "I'll holler at them, getting their attention to that side of the river, giving FJ time to hightail it out of there."

"That sounds dangerous," Stephanie said.

"Piece of cake," FJ assured her. "Once, I almost got caught

in the bedroom of a young married woman. I'll never forget her. She had big -"

"We don't need to know," Stephanie interrupted.

"It'll be okay," Mike continued. "If these guys are innocent, the worst they'll get us for is trespassing."

"What happens when the guy in the truck returns?"

"If I see their truck returning, I'm to honk the horn once. That way FJ will know to get the hell out. I doubt I'll ever have to honk the horn. Stephanie, it will take them twenty minutes to get supper."

"How do you know that?"

"*The Grille* at the marina will be closed. If they head into Savannah, it will take longer, maybe an hour. The closest place for quick carryout is the convenient store by Sundae Café. To drive there, get food, pay and come back twenty minutes minimum. We should be out of there in fifteen."

"When are you leaving?"

Ray walked over to the sliding glass door heading out to the deck. "We should go ahead and head on over to the marina. It's starting to get dark."

Chapter 28

Lisa leaned back in her chair and took a long breath. It had been a long and tiring day. All she wanted now was her pajamas, her slippers, her trusted Min-Pin Cleo, supper, a good murder mystery and a Jack and Coke; two Jack and Cokes. Not much happened on Tybee today. Lisa wished Bubba would find the damn bomb and get this over with. What would happen if he didn't find the bomb? How long would they have to wait before arresting him for murder? Four agents from Atlanta were already scoping out the small island. They had located the boat Bubba rented, and were keeping an eye on it, but were told not to interfere. Bubba would be arrested for murder, for sure, but they wanted the buyer, whoever he was. He was the biggest fish in the net. While they waited, they had done a background check on the other two men associated with Bubba. These guys weren't terrorist, just good old boys, who for some reason or another, weren't going anywhere fast. To Lisa, all these guys wanted was the quick buck. But terrorists, for whatever reason, were terrorists. People were going to die, whether by their hands or someone else's.

"You still here," Matt asked, coming into the room.

"Wrapping up. Glenda and Harry have already gone home. I'm about ready to head out. And you?"

"Same here. I'm ready for beer and pizza, and the *Walking Dead*. By the way, I have some information on who might be interested in a dirty bomb."

"Who? Iran? ISIL? Al-Qaeda?"

"Nope, nope, and nope."

"Who then?"

"Ireland."

"Ireland?"

"The IRA. You've heard of them, I'm sure."

"The Irish Republican Army. Who hasn't? These guys believe all of Ireland should be an independent republic. They're also characterized by the belief that political violence was necessary to achieve that goal. I haven't heard too much from them lately."

"No, but they have taken responsibility for a few minor attacks on British soil in the last few years. Small stuff. A few pipe-bombs. A few car bombs. But they want something bigger. They lust for something bigger. They'd love to get their hands on a dirty bomb."

"You have a name?"

"Sean Murphy."

"Never heard of him."

"No one has. He's small time, but he wants to climb up the corporate ladder. He's been putting out signals, wanting to make a big impact on the U.K. He has the funds. He has the know-how, the knowledge, but lacks the resources."

"So, why him?"

"There are three ships at the Port of Savannah at this moment that are flying Irish flags. One of the ships is owned by an international conglomerate. I have a buddy in the CIA, who came up with a name. Guess who the head of the conglomerate is?"

"Sean Murphy?"

"Bingo. The conglomerate has a ship docked at the Port of Savannah. It makes runs now and then to Ireland. Probably running automatic weapons and ammo. If I was willing to bet my paycheck, and I'm not, I'd put my money on him."

"What about the other two ships?"

"One is contracted to *Doctors Without Borders* and is leaving for Somalia in three days. The other is a cargo liner taking a load of those big aluminum nuggets to a smelting refinery in Northern Ireland."

"Good job, Matt. I'll see if the Assistant Director will put some agents on the ship and the conglomerate."

"There's something else."

"What's that?"

"There's some old timers keeping an eye on Bubba."

"What do you mean by old timers?"

"Yeah, some old Sheriff from Kentucky and his elderly friends. They've been going to Tybee every year for the last five years."

"Why are you calling them elderly?"

"Because they're a lot older than me."

"Someday if you're lucky, you'll be their age."

"Sure, someday."

"So, what are these 'elderly' people doing on Tybee?"

"Playing cards."

"Really?"

"Really. It looks like one of their friends has gone missing and, it seems, they think Bubba and his friends are responsible."

"What makes them think that?"

"Who knows?"

"They could ruin everything. We can't have that happen."

"Agreed. So what should we do about them?"

"Run them through the system and bring them in and see what they're up to."

"I'll get on the horn."

***

The trawler hadn't returned by the time Mike, Ray, and FJ pulled up beside the concrete boardwalk on the opposite side of the marina. The two fishermen who were always there had been joined by two other friends.

"Going to do some night fishing?" one asked.

"Thought I'd try my luck," Ray replied, climbing out of the van.

"Us too. It won't be getting dark for another few minutes. You bring a lamp?"

"It's in the van." *Damn, we forgot a lamp.* "You caught anything?"

"Not really. A few carps and skipjacks. Nothing worth eating.

Maybe you'll bring us luck."

"I hope so."

After a minute or two of fumbling in the back of the van trying to think of what to say, Ray confessed, "Okay guys, I'm a dumbass."

"Why?"

"Because I forgot to bring a lamp."

"That's okay," they laughed, "we'll share ours."

FJ climbed out the side door and took Ray's arm, nodding his head to the side. He wanted to talk with Ray alone, out of hearing of the other fishermen, the four fishermen who at the moment were staring holes through him.

Am I the only little person on Tybee?

"Well, we beat the boat coming back," FJ whispered to Ray. "You want Mike and me to head on over to the other side?"

"Might as well. Make sure Mike parks out of sight."

"Yes, sir," FJ said, standing at attention with his hand on his forehead.

"Screw you, FJ."

As Mike and FJ crossed over the bridge, the trawler was crossing under the bridge.

Mike parked the van on the opposite side of the *Bait and Tackle*, away from the streetlight, away from snooping eyes, but close enough to see the trawler.

"They won't see us here," Mike whispered.

"Why are you whispering? You think they can hear you?"

"No," Mike said louder.

"When should I go aboard?" FJ asked.

"When one of them leaves to get supper. We have to time this really close. You don't want to get caught onboard. If someone comes out on deck, Ray will distract them, allowing you time to escape . . . Are you nervous?"

"Damn straight," FJ replied. "But I can do this."

"You know, once you're onboard, we really can't help you?"

"Mike, you're not making this any easier."

They watched as Bubba climbed into the truck. If Bubba

took a left on Highway 80, then he was going toward Savannah, and wouldn't be back for thirty or forty minutes. If he took a right on the highway, then he was going back into Tybee and would be back in twenty minutes flat. Bubba turned to the right.

"Okay, you've got twenty minutes. Make it fifteen. Get on the boat without the other two seeing you, check things out and then get the hell off. No heroics. Now, it's up to you," Mike stated, as Bubba's headlights disappeared out of sight. "By God FJ, be careful."

"You know I will," FJ said, about to open the door.

"Excuse me," a voice said, knocking on Mike's side window. "You have a minute?"

"Holy Mother of God," Mike exclaimed. "You scared the shit out of me. What do you want?"

"I'm Special Agent David Mulder, FBI," the man answered, showing his badge and credentials. "And this is my partner, Special Agent Helen -"

"Let me guess," FJ interrupted. "Scully, like in Mulder and Scully."

"I have no idea what you're talking about," Special Agent Mulder said.

"Don't tell me you've never watched the *X-Files*?"

Mulder shook his head. "My partner's name is Special Agent Helen McIntire. Show him your badge and credentials."

"Is that real?" FJ asked.

"Yes, it is."

"No kidding?" FJ asked.

"No kidding," agent McIntire replied, smiling.

"Cool."

"What brings you two out here?" Mulder asked.

"We're out for a lover's stroll along the boardwalk," Mike answered.

"Seriously?"

"Hell no," FJ exclaimed, causing Mike to laugh out loud.

"I'm not in the mood, gentlemen. Let me ask again. What brings you two out here at dusk? *The Grille* is closed. So is the *Bait and Tackle.*"

"It's a long story," Mike answered.

"We have time, but not here."

"What do you mean?"

"You're to come with us."

"Why? What have we done?"

"Please, Mr. Roach, let's not make a scene."

"How do you know my name?"

"All will be revealed, when you come with us."

"Now, that sounds like the *X-Files*," FJ whispered.

Mike looked across the river to where Ray was standing, but he couldn't see his friend in the dark.

"If you're looking for Raymond Harris, he has already been taken into custody."

"Raymond Harris?" FJ asked.

"Your friend, the old man who didn't bring a lamp for night fishing."

"Oh, that friend."

"Where are we going?" Mike asked.

"To our field office in Savannah."

"You want me to follow you?"

Agent McIntire laughed. "No. We'll have someone drive your van. Both of you will ride with us."

"I don't like people driving my van."

"Get over it."

"Are we under arrest?" FJ asked.

"No. We have a couple of questions for you."

"And you can't ask them here?" Mike asked.

"Okay, more than a couple of questions," Agent McIntire gave in. "Come on guys. Make this easy on yourselves. Just a few questions."

FJ and Mike settled in the back of a black Lincoln Town Car.

"No handcuffs?" FJ asked.

"You do anything wrong?" Mulder asked.

"No. Not lately."

"Then, no handcuffs. Seriously, we only have a few questions for you. When we're done, you can leave and return to your condo."

"You know where we're staying?" FJ asked Mulder while looking at Mike.

"You're staying at the *My Beach House Rentals.*"

"So, you've been watching us?"

"Yes."

"That sounds like the *X-Files* too," FJ said, looking out the window, making sure they weren't being taken to a dark and deserted warehouse on the edge of town.

"Why have you been watching us?" Mike asked.

"In time, Mr. Roach. In time, Mr. Johnston."

"How do you know my name?" FJ asked.

"In time."

The Town Car drove into Savannah on President Street; took a left then a right onto Louisville Road; continued on Louisville Road to Telfair Road; then left on Chatham Parkway and a left on Chatham Center Drive.

"I'm totally lost," FJ said, looking around. *Thank God, no deserted warehouse in sight.*

"Me too," Mike added.

"That's okay guys," McIntire said. "When we're done, we'll point you in the right direction to get you back to your condo."

"So, why are we here?" Mike asked, climbing out of the car.

"In time."

"You said that already," FJ commented. McIntire gave FJ a hard look. "You're here to talk to our boss, and to answer her questions."

"Her?" FJ asked. "Is she pretty?"

"Good God, FJ!" Mike exclaimed. "Knock it off."

Mulder and McIntire led Mike and FJ to a dark room with a table and five chairs. Ray was already occupying one of the chairs.

"Fancy running into you here, Ray," FJ said, taking a seat. "You come here often?"

Ray shook his head and smiled. On the table was a laptop, a phone, and nothing else. On the wall hung a large screen TV. Special Agent McIntire sat down before the laptop, stroked a few keys, and leaned back. The large screen lit up, and a woman's face appeared in HD.

"Raymond, Michael, and Milton," the Lady said. "Good evening. I'm Special Agent Lisa Clark. I hope you're doing well."

"Why is everyone a 'Special Agent' around here?" FJ asked.

"We're fine," Ray chimed in, hoping agent Clark would disregard what FJ had just asked. "Why are we here? Better yet, how do you know our names?"

"That's a fair question," Lisa answered. "We know because we're the FBI and it's our job to know things. (FJ rolled his eyes.) We know there are six of you staying on Tybee Island. And, you've been coming to the island for the last five years. First, there's Michael and Stephanie Roach. Michael you are, was, a computer analyst before becoming a fiction writer. Your name has popped up on our radar a couple of times."

"How so?"

"On the 'not so private' internet, you've googled words like WMDs, automatic weapons, pipe bombs, pressure cooker bombs, Nazis, KKK, terrorists; those kind of words. We've checked and determined you're not a threat to the country, because of your age and your clean record. Hell, you've never had a speeding ticket. Unheard of. Also, and lucky for you, you've used the results of your searches in the books you write. Just to let you know, if you keep it up, one of these days you're going to get a visit from one of our agents in Kentucky."

"Cool," Mike whispered. FJ nodded his head, giving Mike a thumbs up.

"Your wife, Stephanie, worked for the City of Franklin as an accountant, now retired. Together you have seven grandchildren. Mrs. Charlotte Knott is a widow and a retired librarian in the Franklin School District."

"She doesn't like being called a librarian," FJ corrected. "She prefers media specialist."

"Let's see," Lisa said, hiding a smile by looking down, probably at a sheet of paper. "Mr. and Mrs. Harris. Margaret is retired from the County, former Judicial Assistant. Raymond, it says here, you were a sniper in Vietnam, and once you mustered out, you got into law enforcement. Currently, you're the Sheriff of Franklin, Kentucky. You're kind of old to be an active Sheriff, don't you think?" Before Ray could answer, Lisa continued. "And that leaves you, Mr. Johnston."

"Well, at least, you saved the best for last," FJ said, smiling.

"Milton, you -"

"Call me FJ. All my close friends do."

"Mr. Johnston, you have the most interesting life of all your friends. (FJ gave himself two thumbs up.) Abandoned at birth because you're a little person, you -"

"I prefer dwarf."

Lisa frowned and continued. "Grew up and ran away to the circus, becoming an acrobat, escape artist, and a knife thrower. You were never married, but you and one, Zoe Payne, did have a daughter. Your daughter, Betty, stayed with you in Franklin when you retired. She married and gave you a granddaughter. Zoe Payne stayed with the circus, retired, and is now living in -"

"Don't need to know," FJ interrupted. "I don't want to know."

"Okay. Doesn't matter to us. Now, I think it's time for us to ask you some questions, and your answers gentlemen will determine how long you'll be our guests. Fair enough?"

"Fair enough," Ray replied. "Shoot."

"Don't say 'shoot,' Ray," FJ said. "These guys have guns." Mulder, McIntire, and Lisa laughed.

"You have to excuse him," Mike said. "We do all the time."

"What can you tell me about Joe Ray Henry?" Lisa continued.

"Never heard of him," Ray answered, looking at Mike and FJ, who were both shaking their heads.

"Who has three first names anyway?" FJ asked.

"Okay," Lisa sighed. "How about if I said, Bubba?"

"The big black guy?" Ray asked.

"That's him. What can you tell me about Bubba?"

"Not much. I ran into Bubba's buddy, Pete, the other day at *Publix*, and he introduced himself. He said he was on Tybee with two friends, Frank and Bubba. At the time, they were staying in

185

the condo next to ours. They have since moved out and are now living on a boat. Never saw any of them before last week. That's about it."

"So, why are you stalking him and his friends?"

"Stalking?"

"Ray, go ahead and tell her," FJ said.

"Yes, Ray, go ahead and tell me."

What do I have to lose?

"I think he killed a girl and had something to do with one of our friends who's gone missing."

"You take this to the authorities on Tybee?"

"We tried, but without evidence, they say their hands are tied." Lisa nodded her head.

"That's true . . . If it makes you feel better, we have reasons to believe Bubba did kill Sara Sinclair. But, we -"

"I knew it," Ray interrupted. "So, why hasn't anybody arrested him?"

"But," Lisa continued. "There's no evidence to tie these guys to your friend, Charlotte Knott."

"What do you know about Charlotte?"

"Not much. We read the Tybee Island police report this morning."

"So, you've been in contact with the Tybee police?"

"No. They don't know we're involved."

"Why not?"

"National Security."

"Whatever. I bet Charlotte is on their boat," Ray said. "That's why we were there tonight."

"You were about to go on their boat?"

"I was," FJ answered.

"That could have gotten you, and your friend killed if she's aboard. It could have gotten you killed if she isn't. You're dealing with murderers, Mr. Johnston. Not a bright idea you've come up with."

"It was Mike's idea," FJ chimed in. "But I wouldn't have been caught."

"You're sure about that?"

"Why don't you arrest Bubba for murder, and check out their boat?" Ray asked, changing the subject.

"Sheriff Harris -"

"Ray. Call me Ray."

"Okay, Ray. There could be more going on here than you know."

"Like what?"

"Do you know where Sara Sinclair is from?"

"She told Charlotte, Bowling Green."

"And that's not far from where you live."

"Thirty miles or so. What does that have to do with anything?"

"Maybe nothing. But I find it odd two families from Kentucky who live close together, relatively speaking, both renting homes on Tybee Island right across the street from each other; one's dead; the other's missing."

"And don't forget the three guys, right next door," Ray added. "You said yourself; you think Bubba killed Sara."

"I know what I said."

"So, why did Bubba kill Sara and take Charlotte?"

"The answer to that could be, is, above your paygrade."

"Paygrade my ass. I bet you know where Charlotte is, as well as I, but you're not willing to tell. Listen, Charlotte is aboard that boat, and we want her back."

"How do you know she's aboard their boat when we don't?"

"I don't know. Call it a gut feeling."

"You always trust your gut?"

"Most of the time, no. But, in this case, damn straight."

"Ray, Sara Sinclair is dead. Your friend could very well be dead."

"Bite your tongue, bitch" FJ spat.

Mike slugged FJ on the arm. "Forgive him," Mike apologized. "He gets a little carried away sometimes."

"That's alright. I'd be upset if one of my friends was missing. We really don't know where Charlotte Knott is; take it or leave it. For her sake, I hope she is aboard their boat. Ray, you've been in law enforcement long enough to know, the longer the leads don't come in, the more likely it's going to have a bad outcome."

"Again," Ray said, "why don't you arrest them and check out the boat."

"I'm sorry Sheriff, but -"

"I know. Above my paygrade."

"What do you know about a Preston Mullins and a Parker Davis?" Lisa asked, changing the subject.

"Never heard of them," Ray answered.

"Why? Are they missing too?" FJ asked.

"Why do you say that?" McIntire asked, suspiciously.

"I don't know. It seems like everyone's missing around here."

"For the record," Lisa went on, "they are missing. If you have any information -"

"Damnit," FJ exclaimed, losing his patience. "We've never met them. We've never met the Sinclair's before this week. We've never met Bubba, with his three first names, or his friends. We come here to play cards, eat really good food and enjoy each other's company."

"Agent Clark," Ray pleaded, "we're just trying to find our friend."

"I understand Ray, really I do, but you need to back off and let us do our job."

Chapter 29

The endless, silent sea of grass glowed in the moonlight. Nothing stirred, and the van had the road to itself. It was silent in the van; no music, no talking, each man lost in his thoughts. The only sounds were of the engine and the tires beating the pavement. The headlights caught the remains of the old tree stump along Highway 80, the old tree stump with an American Flag attached to one barren limb.

"That's always cool," FJ said. "Out here in the middle of nowhere, and you find the dead remains of a tree with a flag attached to it. I wonder who put it there."

"Every year, you ask that question," Mike replied. "And the answer has always been the same; we don't know."

"I did notice somebody changed it out this year," Ray said, staring out the window. "Last year the flag was ragged. This year it's brand new. Somebody cares."

The rest of the ride into Tybee was done in silence until they entered the city limits passing the speed indicator machine, which was flashing fifty miles per hour.

"You do know the speed limit is thirty-five? You're going a little fast," FJ commented.

"Oh, sorry. My mind was somewhere else," Mike said, slowing down. "Ray, are we going to back off, as the FBI said?"

"Hell no. The longer we wait, the odds are Charlotte will die. I don't know what the Feds are up to, above our paygrade you know, but I'm not waiting."

"So, we're going back now?"

"No. It's too late tonight. We'll wait till tomorrow morning."

"You mean this morning," FJ corrected. "It's already tomorrow."

"What do you mean?"

"Ray, its 2 a.m. already."

"Shit. Margaret is going to be pissed."

***

The small Hermit Crab raised its large claw in defiance, its antennae twitching right and left trying to determine the best route for retreat. As the giant got closer, the crab spread its front claws and legs thinking it made it look larger. Don't mess with me, it threatened. Scurrying to the right, it froze as a dark shadow appeared. Extending its larger claw, it promised a serious pinch. Suddenly, a storm of sand bombarded the crab, completely covering it.

"Ginny, leave the crab alone," Donald Parson yelled to his five-year-old daughter.

"Okay, Daddy," Ginny replied, throwing what was left of the sand in her tiny hand at the little crustacean.

Dark and threatening clouds raced across the sky, but the air around the Parson family was calm. Even the sea lay still as death. Ginny ran to the edge of the surf and cupped a handful of wet sand. For a moment, she thought about dropping it on the crab.

"How can the sky be so alive and everything else so still," her mother, Mary, asked Donald.

"And notice the color," Donald added. "Everything has a green tint to it."

Pea sized hail began to fall, bouncing off the coolers and blankets, splashing in the water. But, as soon as it began, it was over. Playfully, Ginny ran around picking up the tiny icy pellets, trying to get a handful before they melted.

"We better get inside. Come on Ginny," her father said, picking her up. "When I was little, not much older than you, one day everything turned green as it is now. That afternoon we had a hailstorm, just like that, and a few minutes later, a tornado ripped through town. Luckily, no one got hurt, but dozens of homes were destroyed."

"Was your home destroyed, Daddy?" Ginny asked.

"No sweetie, it wasn't."

"Listen," Mary said, looking out to sea. "What do you hear?"

"It sounds like a train, Mommy." The three and those around them stood looking toward the ocean, the source of the sound.

"There," someone yelled pointing to the southeast. "Look there. What's that?"

At first, it was a white speck, but as it got nearer, it became a white funnel dancing between the dark clouds and the darker sea.

"It's a waterspout," Donald yelled. "Everybody, get inside, now."

"What's a waterspout Daddy?" Ginny asked as her father turned her toward their condo.

"It's a water tornado, baby."

"Is it going to hurt us?"

"No baby. We'll get inside where it's safe. It may not even make it to shore. Don't worry, Mommy and Daddy are here."

"I'm not worried, Daddy."

"Good girl."

Halfway across the beach, Donald stopped, looking down the beach toward the south end of the island. A bright flash of light had just streaked across the horizon, blinding all of them for a moment.

"What was that Daddy?"

Donald wanted to say, I don't know, but he couldn't get his mouth to cooperate. Out of the flash rose a rolling, foaming black and brownish cloud; a boiling cloud that slowly grew into the shape of a mushroom, a mushroom cloud that filled the sky.

The sound wave struck the island at seven hundred and sixty-seven miles per hour, with five times the force of a category five hurricane. Buildings of stone, steel, and wood disintegrated, becoming flying projectiles of toothpicks and rubble. Trees and power poles were ripped from the ground, shattered and broken. The town's water tower exploded. Saint Michaels Catholic Church disintegrated, as did every building and structure on the island. Gone was the lighthouse, IGA, MacElwee's Seafood House, AJ's

Dockside Restaurant, T S Chu Department Store, Lighthouse Pizza, and the Tybee Pier. Cars, trucks and golf carts were tossed around like twisted Matchbox toys. Boats, large and small, were tossed into the air like ping pong balls, disintegrating before striking the water. Everything that was, was gone. Even the forces of nature were no match for the blast wave. The billowing dark clouds were torn and scattered. The waterspout, dancing and twisting, was instantly ripped to shreds. But no one witnessed or heard any of this; not birds, dogs, feral cats, or humans, for they too had disintegrated. Mercifully the sound wave hit Donald, Mary, and Ginny Parson before the heat wave.

Over a million degrees of rolling poisonous gas, traveling at two hundred and fifty miles per hour, engulfed everything. Wooden structures became ash. If it was steel, brick or stone, it melted. The grass, broken trees and power poles burst into flame and, within milliseconds, became dust. The surface of the sea began to boil. The sand on the beach, when it reached 3,090 degrees, became a flowing liquid. After it cooled, which would be days from now, it would be transformed into different shades of glass. The boiling sea and the flowing sand made the beach look like an alien world. The oxygen in the air, fueled by the heat, burned away leaving the air unbreathable. Within seconds, only a barren and parched land remained. There would be no bodies to bury, no structures to be bulldozed, no trees or shrubs to clear. Like a modern-day Sodom and Gomorrah, within seconds Tybee Island was dead, and the growing, widening circle of death marched on toward Savannah, destroying everything in its path.

Heart pounding and filled with dread, Charlotte woke from her nightmare covered in a cold sweat. A dream. No a nightmare. If it had been only a dream, how would she have known their names? It dawned on her; she knew the little girl. It was the same little girl, and her family, she had seen on the beach the day of the fake shark attack.

***

The stars were fading, and the clouds on the eastern horizon were graying up, streaked with shades of orange, pink and red. In a few minutes, the sun would show its head. Another beautiful sunrise – enjoyable – photogenic – comforting – but not today. Ray stood at the water's edge deep in thought, wondering if they were doing the right thing. Agent Clark was right. This was dangerous, no doubt. FJ would be putting his life on the line, and for what? Charlotte, of course. But what if she wasn't on the boat? Were they searching in the wrong direction? What if she was already dead? God forbid. Right now, she could be miles out to sea, resting on the bottom, weighed down in chains. The thought made his stomach turn, like someone just punched him in the gut.

"What are you doing out here?' FJ asked, fighting his way through the sand.

"Thinking."

"About what?"

"What everyone's thinking about. Charlotte . . . I thought you were going to get some sleep."

"Couldn't sleep. Too busy thinking. (Ray nodded his head.) Surely, we'll figure out something this morning."

"No, we won't."

"And why in the hell not?"

"National Security."

"What?"

"That's what Agent Clark said in our meeting. National Security. Think about it, FJ. Why would the murder of a sixteen-year-old from Kentucky involve National Security? It wouldn't. What does a kidnapping of a retired librarian from Kentucky have to do with National Security? Nothing. No, there's more going on here, and we need to find out before we rush out and get ourselves killed."

"Damnit, Ray. The longer we wait the -"

"You don't think I know that. FJ, we need to know the whole story."

"From whom? The Tybee Police? No. The FBI? Hell no."

"And that sticks in my crawl as well."

"What?"

"Why wouldn't the FBI keep the Tybee police in the loop? As police officers, we're all in this together . . . And there's one more thing that's bugging me."

"Only one?"

"Agent Clark said there were two other guys missing . . . I don't remember their names, do you?"

"No, but why does that bother you?"

"We've been coming to Tybee Island for the last five years, why? Because it's quiet and safe. Nothing goes on around here. But, in the last week, they've had a murder and three disappearances. That's not natural. And that's not a coincidence."

"So, what are we going to do about it? You sure as shit can't go to Chief Rogers."

"No, but we could talk with Deputy Brown. He's helped us before."

"So, you going to give him a call?"

"No. We were told to back off, remember? The FBI's probably monitoring our phone calls, and the black Town Car is parked out on the curve in front of our condo."

"Really? I didn't notice."

"I bet they're going to be our shadow for the rest of our stay."

"We can't call Deputy Brown, and we can't go to the police station; so how are you going to get in touch with him?"

"You still have Deputy Grace McClure's cell phone number?"

FJ smiled.

***

Special Agent Mulder felt "out-of-uniform." Instead of his usual black suit, white dress shirt, and skinny black tie, he wore a white hardhat, work-boots, faded jeans and a Georgia Bulldog sweatshirt. As the sun broke the eastern sky, Mulder was taking the exit off the I-516 onto Bourne Avenue. He turned into the Applebee's parking lot. A red Ford F-150, parked beneath the Applebee's sign, flashed his lights. Pulling up beside the Ford, Agent Mulder climbed out of his town car and climbed into the cab of the Ford.

"Good morning John," Mulder said, shaking hands.

"You got me up awful early, David," Special Agent John Chriss said, firing up the engine.

"I need to be somewhere later this morning, and I wanted to see how you plan on taking the trawler."

"Why, you don't trust me?"

"It's not me, but our boss in Washington." John laughed.

Taking Bourne Avenue, the F-150 headed northeast to the Port of Savannah. At the twenty-lane security gate, both men showed their credentials and badges. Without saying a word, the security guard waved them through. As soon as they passed the check point, they were instantly surrounded by hundreds of thousands of large cargo containers, all arranged in neat rows and stacked three to four deep. Large forklifts roared here and there, stacking and unstacking containers. Huge cranes, anchored to the dock and hanging out over the water, were in the process of removing stacked containers or stacking containers.

"How do they keep things straight?" Mulder asked. "I'm lost."

"It takes a while to figure things out. I've been working the Port since 9/11, and it took me a couple of years before I felt comfortable finding my way around. The most important thing to remember, the Port is laid out in three sections, A, B, and C. Section A is the first set of docks coming upstream from the ocean. Our ship is in the middle section, Section B. Also to remember, forklifts have the right-of-way."

Taking the main drag, the F-150 came to a stop by the river, where six cargo ships could be seen loading and unloading containers.

"The ships you see, are the only ones in Section B today. You know anything about cargo ships?" John asked.

"Not that first thing."

"There are two categories that reflect the services cargo ships offer to industry; Liner and Tramp. Those on a fixed published schedule and fixed tariff rates are cargo liners. Tramp ships do not have fixed schedules. They can show up at Port any time, and unannounced. Our conglomerate uses a tramp ship named *The Four Leaves,* like the number of leaves on a shamrock. In the scheme of things, she's considered a small cargo tramp, and will probably be leaving in a day or two, whenever she completes loading. Let's take a walk, and I'll fill you in on what we have planned for taking *The Four Leaves* and the trawler."

Agent Chriss, dressed like Mulder and packing a clipboard, looked like a Port Authority supervisor discussing today's schedule of events with a subordinate. Occasionally, the two men would stop, and Agent Chriss would point out something pertaining to a stack of containers, while in truth, they were watching *The Four Leaves* out of the corner of their eyes.

"The day the trawler comes into Port, we will have three unmarked boats prepared to swoop in, one from downstream, one from upstream, and one from across the river. From our point of view, we will have them surrounded on the water. There will be three SWAT teams, in full body armor, positioned in strategic locations." Using his pencil as a pointer, Agent Chriss indicated the three locations. "A signal from me, and we'll storm *The Four Leaves* and the trawler."

"You do know what will be on the trawler?" Mulder asked. Chriss nodded his head. "Extreme care will be given to the cargo."

"There doesn't seem to be a lot of activity aboard *The Four Leaves,*" Mulder commented.

"Most of the time, when everything is loaded and secure, there's a lot of dead time waiting for all the paperwork to be completed. Once all the T's have been crossed, and the I's all dotted, they'll cast off their lines and roll out on the high tide. We, of course, know why *The Four Leaves* is waiting."

Making their way along the dock, Chriss and Mulder paused before *The Four Leaves.* There was nothing unusual about that. A lot of times, the men working the docks will take their breaks watching Mariners going about their work aboard the giant ships.

"Can I help you with something?" a man, with a heavy Irish accent, asked from the gangplank.

"Just killing time," Chriss answered, lighting up a cigarette and offering the Irishman one. "I've seen you guys in Port before."

"We come here a few times a year," the Irishman nodded, taking a cig.

"What are you hauling this trip?"

"We're taking a few crates to Dublin," the man answered, taking a long drag off his cig.

"What's in the crates?"

"No idea," the man answered, blowing smoke out his mouth and nose. "It doesn't matter to us, as long as we get paid when we arrive in Port."

"I fully understand. It's all about the money," Chriss laughed, throwing his cigarette butt on the ground. "Well, we need to head over to Section A and check out a few things. You guys have a nice day."

"You too," the Irishman replied, turning back to the gangplank.

Back in the truck, Agent Chriss and Agent Mulder went over the mission.

"It looks like you have everything planned out," Mulder said. "I'll let Lisa know. You're to wait on her call before doing anything. I need to head over to Tybee now. I'm busy babysitting a bunch of old people."

"Understood," Chriss laughed. "So, the bomb's been found?"

"To our knowledge, not yet. But we're not taking any chances. Can you imagine a dirty bomb exploding in the center of London? That would be the biggest single event since 9/11."

Chapter 30

The Rentals is one of the few remaining condos on Tybee that has a dinosaur in its parking lot, a coin operated dinosaur. With the invasion of cellphones, payphones for the most part, had become obsolete. *The Rentals* kept theirs for beachcombers to make emergency calls and for partying college kids needing to reverse calls to their parents begging for more money.

"Hello," FJ said, as the phone picked up on the other end.

"FJ," Grace said, "I wondered when you were going to call."

"I'm sorry, but I've been busy."

"I understand."

"We'll get together before I leave, I promise."

"You better. So, if you're not asking me out, why did you call?"

"I know it's early, but is Deputy Brown around?"

"We both worked the late shift last night, but he's still here. I think he's getting ready to head home."

"Could you grab him real quick? I need to have a word."

"Sure, I'll transfer you."

"Thanks."

"FJ, call me."

"Promise."

FJ handed the receiver to Ray. "Hello . . . No one's there," Ray said, looking down at FJ.

"She's transferring you."

"Hello . . . Oh hello, Deputy Brown. It's Ray, Ray Harris."

"I recognized your voice Sheriff. What can I do for you?"

"Deputy, we need to talk."

"Sheriff, nothing new has come forward on your missing friend. I'm afraid I don't have much to offer."

"Deputy, we had a run in with the FBI last night."

"The F.B.I.?"

"Is there more than one? They raised some points, and I need answers."

"You think I can help?"

"I don't know. Maybe. You got a few minutes to talk?"

"Sure. Come on in."

"No can do."

"Why not?"

"The FBI told us to back off, and we're being followed. We can't come to you."

"Then we shouldn't meet here on the island," Brown added.

"Where then?"

"You know where the *Cotton Exchange Tavern* is on River Street, in Savannah?"

"Yes. We ate there the last two times we were down here; good fresh seafood."

"Why don't I meet you there at, say, noon?"

"Sounds like a plan."

The line went dead.

"Well?" FJ asked as Ray hung up the receiver.

"We're going to meet him at noon."

"How are you going to do that with the FBI following you?"

"We'll have to think about that."

***

The hatch opened with its usual bang.

"You can come on up Charlotte," Pete called below. "We're south of Tybee now."

Charlotte climbed out of the hold on stiff legs. The eastern sky was beautiful with its reds and oranges, and the sun glowed a bright orange on the horizon.

"You guys are out early," she commented.

200

"We have to be. Today's the deadline we were given to find the bomb."

"And if you don't find it?"

"None of your concern . . . Charlotte, you look like shit."

"I feel like shit." Charlotte was covered in mud and blood from the tiny wounds the sawgrass had inflicted. Her hair was matted to her scalp. The color of her clothes was unrecognizable. She did look like shit.

"Step around here," Pete pointed.

Beside the boat's rail sat a small generator thingy, with two long hoses attached.

"What's that?" she asked.

"That's a heavy-duty saltwater pump," Pete replied. "One hose goes in the ocean; the other hose can be used to spray off the deck."

"From the looks of this deck, it's never been used."

"Funny, Charlotte, real funny. No, we rented it last night just for you."

"For me?"

"Yes, you really need a shower."

"Thank God," she sighed. "A shower, even a saltwater shower, would be heavenly."

The strong spray hurt like hell, and the saltwater burned her wounds, but it was the best shower Charlotte had ever taken. At first, Pete aimed the hose directly at her, knocking off the dried and cracked mud, almost knocking her off her feet. Afterwards, he pointed the nozzle straight up, letting the water fall like a gentle rain shower.

"Here," he said, handing Charlotte a bar of soap and a bottle of Head and Shoulders. "It's mine, and if it works for me, it'll work for you. You'll still have to air dry."

"Not a problem."

Fifteen minutes later and Charlotte felt like a new person. Every inch of her exposed skin was covered in tiny cuts from the sawgrass or insect bites. The left side of her face was still a little swollen and bruised; her eye was slowly clearing up.

"You look a hell of a lot better," Pete laughed.

"I feel a lot better . . . Pete, we need to talk."

"About what?"

"About Frank."

"There's nothing to talk about."

"Pete, I liked Frank. With his simple mind, he had no idea what was going on. I didn't want anything to happen to him."

"Not like Bubba and me?"

"Bubba, yes. He killed Sara. He's responsible for the other two men. Bubba, yes, but not you. You were dragged into this. You didn't want any of this to happen. I truly believe that. Pete, there's still time for you." Pete shook his head.

"No, Charlotte. Bubba made the bed, but I'll have to lay in it with him."

"I could tell what I've overheard, how you treated me, how Bubba wanted to kill me. Pete, you're the only one keeping me alive. They would go lenient on you."

"That's bullshit, and you know it. You're talking about a young girl."

"Pete," Charlotte pleaded.

"Go around and take your seat," Pete said sadly, turning away. "It's going to be another hot day."

***

"I hate stakeouts," Special Agent Mulder said, yawning.

"I wouldn't call this a stakeout," Special Agent McIntire added. "If they look out their window, they'd see us."

"Lisa wants them to see us. We're here to remind them not to do anything stupid."

"Well, this is odd. Look coming here."

Across the lawn a woman was walking toward the car, carrying two paper cups. Mulder looked through a stack of 4x6 photos. "That's Margaret Harris, Ray's wife."

"Good morning," Margaret said, as Mulder rolled down his window. "We thought you might like some coffee. Didn't know how you take it, so both are black."

"That works for me," McIntire said, leaning over to be seen. "You're a lifesaver. Thank you so much Margaret."

"Our pleasure. You going to be following us around all day?"

"Afraid so, ma'am," Mulder said, taking a sip. "It's not our idea."

"I know. Orders are orders."

"Yes, ma'am."

"Ray wanted me to tell you; we're going to Savannah this morning. We're heading down to the riverfront to get some gifts for the grandkids."

"Why would Ray want us to know that?"

"In case you lose us on the way there."

Chapter 31

Mike pulled off Bay Street onto Williamson Street, next to the Quality Inn, lucky finding an empty handicap parking spot. Putting Margaret's sticker on the rearview mirror, he asked the others, "They still with us?"

"Yes," Ray replied. "Mulder just parked over on Barnard Street. Hell, he just waved at us."

"Well, wave back. We're friendly people. Okay, we don't have much time before we have to meet Deputy Brown, everyone ready?" Everyone nodded.

Exiting the van, the five huddled together for a moment, getting their bearings. Mulder and McIntire got out of their car, waiting, watching. Suddenly, the five turned and walked off, in different directions.

"What the hell," Mulder laughed. "Ray is one smart son-of-a-bitch."

"What do you mean?" McIntire asked.

"There are five of them and only two of us. Who are we going to follow? We sure as shit can't follow all five of them."

"I'll take Mike," McIntire said as Mike passed them, smiling, nodding his head.

"I'll take Ray and Milton," Mulder commented. "It looks like they're going together. Keep your walky-talky handy. I'll give you a call if something happens."

Mike leisurely made his way over to Emmet Park, stopping every now and then to look at the concrete monuments. Finding a vacant park bench, Mike took a seat under the hundred-year-old trees, all of which were covered in Spanish-moss. *Kodak Moment,* he thought. The dense canopy dropped the temperature several comforting degrees. *I could sit here all day.* Once known as the Strand and later as Irish Green because of its proximity to the Irish residents of Savannah's Old Fort neighborhood, Emmet Park was renamed in 1902 for the Irish patriot Robert Emmet (1778-1803) to commemorate the centennial of his death. Emmet, who led an unsuccessful Dublin uprising for Irish independence and was executed for treason, was a hero to Savannah's Irish community. Emmet is best known for the speech in which he asked that his epitaph not be written until "my country takes her place among the nations of the earth."

"What's he doing," McIntire's walky-talky squawked.

"He's sitting on a park bench."

"Doing what?"

"Sitting. He could be waiting for someone. He keeps looking around. He could also be waiting for me to give up and leave."

"For God's sake, don't leave."

"Roger that. What's Ray and Milton up to?"

"They just sat down at the bar at *Vic's On the River*. Looks like they're ordering drinks and are waiting for someone."

"You see the other two?"

Mulder scanned River Street trying to locate Margaret and Stephanie. The street overflowed with tourists making their way to the *Riverboat Tours, Savannah's Candy Kitchen, The Shrimp Factory, The Five and Dime General Store, Bob's Your Uncle* and *Fannie's Your Aunt*. With all the movement, noise and colors, Mulder found it was hard to focus on one individual.

"Margaret just now walked into *Fabulous Finds*. Stephanie, I haven't seen. She may have entered before Margaret. I don't know. I was too busy watching Ray and Milton."

"You want me to leave Mike and go check?"

"Negative. That could be just what they want. I believe the three men are the ones to watch."

"Why is that? Because they're men?"

"Oh, hell no. But it was the three men who staked out the boat. You stay with Mike. I'll keep an eye on Ray and Milton."

"Roger that."

Stephanie entered the *Cotton Exchange Tavern* through their side door. Because the building is at the intersection of River Street and a steep access road to Bay Street, Stephanie found herself in the second story of the tavern. Locating the stairs down to the main level on River Street, Stephanie descended looking for the bar. It was there in the corner booth she found Deputy Brown.

"Good day, Deputy Brown," she said, as she walked up. "I almost didn't see you back here."

"That's what Ray wanted," he said standing up. "He doesn't want anyone seeing us together."

"Please sit down," Stephanie said. "Ray wants me to bring you up-to-date on his meeting with the FBI, and he has a couple of questions."

"That's fine. I'm not sure how much help I'll be, but go ahead."

"The other night at the -"

"Would you like something to drink?" a young lady asked, interrupting.

"I'll have sweet tea," Brown replied.

"Do you make dirty martinis, really good dirty martinis?" Stephanie asked.

"I don't drink, but everyone that does, says they're the best."

"Then I'll have one, please. Make it extra dirty."

"Extra dirty? How do you do that?"

"You add more olive juice."

After the drinks arrived and the girl disappeared, Stephanie retold the men's ordeal in Savannah, leaving out nothing. Brown sat there nodding his head every now and then.

"That's about it," Stephanie said, taking a sip of her dirty martini. The girl had been right. It was the best.

"So, Ray was right about Bubba," Brown said, shaking his head. "Bubba killed Sara Sinclair. But, without their evidence, we can't do a damn thing. What's up with that?" Stephanie shook her head. "The FBI is taking it seriously, and they say we should stay out of it. They have two agents following us. That's why I'm here and not the others. They can't follow all of us."

"They could have if they brought more men."

"Why bring more men to watch over five old people. They had no idea we were coming here until we told them this morning, and we split up the moment we got here."

"So, you said you had questions."

"The Feds said you guys on Tybee weren't contacted because of 'National Security.' Why is that?"

"I have no idea," Brown replied. "Homeland talks with us all the time. We're the first responders if something happens on the river. It doesn't make sense."

"And what's up with these other missing men?"

"That I can answer. There are two men missing. Retired Marine Preston Mullins and his son-in-law, Parker Davis. Good men. They've been coming here for years looking for the lost bomb. Have you heard the story about the missing bomb?"

"AJ told us at his restaurant the other day. You think the government really lost a bomb?"

"I don't know. There are a lot of people who believe, but there's just as many who don't."

"Maybe the FBI thinks it happened," Stephanie whispered. "That could be the reason why all of this falls under National Security. They're waiting for Bubba to find the bomb."

"Or maybe, Bubba's buyer," Brown added. "I mean, Bubba is not the sharpest tool in the shed. What's he going to do with a bomb, even if he finds it? No. If he finds it, he'll want to sell it. That's who the FBI wants, the buyer. Stephanie, if Bubba and his friends had anything to do with your friend and the other two, they are very dangerous. Maybe, you guys should back off."

"No way. Charlotte's too close a friend for us to sit back on our hands and do nothing."

"You're not going to get much help from Chief Rogers. With everyone wanting his head, Lord knows, all he needs now is the FBI coming down on him. But, that doesn't mean I can't help. What can I do for you?"

"First off, you can give us your cellphone number. That way, we won't have to be calling the police station all the time."

***

The rusty trawler passed Wassaw Sound, heading south along the coast. Pete, with his hand across his forehead, scanned the shoreline, trying to tie down their current location.

"What are you doing?" Charlotte asked.

"I think it was somewhere around here we sunk the oyster boat."

Charlotte searched the surrounding murky water, knowing she wouldn't see anything. The bubbles were long gone. *May they rest in peace,* she thought. Charlotte knew, their families would never find peace; would never have closure.

"Bubba, where're we going?" Pete called up from the main deck.

"We've searched every river, creek, ditch, and mud hole coming out of the Sound. It's time to move on."

"So, where are we going?"

"The Little Ogeechee River is just south of the Sound. We haven't tried there."

"Bubba, you know what today is?"

"I know Pete. Don't start reminding me of it."

"I'm going up to the wheelhouse," Pete said to Charlotte. "With the chain around your neck, you're not going anywhere. If I see a boat, I'll yell and -"

"I'll get in the hold. Yah, yah, yah, I know the drill . . . Pete, what's really going to happen today."

"This is the last day Wally gave us to find the bomb."

"And if you don't find it?"

"Then Frank would have gotten off easier than Bubba and me." Pete lowered the metal detector into the water as the boat slowly made its way along the coast. Then he joined Bubba in the wheelhouse.

"You leave her down there alone?" Bubba asked.

"She can't slip out with the chain around her neck, no matter how much grease she uses. She's not going anywhere. Don't worry about her," Pete answered, turning on the detector's computer.

"I'm not worried about her. But I will say this; we should go ahead and put a bullet between her eyes."

"Damnit Bubba, is that the answer to all your problems, put a bullet in it? I'm telling you, there will come a time when you're going to need her."

"What's that ahead?" Bubba asked, pointing. "Looks like a pier sticking out into the ocean. I didn't know there were any down this way."

As the boat neared the wooden pier, Pete yelled to Charlotte to get below. As they passed, Pete noticed a large faded sign – Wassaw National Wildlife Refuge. *The pier must be used as the access to the refuge*, Pete thought. Currently, there were no boats, no one on the pier or on the shore that they could see, so Pete yelled to Charlotte to come on up. A few miles and minutes later the trawler turned into the Little Ogeechee River.

"Where to Bubba?"

"We'll take the first river up ahead, to the right. That's the Moon River. You have the metal detector going?"

"It's scanning the bottom, even as we speak." Bubba nodded his head.

As the sun rose that morning, along with it, rose the temperature. By noon, Charlotte was dripping with sweat. The buzzing, biting bugs had grown to no more than a nuisance. And to make matters worse, with the sun directly overhead, there was little to no shade to hide in. Before they left that morning, Bubba went into Tybee and stopped at the *B&P Gas Station,* beside the *Sundae Café,* for donuts and coffee, along with the makings for sandwiches. Lunch that day consisted of pimento cheese sandwiches, chips and warm water. In the early afternoon, because of the intense heat, Pete hosed Charlotte down with saltwater using the sump pump again. To Charlotte, it was refreshing. The bruises on the left side of her face were now a pale brown, and she could focus her left eye, somewhat. The wound was starting to heal but would leave a nasty scar. Pete assured her, cosmetic surgery could fix it.

"Pete, could I use the hose to rinse my clothes off. I haven't taken them off for days."

"I don't see why not."

"Show me how to use the pump, and then you can get lost."

"What do you mean by that?"

"I'm not taking my clothes off while you're watching."

"Oh, yeah," Pete said, blushing. "I'll go up with Bubba. When I hear the sump pump shutdown, I'll give you a few minutes to get dressed before I come down to put the pump up."

"Thanks, Pete."

Charlotte felt odd, standing out in the open in her birthday suit. But her clothes needed attending. After several minutes of spraying, she could see the natural color of her tank-top and shorts slowly starting to appear. Using Pete's soap, she lathered and then rinsed her clothes again. After wringing the clothes by hand, she redressed. They were damp but smelled a hell of a lot better.

***

"Your time is running out," Charlotte said to Pete, as he rolled up the sump pump hose. "You have less than a day."

"I know," Pete said, looking up at the wheelhouse.

"Are you going to let me go?"

"That's my plan, Charlotte."

"You think Bubba's going to let you?"

"Doesn't matter what Bubba will or will not let me do. I will try and keep my promise."

"Pete, get up here," Bubba yelled from above. "The detector is going crazy."

Pete turned and walked off but stopped before the stairs. "Charlotte, I will not be caught. I'd rather die before going to prison."

"Pete, don't talk like that."

"Charlotte, I -"

"Pete, get your ass up here," Bubba screamed.

Bubba stood by the detector monitor, as Pete entered the

wheelhouse.

"Took you long enough," Bubba said. "Focus this damn thing. You know I can't make heads nor tails out of all these knobs and buttons."

Pete bent over and adjusted a few sliders, and the screen came into focus.

"Looks like more oil drums," Pete said, turning away.

"Shit," Bubba exclaimed, kicking a wooden crate across the room. "We've got to find that damn bomb today."

"And if we don't?"

Bubba thought a moment. "I'll call Wally and tell him we found it anyway. That should give us a day or so to get out of the country."

"And then what? Live on our good looks?"

"Damnit, I don't know," Bubba admitted. "But it'll be better than staying here. You know that, as well as I. If we have problems at the border, we'll have our hostage."

"You're taking her with us?"

"You said we might need her someday. Well, I think that day has come."

"Let's keep looking for your bomb," Pete said, walking to the doorway. "We still have a few more hours before it gets too dark."

"What did you mean, 'your bomb'? You've really given up on me?"

"Bubba, I'm tired. Frank is dead, and my heart isn't into it anymore. I'll help you, but I don't want any part of the money. Maybe you can give my part and Frank's part to his parents."

"I could do that," Bubba said smiling. From the look in Bubba's eyes, Pete knew he didn't mean it. They would never see a penny.

Chapter 32

Moon River turned out to be a dud, and Bubba was starting to sweat, not from the heat but from what Wally was going to say when he called him later that afternoon. The tide was slowly going out and Bubba knew they had to turn back before they got stuck in the mud waiting for the rising tide, wasting precious hours waiting for the rising tide.

"Where to now?" Pete asked.

"We'll try Shipyard Creek."

"You think we've got time?"

"We've got maybe forty minutes or so before low tide. The creek's not long. We'll be in and out before low tide."

Shipyard Creek wasn't wide, and at its end, there would be no place to turn the trawler around. With the rust-bucket's bow pointing toward Moon River, Bubba put the boat in reverse and slowly began backing into the creek.

"Watch our backend," Bubba yelled to Pete, who was standing at the stern. Charlotte watched as both men gently guided the big boat through the sawgrass.

"How deep is the water here?" Pete yelled, getting nervous.

"The depth gauge says nine feet."

"Is that enough to keep us from dragging our bottom?"

"Just barely."

"How long is the creek?"

"A couple of miles, according to the charts. Why?"

"You better shut down and have a look."

Bubba killed the engine and left the wheelhouse. From his vantage point on the upper deck, Bubba had a clear view of the creek, which ended a few hundred yards away. "What the shit?" Bubba said as Pete joined him.

The creek didn't look like a creek with two banks, and water flowing in between. The creek's channel was spotted with hundreds of small muddy patches, none more than a couple of feet in diameter. A few logs covered some of the patches, but most of the patches were barren.

"That's odd," Bubba said, trying to see over the grass. "I wonder what caused all of this."

"I have an idea," Pete said, looking at the sea charts.

"Well?"

"Hurricane Miles did this when it came through here a few weeks ago. The banks of the creek couldn't handle the sustained winds and caved in on each other. The roots of some of the grasses couldn't maintain a grip and were blown away, to who knows where. So, what are we going to do? Find another creek?"

Bubba stood there shaking his head. "I don't know. Jesus Pete, Wally's going to kill us."

"We should have planned for that," Pete said, looking around at the tall grass and the muddy log covered mini islands. "If we leave now, maybe we can get a jump on Wally. You'll call him acting excited, and tell him we found the bomb, but it's going to take us a few days to get it out of the mud. That will surely give us time to get out of the country."

"Pete, we may have a problem with that."

"What do you mean?"

"I don't have a passport."

"What do you mean, you don't have a passport. Then, how in the hell were you planning on getting out of the country?"

"I hadn't planned that far in advance."

"Damnit Bubba . . . Okay. If illegals can get in, surely we can get out. We'll cross that bridge when we get to it."

"Pete, what if Wally doesn't believe we found the bomb and asks for a photo?"

"Tell him it's under water, but assure him it's there . . . Hell, I don't know. I'm making this up as we go."

Suddenly, the boat tilted to port.

"What the hell," Pete exclaimed, catching himself by grabbing the rail.

"Shit," Bubba said, looking over the side. "The tide went out sooner than I thought, and we've settled on the bottom."

"You mean to tell me, we're stuck in the mud?"

"Until the tide comes back in. It won't take long. When should we call Wally?"

"I wouldn't call him now, while we're stuck. We'll need all the time we can to escape."

"So, what are we supposed to do now?"

"Find a place to sit and wait it out. Me, I'm getting out of the sun," Pete said walking into the wheelhouse.

"Pete, what just happened?" Charlotte yelled from below.

"Low tide, Charlotte. Make yourself as comfortable as you can. It's going to take a while."

The small mini islands of mud were now connected, forming one large mudflat. From the wheelhouse, Pete shook his head. This was turning out to be one hell of a bad day. Scanning the horizon revealed no other boats.

They were smart enough to remember low tide was coming, Pete thought, smiling at himself. From the wheelhouse, Pete could see this portion of Moon River wasn't much more than a mud hole with a small narrow stream trickling down its middle. At the junction of Moon River and Shipyard Creek, on the opposite bank, Pete saw something odd lying at the low water line, something large and muddy lying at the low water line. *A log?* Pete thought. *I don't think so.*

***

Lisa looked at her watch. 3:30 p.m. Looking around the room, she smiled. Matt had earbuds in his ears listening to Rock and Roll while pounding on his keyboard. Glenda was busy researching the Port of Savannah. Harry was napping.

I wonder why he doesn't retire.

Lisa's phone lit up, and she answered it by pressing the speaker button.

"We intersected this one," a strange voice said. "This is real time. Thought you might be interested."

Speaker 1:"I wondered if you would have the balls to call me."

"That's Wally," Harry said rousing from his nap.

Speaker 2: "You're not going to believe this, but we found it."

"That's Bubba."

Wally: "You're fucking with me. You're lying, and you know it. No one's found the bomb in all these years, and you're telling me a bunch of goofballs did."

Bubba: "Swear to God."

Wally: "Proof. Send me proof."

Bubba: "I'll take a photo and text it to you. The bomb was covered in mud, but Pete wiped some of it off. You can see the pointy end. Wally, this is the real deal."

Wally: "Okay, send me the picture. If it looks like the item, I'll set up a meeting in Savannah."

Bubba: "Which ship will we be meeting?"

Wally: "I'll get back to you on that. Text me the picture. If it checks out, you three boys are going to be rich."

Bubba: "Two of us. Frank is dead."

Wally: "How in the hell did that happen?"

Bubba: "Our hostage tried to escape by going into the sawgrass. Frank went after her. Next thing you know, our hostage pops out of the marsh with Frank on her tail."

Wally: "So how did he die?"

Bubba: "A monster gator was chasing them. It got Frank."

Wally: "Damn."

Bubba: "When we found the bomb, Pete was even afraid to get into the water."

Wally: "You blame him?"

Bubba: "No, not really. Wally, there was nothing we could do for Frank. He was there one moment and gone the next."

Wally: "That's a shame."

Bubba: "Pete says, we should give Frank's share to his parents."

Wally: "I don't give a shit what you do with it. Send me the photo, and I'll get back to you."

[Line dropped.]

"Wow, that was exciting," Lisa said, pressing the speaker button, cutting her end of the connection. "What do you make of it?"

"There's so much," Glenda replied. "Where to start?"

"Anywhere," Lisa commented.

"Well, according to Bubba, they found the bomb, and they're texting a picture."

"I'm monitoring text messages from Tybee," Matt chimed in.

"I'm looking for anything with a Jpeg attached.".

"One of their comrades was eaten by an alligator," Harry added. "Hell of a way to die. Did you know, mankind's worst fear is that of being eaten alive? It all started back in our caveman days when we hid in caves in fear of the dark, big cats and cave-bears. You hear or read about a shark attack, and it makes your skin crawl. You let someone get shot and die, in todays' world that's not a big deal. But let something eat you, well that's different. It's a normal reaction."

"Did you notice, their hostage is still alive?" Lisa asked, changing the subject. All three nodded their heads. "That has to be Charlotte Knott."

"Are we going to tell them?" Glenda asked.

"Who?"

"The Tybee Police or her friends."

"Not today."

"Are we going to be able to take them in Savannah without collateral damage?" Glenda asked.

"You're talking about the hostage? (Glenda nodded.) We'll do our best, but the number one priority is the bomb."

"You're really not going to let the Tybee Police and the Coast Guard in on this now?" Matt asked.

"The Assistant Director says no. We'll get them all, Bubba and his friend, and the buyer in Savannah."

"And the hostage?"

"And the hostage."

"Gotcha," Matt exclaimed from his desk.

"What?" Lisa asked.

"The photo," Matt replied. "It was easier than I thought. Bubba's using his own cell phone, remember? All I had to do was monitor his cell number. And here for you enjoyment, ladies and gentleman, is the bomb."

Instantly all the monitors in the room lit up displaying a fuzzy photo.

"Not very clear," Harry complained. "It looks like one of those pictures people take of Bigfoot. You know the ones, a blurry picture of something big, something unrecognizable and the photographer swears up and down its Bigfoot. And to top it off, he or she was its sex slave."

"That happened to my aunt," Glenda said seriously. "Said she got pregnant by Bigfoot, but aliens took her aboard their spacecraft and aborted it. She has the scar and everything." There was intense silence as everyone stared at Glenda. Glenda continued. "My mom said the scar was from gallbladder surgery. My aunt says mom is one of *them*. Mom and my aunt were never really close after that."

"Wally's not going to like that," Lisa said.

"About my mom and aunt?"

"No," Lisa said, fighting back a laugh. "I'm talking about the blurry picture."

"Bubba knows that," Matt stated, "because he just sent another one. That's better."

On their screen was a picture of what looked like a massive bomb and a man standing beside it.

"Looks like a bomb to me," Lisa stated.

The monitor screen split into two views.

"I did that," Harry said, proudly.

Screen left was the second photo Bubba sent to Wally. Screen right was an old black and white photo of a hydrogen bomb from the late fifties. The ends of the bombs looked identical.

"That's the bomb alright," Lisa said. "You know if these guys were on the up and up, they would have gotten rich off the talk shows and book deals."

"Now, they're going down for murder and treason," Harry sighed. "What a waste."

"Speaking of going down," Matt added. "If for some reason this goes south and we didn't notify the other authorities for their help, our asses are grass."

"Then it better not go south," Lisa said, picking up her phone. "I'm calling the guys in Savannah. We need to let them know the bomb will be heading their way tonight or tomorrow."

Chapter 33

"Well, we're floating again," Pete said, noticing the gentle swaying of the trawler.

"We're more than floating, Pete old boy. We're rolling, rolling in the money," Bubba laughed. "All we have to do is get her aboard without blowing up."

"You told me touching it could set it off," Charlotte said, standing beside Pete in the wheelhouse.

"Well, when I took the picture, Pete had to touch it to wipe the mud off, and it didn't blow up."

"Good God Almighty, I didn't think about that." Pete's knees suddenly went weak. He could be dead right now. All of them could be dead. Tybee Island could be dead.

"So, how are we going to get it out of the mud and aboard the boat?" Bubba asked.

Only the front quarter of the bomb was covered in water. The other three quarters were lying on the mud bank, covered and surrounded by sawgrass. The thing was about the same length, but larger in diameter than the replica at AJs.

"What if we dig a trench under the middle of the bomb and slide a strap under her?" Bubba asked. "We could attach the strap to the crane hook and lift her aboard."

"That's a dumb idea," Charlotte said calmly and softly, so as not to piss off Bubba.

"How so?"

"You're talking about balancing the bomb in the middle. What if you're wrong and halfway on board, it slips? If the nose makes hard contact with the metal deck, we could die. And, as old as its metal is, it could split in half."

"Well, you have something better?"

"You could attach a strap about a quarter of the way from each end. That way when you pick it up, it would hang between the two straps."

"Not bad, Charlotte," Pete agreed. "But you would be concentrating all its weight in the middle. What if the bomb's casting has weakened? It could split open, spilling radioactive material everywhere. I don't know about you, but I'm planning on having children someday. Building on your idea, why don't we add a third strap, one around the middle? We would be spreading its weight along the entire length of the bomb."

"You're talking about three straps," Bubba said. "How are we going to attach three straps to the crane hook? They would be spaced too far apart."

"There's a ton of pipe joints aboard. They were used for oil drilling cases. We could lay a joint beside the bomb and attach the three straps to it. We would then add an additional strap to the middle of the pipe and attach it to the crane hook."

"That's a hell of a lot of work," Bubba whispered.

"There's more," Pete added. "We need to make a frame, a cradle, for it to lay in. We don't want it to go rolling around the deck."

"Again, a hell of a lot of work."

"Finding the bomb was only the first part," Pete said, searching the deck for the raw materials for making the sling. "The three of us will clear the sawgrass from around the bomb, dig the trenches and attach the straps."

"Good plan, Pete," Bubba said.

"Not a good plan, Pete," Charlotte chimed in.

"Why not," Pete asked.

"You're asking me, your hostage, to help you. I mean really. After what you two have put me through, and you want me to help you?"

"You want this to end?"

"You know I do."

"Then help me."

"There's one other thing."

"What's that Charlotte?"

"The alligator."

"Oh yeah. That could be a problem."

"Why don't we take handguns with us," Bubba suggested. "A couple of rounds in its mouth would change its mind about eating us."

"Good idea, Bubba," Charlotte added. "You'll have to show me how to use a gun."

"Good try Charlotte," Pete laughed. "Just Bubba and I need a weapon. Who's to say you won't shoot one of us, thinking we're the gator."

"I would never do that," Charlotte said, staring hard at Bubba.

"We better get started," Pete sighed. "It's going to be dark in a few hours. I'd like to get the bomb suspended in its sling before nightfall. We don't have to have it aboard then. We don't even have to have the cradle made by dark. That can wait till tomorrow morning."

Bubba ran up to the wheelhouse and returned with two handguns, a rusty fire axe, machete and shovel.

"I found these the other day. We'll need the axe and machete to clear away the grass and weeds; the shovel to dig the trenches under the bomb."

"I hope you didn't pay extra for those," Charlotte laughed.

"Smartass," Bubba laughed. "You'll get to use the shovel. We'll be keeping an eye on you. I don't want a smack upside the head."

The three stood at the rail, staring down at the bomb.

"Who's going over first?" Bubba asked, searching the dark areas beneath the grass; searching, thinking about the alligator.

"Not me," Pete answered, thinking the same thing.

Both men looked at Charlotte. "Hell no," she exclaimed. "It's not my damn bomb. I'm the hostage, remember?" "Okay then," Pete said, throwing a leg over the rail. "Bubba, have that gun handy. If the grass moves, kill it. But by God, don't shoot me." Bubba laughed.

"I'm not being funny."

Pete dropped into the waist deep water, his mind full of alligators.

"Bubba?"

"Nothing Pete."

"Okay. Hand me the machete."

The bomb was completely entwined with weeds and vines. "Bubba, get down here and help. It's going to take longer than I thought. Charlotte, you come on down too."

"Why?" she asked.

"I don't want both of us down here and you up there. You might decide to drive off and leave us here stranded . . . No. Climb on over. There's nothing down here."

"How about leeches," Charlotte said, remembering the other day.

"Oh, there will be leeches. Can't help it. But, we can take care of those later. Charlotte, get your ass down here."

The task was back breaking, and the grass suffocating, hot and humid. Within minutes they were soaked from sweat and their legs caked in mud. It took forever for Pete and Bubba to clear the vines, weeds and grass from around the bomb. Not for a moment did Bubba and Pete take their eyes off Charlotte. She wasn't going to get the chance to use the shovel as a weapon.

"Alright, that's done," Pete said, out of breath. "Charlotte, come here. This is about the middle of the bomb. Start digging on this side. I'll get on the other side and once you're halfway under, you can pass the shovel on over to me."

While the two dug the trenches, Bubba placed the joint of pipe beside the bomb and the straps across it. A clang rang out, causing Charlotte to jump back, dropping the shovel and placing her hands beside her head.

"What was that?" Pete yelled.

"I accidentally hit the bomb with the shovel," Charlotte yelled back. "I'm sorry."

"Well it didn't go off," Pete sighed. "Be more careful. Okay?"

Charlotte shook her head.

It took close to two hours before everything was in place, and it was well past dark. Bubba had climbed back on the trawler and turned on one of the search lights, aiming it at the bomb. From the railing, Pete surveyed their handy work. "Looks pretty good," he said. "Okay, Bubba, start the crane, but don't raise anything."

Once the engine started, Bubba went to the crane controls. "Okay, Bubba, take the slack out of the cable," Pete said, pointing. Soon the cable was tight. "Slowly start raising the cable. Once the bomb is free of the mud, stop. Don't raise it higher than a foot."

"Why not?" Bubba asked.

"I want to make sure the bomb is balanced, and it doesn't break up."

The sound of gears grinding filled the darkness. At some point, the cable stopped, and the whining of the gears increased.

"Hold it there," Pete yelled. "Something's holding her down."

Grabbing the machete, Pete dropped over the side. It took a few minutes before he found the cause of the delay.

"There's a vine wrapped around the middle strap . . . Give me a minute . . . There that should free it."

Climbing back on board, Pete motioned for Bubba to resume. The cable went tight again and slowly the bomb rose from the mud with a sucking sound. When the bomb was about a foot off the mudflat, Pete waved his arms, yelling, "Stop there."

Pete waited a full minute, checking for any sagging, any cracks, and if the bomb was balanced. "Okay, Bubba raise it up, so it will clear the railing."

Bubba stopped the crane a foot and a half above the railing, still no sagging or cracking.

"Okay, slowly swing it over to the middle of the deck."

The massive bomb slowly rotated, with Pete's eyes never leaving it. "Stop," Pete yelled. "We're good." All three let out a big sigh. "We did it," Charlotte said, dropping down on her chair.

"We did," Pete said. "All of us did."

In his hands was the end of the chain and the lock.

"Seriously?" Charlotte asked. Pete nodded his head. "Afraid

so . . . Walk out into the light and let's get this attached and then we'll check for leeches."

Charlotte had a dozen; Pete just as many; Bubba was the winner with a dozen and a half.

"Tomorrow I'll clean us up with the sump pump. I'm too tired tonight," Pete commented, staring at the bomb. "You did it, Bubba. Where others swore it didn't exist, and those that believed, couldn't find it for fifty years and you found it. You should probably get on the phone and tell Wally we have it aboard."

**

Lisa reclined in bed, watching an old rerun of *SVU – Law & Order Special Victims Unit.* She had already finished supper and her two-drink limit of Jack and Coke. Cleo lay beside her, as always, licking her paws and privates. Lisa was tired and more than ready for bed. She hoped she didn't fall asleep before the end of the show. Most nights she did. All the lights were out, with the only light coming from the soft glow of the TV screen. Cleo yawned.

"I'm with you girl," Lisa said, yawning in return. Then the phone rang.

"Now what?" Lisa whispered to Cleo as she searched for her cell phone on the crowded end table. "Hello."

"Lisa, Matt," the familiar voice said on the other end.

"This better be good," Lisa sighed. "I was just dozing off."

"Sorry, but Bubba just called Wally." Lisa was instantly awake.

"It's awful late for him to be calling, don't you think?" she asked.

"I know. But, if I had been Bubba, I would have called. You know today was the deadline."

"I remember. So?"

"He did it. He got the bomb aboard his ship, and he's proud. That's why he called Wally so late."

"Okay . . . So, if Wally can get hold of his buyer tonight, then the deal should go down tomorrow."

"That's the way I see it."

"I'll call Mulder in Savannah and give him a heads up. I want him at the southern end of the island when Bubba comes up the coast. I'll have him follow their boat all the way to Port. He'll be able to keep our team up to date on their where-a-bouts. Good job, Matt."

"Thanks, boss."

"Matt, is there any way we can get eyes on the trawler?"

"You mean right now, while she's out there in the marsh?"

"Yes."

"I'll have to think about it, Boss."

"Great. I'll call Mulder now . . . Wait a minute Matt."

"What's up, Boss?"

"You're working awful late. You still in the office?"

"Uh, no. I'm at home."

"Then how did you get the phone call?"

"It is a long story."

"Could it be you have an unauthorized server at home, and you're monitoring from there? No, don't tell me. I really don't want to know."

"Okay, Boss, I won't tell you."

"I'll be in earlier in the morning. We're going to have a busy day."

Chapter 34

Jennifer Clinton was a senior at Butler University in Charleston. She loved going to Savannah for extended weekends. She and her friends enjoyed hanging out at *Club 51 Degrees*, a massive nightclub with three floors of DJs spinning tunes, drink specials, and special themed events. There was also the boisterous *Club One* multi-level night club, that was known for its dancing, drag shows, and a basement video bar. Mostly, she and friends loved being picked up by men with speedboats and a good deal of weed.

To Jennifer, there was no better weekend than being on the water, nude sunbathing and getting high on drugs. Of course, the men would expect something in return. But Jennifer enjoyed that as well. She was, by definition, a slut. Her saintly mother would have a cow if she knew of her daughter's sinful behavior. Maybe that was the reason Jennifer was the way she was.

"Girls, sadly, our weekend is drawing to a close," a tall, shirtless, muscular man said starting the inboard engine. "The tide's finally high enough and we need to head on back to AJ's dock. Our wives think we've been fishing all weekend and are expecting us to be home by supper."

Jennifer couldn't remember if his name was George or John. "I like your idea of coming out here in the marsh while the tide is low," she said. "Keeps prying eyes from catching you while you're smoking pot."

"We do this all the time," the man said, watching Jennifer put on her bra. "Maybe we can do this again?"

"We'd love too."

George or John put the boat in gear and slowly pushed the

throttle forward. "You guys can light up while we're going back," he said.

"How do you keep track of where you are in the marsh, especially when it's getting dark?" Jennifer asked.

"As you go in, always take the channels to the left. Keep turning left. When you come out, always take the channels to the right. Just the opposite of how you went in, and you will end up where you started."

"That's genius. Pure genius," she laughed, sucking hard on a joint.

After a few minutes, Jennifer noticed lights ahead.

"I wonder what those are."

"I don't know this late in the day. Pick up around here a little. Hide the pot. The beer, I don't care about."

A boat drew slowly out of the darkness. From the spotlights on the bow and the stern, Jennifer could see it was an old rusty boat. Two men stood on an upper deck watching as they approached, one black, the other white, both were covered in mud from the waist down. They didn't look like cops.

"Good evening," George or John said, being friendly.

The black man nodded.

"You guys are out kind of late," the white guy said, walking along the catwalk as the speedboat slowly passed.

"We've been partying all weekend, farther up Moon River, on one of its side creeks," George or John replied.

"We never heard you," the white guy commented.

"We try to keep the noise down. Don't want the cops showing up. You know what I mean."

The white guy smiled and nodded. "I know what you mean."

"What's that?" Jennifer asked, noticing the long cylinder thing hanging above the deck.

"That?" the white guy asked. "That's an old army shell casing. We uncovered it this afternoon."

"Is it worth something," she asked.

"Only a few hundred dollars, I'm afraid."

"So, why did you dig it up?"

"For the fun, I guess. We've been hunting old stuff like that for years."

"Well, you guys take it easy," George or John said, as they passed the stern of the rusty boat. "We need to get on in to Tybee."

Pete and Bubba gave them a friendly wave as they disappeared.

***

Mike and FJ couldn't see Ray on the other side of the marina. It was getting too dark.

"I wonder where they are," Mike said, turning to FJ. "They're always back here by now."

FJ shrugged his shoulders. "Maybe there was a traffic jam."

"A traffic jam on the ocean?" Mike laughed.

"I don't know . . . Somebody's coming. I hope it's not the F.B.I."

"Roll your window down and let's see what he wants," Mike said softy.

"Evening gentlemen," the stranger said as he approached FJ's window. "You guys have been out here a long time."

"We were just looking at your marina."

"It's not my marina, but the *Bait and Tackle* is mine. We're closing up in about fifteen minutes and we don't like people hanging out around here when we're gone. We had a few problems with kids smoking pot and destroying property."

"I understand," Mike replied. "Maybe we can come in before you close. Maybe do a little shopping."

"You got fifteen minutes."

"That'll give us time to look around."

"There's no harm in that."

"You really want to go in there?" FJ whispered as the owner walked away.

"I'm bored," Mike whispered back. "It'll give us something to do while we wait."

The *Bait and Tackle* was like any other bait shop; a section with live bait – peeler crabs, sardines, minnows, bloodworms and night crawlers; a section with lures, rods and reels; a section with fishing accessories and apparel. Mike stopped at a display and picked up a rod, testing its flexibility.

"You interested in a rod?" the owner asked, walking over.

"No, not really. My mom was a fisherman. She used to get up at three or four in the morning to get her chores done, so she could be on the bank when the sun came up. She'd drag me out to a Pay Lake and -"

"Excuse me, but what is a Pay Lake?"

"Let's see how I can explain it. If you had several small lakes and you stock them with fish, mainly catfish, then you charge people to fish there. The more fish you stocked in one lake, the more you could charge. Get it?" The man nodded his head.

"My mom would drag me out to a Pay Lake, and together we'd sit on the bank fishing. Well, she called it fishing; I called it sitting on the bank. You see, we used the same tackle: a cane pole, line with bobber, worm on a hook, and she'd catch fish, me nothing. I asked her how she did it; how she caught fish."

"And did she tell you?"

"She asked me if I spit on the worm before I flung out the line."

"You're kidding?"

"Nope. That's what she said. So, I tried spitting on the worm."

"Did it work?"

"Not at all. Not that first damn fish." The owner laughed. "That's funny. I'm going to go around now and start locking up. You'll have a few more minutes. If you need anything give me a holler."

Mike made his way down the long line of rods, coming close to where FJ was talking with a pretty young salesgirl.

"You seriously haven't heard of Peter Dinklage?" FJ asked.

"Nope," she replied.

"And you've never heard of *Game of Thrones*?"

"Nope."

"It's on HBO."

"Oh, I've heard of that, but I've never watched it."

"And why not? It's a great channel."

"I've heard it is, but it's on premium, and I don't get premium."

Mike's cell rang. "Hello . . . Okay . . . We'll be there in a minute."

"What's up?" FJ asked, coming over.

"Not your ego, from what I overheard."

"Screw you, Mike."

"Ray wants us to pick him up. Deputy Brown called. Wants us to meet him over at AJ's dock."

***

"Where's the trawler?" FJ asked as Ray climbed into the van.

"And how in the hell should I know?"

"Maybe Special Agent Mulder told you."

"He warned me, said what we're doing could get us killed."

"And you said?"

"It's a free country."

"Great response, Ray. Great response."

"Screw you, FJ."

"So are we heading over to AJ's now?" Mike asked.

"Deputy Brown said he wants to see us now."

"Even with agent Mulder following us?"

"I told Brown that and he said come on. He says, something's going down, but he couldn't talk about it over the phone."

Chapter 34

AJ's was packed, forcing Mike to park on the next street, in an empty lot with a yellow surfboard with letters stating – AJ's Parking.

"Man, I wished I had some stock in AJ's business," FJ said, crossing the street.

A crowd, waiting their turn, stood outside the restaurant. Children were climbing on the fake bomb; groups of people were talking; a few grownups were smoking; a couple of people were waving their hands in front of their faces because the smoke was bothering them.

Why don't you stand somewhere else? FJ thought, passing them.

A teenage couple stood off to the side, lost in each other's eyes. Both were dressed in gothic black outfits. FJ recognized the girl as the girl from *T S Chu Department Store.* As the three approached, FJ could feel adult eyes staring at him. Children stopped playing and waved. The whispered name, Peter Dinklage, came from a few. FJ waved his hand like royalty, as they made their way to check-in.

"How many in your party," a young woman with a clipboard asked.

"Deputy Brown asked us to meet him here," Ray replied.

"You mean Marvin?"

Ray nodded his head.

"Follow me please."

As they walked through the restaurant, FJ tugged on Ray's arm. "Did you know his name was Marvin?"

"Nope," Ray replied. "But how many Deputy Brown's does Tybee have?"

"I don't see Agent Mulder behind us," Mike whispered as they

235

turned a corner, entering the outside dining area.

"Oh, he's back there somewhere," Ray assured him.

The young woman led them across the outside dining area and through a gate with a sign that read, "Employees Only." A narrow, railed, wooden boardwalk led them down to the dock.

"This is the employee's access to AJ's dock. We use it to bring food, ice, and package liquors to those spending time on the water. The Tybee Police Department has a boat moored here."

Deputy Brown, standing on the covered deck of a smart looking cruiser, waved them aboard.

"Welcome," he said. "Would you like something to drink or eat?"

"Both," FJ replied. "I'd like a cheeseburger through the garden, fries and a tall beer, any kind of beer."

Ray and Mike ordered the same. It had been a long time since lunch. Margaret and Stephanie knew they would be late, so they planned on walking over to MacElwee's. The four men took cast iron seats around a cast iron table with a Plexiglas top.

"This is nice," Mike said, looking at the boat and their surroundings. The police had the first mooring spot on the dock reserved, making it easier for them to exit the area in a hurry. The sun had long set, but the full moon illuminated the surrounding water and marsh. Music drifted across the water from AJ's.

"Well, Deputy Brown, what do you have for us?" Ray asked after their beers arrived.

"First off, call me Marvin."

"Okay, Marvin, lay it on us."

"Every other afternoon, I come down here and monitor the returning boaters. If any are drunk or under the influence, I give them a warning. Now don't get me wrong, I enjoy a beer or two while fishing, but on the ocean and in the marsh, drinking could get you killed . . . Late this afternoon, a local guy pulled in. He and a few friends had been partying all weekend on the marsh. They all think they're smart. They wait till low tide when the water's out, thinking no one will sneak up and surprise them. Then, they smoke pot, get drunk and have orgies. Anyway, this afternoon George said they passed a rusty old boat anchored in the marsh. I asked what he meant by rusty boat. He said it looked like the one that's normally moored at the *Bait and Tackle*. He -"

"That's their boat," Mike interrupted. Marvin nodded his head. "He went on to say there were two men onboard, a black guy and a white guy."

"They didn't see the third guy."

"He must have been below guarding Charlotte," FJ stated.

"If she's aboard," Marvin reminded him.

"Yeah, right."

"Are they and you really sure it was Bubba's boat?" Ray asked.

"By their description, it has to be. It's the only rust-bucket parked at the *B and T*. Now here's the kicker. They saw a circular metal shell casing, as the man called it, hanging from a crane onboard the boat. Ray, it has to be the bomb."

"You know what that means?" Ray asked.

"No," Mike answered.

"It means, they're close to their objective, and they don't have much of a need for Charlotte anymore."

"They'll let her go, right?" FJ asked.

Ray didn't answer but stood there staring at the dark waters, thinking of Sara Sinclair. After a few moments, Ray turned to Deputy Brown. "So, Marvin, what can we do?"

Marvin stood and walked over to the rail, pulling a pack of cigarettes from his shirt pocket. A minute later, he was lit up.

"I didn't know you smoked," Ray said.

"Only when I'm nervous, and right now I'm nervous," Marvin said, taking a long pull off the cig. "I'm about to suggest something that could get us all in trouble, something that could get us killed."

"I'm all for that," FJ said, sarcastically.

"As big as the marsh is, do you know where they are?" Ray asked, trying to take their mind off of dying.

"They're on Moon River," Marvin said. "I used to fish there a lot when I was a teenager. I won't have a problem finding them."

"Can we go and check them out?" Mike asked.

"Not all of us," Marvin replied.

"Why not? This boat seems big enough."

"We can't take the department's boat. I have a personal craft we could use, but it would only handle three of us."

"What kind of craft is that?"

"It's a Panther model airboat. If you're done with your burgers, I'll show it to you."

Marvin led them along the dock to the last mooring station. There floated an older model airboat, one of those with a big fan on the back. It had three seats, a tall one in the back for the driver, and two shorter in front, side by side, for the passengers.

"Here's my baby," Marvin said proudly. "She doesn't look like much, but she can haul ass. In her former life, she used to carry up to nine tourists through the Everglades. I removed all the seats but two. With her lighter load and her 850 HP fuel injected engine, she can push her way through the tallest grass and mud. The kids love zipping through the water and gliding across mudflats. The best part, I don't have to worry about low tide."

"That's nice," FJ said, "but what has that to do with us?"

"I'd like to have a look at the bomb," Marvin said. "I thought you would too."

"Now? In the dark?" FJ asked. "Would you be able to find them . . . in the dark?"

"The witnesses told me they were on Moon River, and the trawler had search lights on their boat. I bet they'll leave the lights on, to make sure no one rams them in the dark. Wouldn't want the bomb to explode."

"Great. You had to bring that up," FJ exclaimed. "So, who goes with you?"

"That's up to you," Marvin replied. "Don't matter to me. Draw straws. The short straw stays here."

"Hey, I resent that," FJ chimed.

"What?" Marvin asked.

"Ignore him," Mike replied, laughing.

"I'm not hanging around here wasting time while you three go off into the dark," FJ commented flatly. "Besides, Mike won't let me drive his van."

"You can't drive my van anyway. It's not set up for little people."

"And you won't let me drive your van either," Ray added.

"That's true," Mike admitted. "So, I guess I'm the short straw."

"Now you know how I feel," FJ laughed.

***

"It's getting late," Pete said, looking at the full moon and stars. "We should probably hit the hay. We have a lot to do in the morning . . . Charlotte, out here in the marsh, we won't have to worry about anyone sneaking up on us. So tonight, we'll leave the hatch open for you."

"Thanks, Pete."

"You think that's a good idea?" Bubba asked.

"Where's she going?" Pete replied. "She can't slip out of the chain . . . To help us all sleep, I'll turn off the bow searchlight and only leave on the stern. We'll get up early and build the cradle for the bomb. Bubba will call Wally letting him know we're coming in. By this time tomorrow, this will all be over." Charlotte stared at Pete, searching his eyes. What did he mean – By this time tomorrow, this will all be over? Bubba stared at Charlotte, thinking the same thing. Pete went to his cot.

***

Call or not call? That was the question playing around in Wally's head. Since Bubba called earlier, Wally was dying to tell Sean the good news, but with a four-hour difference in time zones between Atlanta and Ireland, the person who picked up on the other end wasn't going to be happy being woke up this early. Wally gave in and slowly dialed the number.

"Hello," a sleepy voice said.

"Is this Sean?" Wally asked, nervously.

"No. I'm his . . . Answering service. Who wants to know?"

"This is Wally Wilkins. I talked with Sean the other day. I

have something for him."

"What?"

"That's between Sean and me."

"Go screw yourself," the voice said. "Anything you have to say to Mr. Murphy goes through me first. So, let me ask again, what do you have for Mr. Murphy?" There was a pause. "Well, shithead, you going to tell me or not?" Another pause.

"I found the frickin hydrogen bomb!" Wally blurted out.

"Say again."

"You heard me the first time, dumbass. Get the cobwebs out of your eyes, ears and ass, and listen up. Sean and I are friends. So, you better move your ass and wake him up right this God damn minute, or you'll be the one being screwed."

"Do you know who you're talking to?"

"Yeah, his damn answering service. But you know what? I really don't give a shit who I'm talking too. You have a minute to get him on the line, or I'm finding another buyer. You have one minute and counting."

Wally waited, watching his watch. He wasn't kidding. Sean's 'Answering Service' had really pissed him off. Wally wasn't worried about finding another buyer. The world was full of terrorists. Forty-seven seconds later another sleepy voice came online.

"You have some balls, Wally."

"Sorry Sean, but it seems I had a problem with your 'Answering Service.'" Sean laughed. "So, you found the item in question?"

"Yes, Sir."

"And it's still intact?"

"Yes, Sir. And ready for pickup tomorrow afternoon."

"That's good, really good. When you make delivery, I'll have the money transferred to your account."

"That's what I wanted to hear. I'll be at the Port when the boat pulls in. (Silence) Tomorrow then?"

"Tomorrow." The line went dead.

Sean picked up another burner phone and pressed a single key.

"You alone?" Sean asked.

"Yeah, Boss. What's up with calling so early?"

"I got a job for you."

"You want someone to not show up for work one of these mornings?"

"That's why I hired you."

"So, who is it?"

"Not one, but a smartass who had the balls to wake me, and his friends. I'll send you details later. The smartass I want dead by tomorrow morning. The others when they pull into port."

Sean pressed a button, and the line went dead.

Chapter 36

"So, how do you drive this thing?" FJ asked, strapping himself in to one of the passenger seats onboard the airboat.

"Pretty easy," Marvin replied. "You see the 'stick' on the left side of the captain's chair? It controls all the movements of the boat. The further you push it forward, the faster the boat goes. If you suddenly jerk it forward, it will almost throw you out of the boat, launching itself forward. Pull it back, and the boat slows to a stop. Jerk it back, and the boat will stop on a dime. Push it to the left, and the boat turns to the left. Pull to the right, toward you, and the boat turns to the right. It's kind of like the old-time airplanes."

"What's the little stick behind the left one?"

"That little stick is for the trolling motor I installed. When I go fishing, I use it for small maneuvers up close to the marsh. And it's silent. Don't want to scare off the fish."

"I bet it gets noisy with that big fan behind you," Ray said, pointing.

"That's why you'll be wearing these," Marvin said, handing each man a set of ear protectors.

Once everyone was strapped in, Marvin fired up the engine. It was loud, even with the ear protectors on. A flick of a switch turned on a row of lights attached to the front and sides of the boat, lighting the water for forty feet or more.

"Hang on," Marvin said, even though he knew the men couldn't hear him.

Mike watched as the airboat disappeared into the darkness. There was no reason for him to stay here now. When they got back,

Ray would call him to come and pick them up.

"Where're they going?" Mulder said, startling Mike.

"Fishing."

"Fishing, my ass. They're going to look for the boat. I need to call this in."

"Wait a minute Mulder. There's no hurry. Let's you and I go and have a beer. My treat. We can talk, and if you still feel the same way when I'm done talking, you can call it in."

"Your treat?"

"My treat."

Airboats are ideal for marsh travel because there is nothing below the deck that could get hung on something. Ocean travel is just the opposite. Airboats aren't made for heavy waves. So, their journey had to be completely within the marsh. Heading west along Tybee Creek for a few miles, Marvin turned onto the Bull River, heading south to Wassaw Sound. From there, he headed upstream along the Wilmington River. After a few minutes, he turned a left onto Skidaway River. Another few minutes and he bought the airboat to a standstill, shutting the engine and lights off.

"That was exciting," FJ exclaimed, taking off his ear protectors. "I couldn't see shit in front of me, but it was exciting. I'd like to try that in the daylight."

Marvin laughed. "Someday I'll take you out."

"Why did we stop?" Ray asked.

"Just ahead is Moon River, where they are. I'm afraid if we get any closer, they'll hear the engine or see the lights. I suggest we use the trolling motor." Ray and FJ nodded. "It's going to be slow going. The trolling motor isn't fast, and we'll have to use a flashlight to see. Ray, take the light and keep it pointed down at the water in front of us. Don't let them see the shine."

It took almost as much time to travel the length of the Skidaway River as it did getting to the Skidaway. Finally, Marvin shut down. "Look ahead and to the left. Isn't that a light?"

"I can't see anything," FJ replied, standing on tiptoes.

"It's because you're too short," Ray laughed. "But I can see it."

"Screw you, Ray," FJ spat.

"Let's get a little closer," Marvin answered. "At some point, we'll have to stop. I don't want them seeing us."

Thirty minutes later and the airboat was resting in a small drainage ditch a hundred yards from the rusty trawler.

"Is that what I think it is?" FJ whispered.

"I bet it is," Marvin replied.

"It looks nothing like the bomb at AJs," FJ added.

"I don't see anyone on deck," Ray whispered. "I bet they're inside sleeping. Can we get closer?"

"You want to take the chance of getting caught?" Marvin asked.

"I think they're asleep," Ray assured him. "Let's get a little closer."

"I don't like it, but okay."

Silently, they made their way alongside the marsh, staying as close to the sawgrass and shadows as they could. Within twenty feet, Marvin stopped. "Jesus, guys, I don't like this one bit."

"We're okay," Ray whispered. "Their light is on the stern, and its casting shadows our way. If you pull up next to the side of the boat, they can't see us for sure."

"And why would we want to do that?"

"Maybe we can hear something," Ray answered.

Using his hands, Ray stopped the airboat from bumping into the larger boat. He noticed his hands were shaking. *If we're caught now . . .* He shook his head, forcing his mind not to finish his thought. Marvin held the anchor chain steadying the boat while Ray placed his head against the cool metal, listening, but hearing nothing. *What now?* They couldn't stay here all night. FJ leaned in as close as he could to Marvin's ear and whispered, "I'll be right back."

Marvin wanted to scream as FJ stood, grabbed the anchor chain and began climbing up hand over hand. As FJ passed Ray, he bumped him with his foot, almost causing Ray to piss his pants.

What are you doing, you little fart? Marvin thought as FJ made it to the small hole the anchor line disappeared into.

Are you out of your frickin mind? Ray thought, as FJ swung a leg up over the chain and grabbed the lip of the deck with a free hand. With a twist of his body, FJ was sitting atop the chain, straddling it like a horse. Once balanced, FJ slowly shimmied up the chain and crawled up under the railing. He sat there breathing hard from the climb; heart beating even harder from fear.

Suddenly, Marvin put the trolling motor in reverse, silently backing the airboat away from the trawler. Ray wanted to yell, "What the hell? FJ's up there." As soon as they backed far enough away, Ray could see the light on through a porthole. Somebody was up. The runoff ditch was a safe haven.

"You think they heard us?" Ray whispered.

"I doubt it."

In the moonlight, they saw Bubba come out on the deck, stopping by the rail.

"What's he doing?" Marvin asked. "It's hard to see in the dark."

Ray almost laughed. "He's taking a piss."

"FJ's right by him," Marvin exclaimed, in a whisper. "How can he keep from not seeing him?"

"It's dark, and Bubba has no reason to look for anyone. As long as he doesn't turn and step on FJ, everything's good."

"What made the little shit do that?" Marvin asked.

"He loves Charlotte, like the rest of us. And, he's been wanting to look inside the boat since day one."

"It could be the last thing he does."

Bubba returned the way he came. Soon the light switched off. Marvin and Ray, both let out a sigh. FJ let out a sigh. Rising, he made his way over to the open hatch. *Are you down there, or in the crew quarters?* In the moon light, he could see the end of a chain attached to the top step. *You're down there?* Slowly, he lowered his foot to the first step, then the next.

"What's he doing?" Marvin asked.

"I think he's going into the hold."

"That's crazy. Why doesn't he shine a light down there?"

"Because he doesn't have a flashlight."

"Shit."

Halfway down the ladder, a flashlight came on from below, blinding FJ.

I'm dead, he thought to himself.

"FJ?" Charlotte whispered. FJ smiled, as Charlotte grabbed him up, crushing him to her chest. "I thought I'd never see you again," Charlotte said, sobbing.

"We knew we would find you," FJ whispered, sobbing as well. "You can let me go now . . . Really, Charlotte. You can let me go . . . Charlotte, you're hurting me."

"How did you get here?" Charlotte asked, turning him loose.

"It's a long story, but Ray and Deputy Brown are waiting for us up there . . . My God, Charlotte, you look like hell."

"I feel like I've been through hell."

"Those bastards. Charlotte, let's get you out of here."

"I can't," Charlotte said, pointing the flashlight at the chain around her neck.

Looking at the lock, FJ shook his head. "That's an easy one," he said, looking around. "Let me have your light."

With the flashlight, it didn't take FJ long to find what he was looking for, a small piece of a welding rod. With Charlotte holding the light, FJ twisted the wire inside the opening in the lock. It took a minute, but suddenly there was a small click. With a smile, FJ removed the lock. "You're free."

"You have no idea how good that feels," Charlotte said, rubbing her neck.

"Now, let's get the hell out," FJ said, taking Charlotte's hand.

Halfway up the ladder, they heard footsteps on the deck above.

"Back down," FJ whispered.

***

"What's he doing?" Marvin asked as he watched Bubba nearing the open hatch. "You think he heard something?"

"How the hell should I know," Ray asked, drawing his revolver.

"Is that wise?" Marvin asked, looking at the gun.

"Probably not, but if he starts to go down, I will shoot him."

"Why? Right now, we're the bad guys, remember. We're trespassing, and Bubba has the right to go down. You shoot him, and I'll have to arrest you."

"You're kidding? If you remember, Bubba killed Sara Sinclair."

"Shit, that's right. If he starts down, shoot him."

Bubba paused above the hatch, looking around at the dark and still waters. "Charlotte, you down there?" he asked.

"Where else would I be?"

"Good," Bubba replied, closing and latching the hatch. "I know what Pete said about leaving the hatch open, but I don't trust you." Satisfied, Bubba went back to his cot.

Chapter 37

I stand in the doorway looking out into the compound. I see it's drizzling, and the gentle rain is striking the warm earth, creating a mist that shields the surroundings in an eerie fog. Its early morning, right before the dawn. Off to my left, a single light-pole casts a soft glow barely fighting its way through the ghostly mist.

Two hooded men, dressed in black robes, stand one on either side of me. Their black gloved hands holding me firmly by the arms. The chains encircling my wrists rattle from my nervousness. A gentle push and the three of us step out into the rain. No word is spoken, nor would there be during the next few minutes. They let me pause, but for a moment, lifting my head to the falling droplets, letting the rain refresh my face. Letting the droplets mix with the tears on my cheeks. The chain strung between the shackles around my ankles drags nosily across the concrete walkway. It's the only sound. Stopping before the steps leading up to the top of the platform, my jailers wait, waiting for the nod from the executioner to continue.

In black hood and robe, he stands at the top of the steps, a dark, menacing silhouette with gloved hands on hips. Behind him the silhouette of the hangman's rope looms, looped with its thirteen wraps. Raindrops slowly drip from the bottom of the loop, like tiny drops of blood. With a bow and a slow downward wave of his hand, the executioner motions us to come forward. I count the steps as the three of us ascend. There are thirteen.

The executioner steps out of the way and points to the spot where he wants me to stand. It's a three foot by three-foot trapdoor. As I step onto it, it gives a little under my weight. I take a deep breath. My heart is pounding. With a hand on my shoulder, the executioner stops me and turns me to face my victims. There they stand below me, staring up and silent.

Sara Sinclair, her hair matted to her scalp from the rain, her bikini top strap broken on one side, her skin deathly pale except for the black rings around her neck. I can't see her eyes; only two black orbs. She mouths the word – guilty. Beside her, Sergeant-Major Preston Mullins and his son-in-law, Parker Davis, their bodies bloated, with blood oozing from bullet wounds and the bites from the scavengers of the sea. They both mouth the word – guilty.

Behind Sara, stands Charlotte Knott with one hand resting on Sara's shoulders. The left side of Charlotte's face is missing, leaving a gaping, bloody hole. Her pale skin covered in bloated leeches. With half a mouth, she mouths the word – guilty. Frank stands behind Charlotte, bloated, one arm is missing, as is half of his right side. He smiles at me, his friend, and then, sadly mouths the word – guilty. Surrounding the five are the silhouettes of thousands of the unknown dead – men, women, children and babies, young and old – those who died in the massive radioactive explosion. From their mouths comes the only spoken word that day – guilty. That single word floats through the air, slashing and tearing through my very soul.

The executioner steps in front of me now, and I can see his eyes and only his eyes. They are yellow serpentine with black slits, like the eyes of the Beast of Eden. In those eyes, I see no anger, no sympathy.

He reaches out taking the rope and places the loop over my head. It is water soaked, and the cool water sends a chill down my spine. The end is nearing. He tightens the hangman's noose and balances the knotted end on my left shoulder, and then steps back to survey his handiwork. Three feet of extra rope hangs down beside my body. That will be the distance I drop. Reaching behind him, he removes a spare hood and places it over my head. I sucked in a breath, becoming claustrophobic. There is only darkness now.

I hear his footsteps as he steps off the trapdoor and makes his way to the bar holding the trap in place. It's a simple mechanism.

Pull the bar, and the trapdoor is released. In a heartbeat, several sandbags attached to the trapdoor, jerk the door down and out of the way. The body freefalls, coming to a sudden stop three feet later, breaking the neck.

Inside my black hooded domain, I see nothing; I hear nothing; I wait. My legs start to tremble. I feel like I'm about to puke. I feel my muscles tightening from fear. I'm truly sorry, but that doesn't matter to them. They demand justice, and this morning they will get it. Suddenly, there comes a ping and the sound of pulleys spinning. The trapdoor springs open. I'm falling.

Pete shot up from his cot, trying to catch his breath. He was hyperventilating, and his chest felt like it was being crushed. He forced himself to slow down and take long breaths. His forehead and shirt were soaked in sweat. There would be no sleep for him the rest of the night.

Chapter 38

"Now, what are we going to do?" Charlotte asked. "We're locked in. I've looked, and there's no way to open the hatch from down here."

"Let me think a minute . . . Is there another hatch?"

"I don't know. Maybe at the stern. The chain won't allow me to go back there."

"Let me have your light."

FJ shined the beam around the hold. "Oh, God. What a frickin mess."

The black water was covered in slime, oil, trash from meals and feces.

"Is that?"

"Yes," Charlotte answered. "Frank used to empty my shit bucket here instead of dumping it overboard.

"Is the water deep?"

"I don't think so. I've never tried to find out."

"Great," FJ said, sitting down on the metal platform with his legs dangling in the black and smelly water. Sliding off, he found the bottom. The water was coming up around his neck. He had to bob to keep from going under. "This is some nasty shit. I hope there's no monsters or crawly things. I'd die if something grabbed me."

Slowly, he disappeared in the darkness. Once, Charlotte heard a splash, followed by the muffled word – shit. Minutes later, FJ returned covered in slime.

"That was the most horrible thing I have ever done in my entire frickin life," he whispered, the slime covering his face. After

Charlotte helped him back on the platform, he whispered, "There's another hatch back there all right, but it's latched as well."

"We're never going to get out," Charlotte sobbed. "I wish you hadn't found me. FJ, these guys mean business. They killed Sara."

"I know," FJ whispered. Charlotte gave him a weird look.

"The FBI told us," he added.

"The FBI. Then why aren't they here?"

"They say, it's a matter of National Security. We don't see it that way. So here I am. Your knight in slimy armor."

"FJ, truth be known, we're never getting out of here. You can climb out through the vent. You said Ray and the Deputy are out there. Go to them. Save yourself."

"No fuckin way. Excuse my French, but we're not done yet. Not by a long shot . . . Charlotte, you just said vent. What did you mean by that?"

Charlotte pointed to the opening above them. "Pete told me that's a vent. At the other end, it's shaped like a tuba. It opens onto the deck."

"I've seen those things in the movies."

"It's supposed to funnel fresh air down here when the boat is moving, but it doesn't help much."

"Shine your light up there."

From their point of view, they could see up to the bend.

"Help me get up there," FJ said.

Charlotte cupped her hands near her knees, in which FJ placed a foot. Then he hopped, with Charlotte raising her hands. Catching the sides of the tube with his hands, he supported himself, taking some of his weight off Charlotte. Then Charlotte, from below, pushed up. Soon, FJ was supporting himself with both hands and feet. Working back and forth like a rock climber climbing a rock chimney, he inched his way to the bend and beyond. It wasn't long before his head popped out the opening. FJ thought about climbing out and opening the hatch, but with all the noise it made closing, he knew the others would hear it. The only thing to do was to rejoin Charlotte. He would not leave her alone. He would die first. He would let Ray figure this out.

***

"So, what are we going to do?" Marvin asked.

"I have no idea," Ray confessed. "Maybe, I can get aboard and hold Bubba, Pete and Frank off while you open the hatch for FJ and Charlotte."

"You think you can do all that?"

"You have a better idea? It won't be long before they find both of them in the hold."

"I don't think you're going to get the chance."

"Why do you say that?"

"Look."

The lights were on in the crew quarters, which meant the three men were up.

***

Soon the outline of Bubba could be seen climbing the steps to the wheelhouse. A moment later, the spotlight on the bow came on, flooding the bow and the surrounding water in a bright light. Pete could be seen standing above the now opened hatch.

"You look like shit," Bubba said, eyeing Pete.

"I didn't sleep well last night."

"You can come on up, Charlotte," Pete yelled below. "We need to get started. I'd like to have the cradle built before sunrise."

"What are we going to do?" Charlotte whispered to FJ, who shrugged his shoulders.

"Pete, I'm not feeling well," Charlotte said from below. "At my age, yesterday just about wore me out. I'd like to rest if I can."

"I understand. You are the hostage after all. I'll check on you later."

"Thanks, Pete."

"Not a problem Charlotte," he said, closing and latching the hatch.

"He seems like a nice guy," FJ whispered.

"He really is. Bubba's the asshole."

"What about Frank?"

"Frank's dead."

"Dead. How?"

"An alligator got him."

"That's so wrong."

"FJ, if it weren't for Pete, I'd be dead now. Bubba makes no bones about killing me."

"Asshole."

Ray and Marvin watched as Pete closed the hatch.

"I bet he locked it . . . Damnit," Ray whispered.

"Well?" Marvin asked. Ray shook his head. "I don't know. We'll have to wait."

"For what?"

"Divine intervention. I don't know, but with FJ aboard, anything could happen. We'll have to let FJ figure it out."

Chapter 39

Pete stood there staring at the bomb. He placed his hand softly on its side, making sure it was real. Even in early July, the metal felt cool to the touch. He couldn't believe it. They actually found the damn thing. Now, all they had to do was get it to the Port of Savannah, get Bubba's money and leave the country. He wondered if Bubba would keep his promise and give his and Frank's share to Frank's parents. No, Damnit! He wouldn't. Pete made a promise to himself. Bubba would give the money to Frank's parents, or Bubba would die. Frank, in his simple way, lost his life trying to help Bubba live out his dream. Pete made another promise. Charlotte would not die as well. She'd been through hell, and by no fault of her own. Somehow, she would live. Too many people had died in the last few days.

"What are you doing?" Bubba asked, bringing Pete out of his daze.

"Just looking at it," Pete replied. "It's been missing for so long. You should be proud finding it."

"I'll be happier when we get our money. What do we need to do?"

"We need to make some kind of cradle, to keep it from rolling around the deck. We could use the pipe joints and the empty oil drums. Once in place, we can strap it down."

"Sounds like a plan."

It took longer to build the cradle than they thought. By the time they finished, the sun was up, as was the temperature.

"Bubba, lower the bomb slowly and let's see if the cradle holds. If I wave and scream, stop lowering it."

"Yes Sir," Bubba laughed.

For the next few minutes Pete held his breath. It wasn't until the cable line went limp, did Pete let out his breath. "Looks good. Leave the cable attached so it can be unloaded at Port. But, let's strap it down real well. I don't want it moving an inch."

Another thirty minutes and the job was done. Pete wiped the sweat from his eyes. They won't have to move or touch it again. They would leave that job up to Wally's buyer. His part of this shitty ordeal was over.

"Are we ready?" Pete asked.

"Ready," Bubba replied.

"Then take us to Savannah."

***

From three hundred feet, the small electric hover drone couldn't be seen or heard. Matt and his friends at Hunter Air Force Base, near Savannah, had souped-up the drone's WIFI to handle controls from a hands-on pilot at the Air Force base miles away. Together with Lisa's eyes and his hands, they guided the small craft across the marsh to Moon River. In the dark, even with night vision, it took most of the night to locate the rusty trawler. For the last few hours, Lisa and her team had watched Pete and Bubba build the cradle and strap down the bomb. They also watched Deputy Brown and Ray hiding in the marsh a few hundred feet away.

"They've been out there all night," Glenda said, "on a small airboat with nothing to do. Can you say boring?"

"Something's wrong," Lisa said, pointing at the airboat.

"Like what?" Matt asked.

"We can easily see two men on the airboat."

"So?"

"Mulder said three men went off in the airboat. The Deputy, Ray and Frederick. Where's the little person?"

"You don't think?" Harry asked.

"He's not on the airboat; that leaves only one place."

"Why in the hell would he do that?" Glenda asked. Lisa

shook her head.

"They could have taken him back to the dock," Matt commented.

"They could have," Lisa agreed. "But right now, we'll have to assume he's on the boat. If he's on the boat when it pulls into Port, he could become collateral damage as well."

"So, what should we do?"

"We'll have to play it by ear."

***

Captain Alfred "Al" Landau, skipper of the *Starfish*, had been a shrimper close to thirty years, hunting the elusive shrimp, also known as 'pink gold.' He started as a deckhand on his grandfather's boat at the ripe old age of thirteen. Shrimpers work during the night and clean their catch during the day. After a tiring night, and during the long trip back to port, Al would nap in his grandfather's wheelhouse. Once back in port, Al's grandmother would pick him up and take him to school.

Al's shrimp boat is the type that has two large nets, which his crew tosses over the side, one to port and the other to starboard. Attached to the ends of the nets are grates which drag the muddy bottom, stirring up the shrimp, plus a lot of other critters that happen to be swimming along. This is called the 'by-catch' and the stuff they hose off the boat once the shrimping is done for the night. Among the 'by-catch' are Crustaceans, fish, seashells, and sea urchins.

Once the nets are raised from the bottom, shrimpers need to be careful as the cables and grates coming on deck can be dangerous. Al once saw an experienced shrimper lose a leg when he got it tangled up in a cable on the slippery deck. The entire catch is dumped on the deck and picked through carefully. Small shrimp can be among other dangerous sea life, so shrimpers use something to pick through the huge catch, like a wooden stake. Then the shrimp are beheaded, weighed and stored in freezers.

A friend, another shrimper, retired two years ago and opened his boat as a tourist attraction. People could come aboard and learn how shrimping has been done for generations and listen to a few salty sea stories. Al was getting on in years and dreamed of a time when he wouldn't be spending long backbreaking hours on the marsh. Today was not going to be that day.

***

With sunrise, the drone's visible light lens was switched on, giving them a better view of the bomb.

"I don't believe it, but they really found it," Lisa said. "Now, I guess, they'll be heading to the Port of Savannah."

"Do we have everything ready at the Port?" Harry asked.

"More than ready," Lisa replied. "We've got the Irish boat surrounded by two dozen agents. When the time comes, we'll kick their -"

"They're moving," Glenda interrupted, pointing at the large screen. "Looks like the trawler is heading south to the Little Ogeechee River, and then on to the ocean. From there it's a straight shot up the coast, past Tybee Island to the Savannah River and then the Port."

"What's the Deputy and the Sheriff doing?" Matt asked.

"Just sitting there," Lisa commented. "I bet they're wondering what to do next."

"What would you do?" Glenda asked.

"Truthfully, I don't know. One of their friends is aboard the trawler, and they can't do anything about it without getting him killed. I'm sure they know that. I bet they're feeling pretty frantic right about now. I know I would be."

"Well, they're moving," Harry chimed in.

"They're heading back up Moon River toward the Skidaway River," Glenda said, walking up next to the large screen. "I wonder why? That's the long way around."

"They can't take the airboat out on the ocean," Harry said, with one finger across his lips.

"So, they're forced to take the long way," Lisa added. "We

know where the trawler is going. So, let's have the drone track the airboat for a while. I'm curious as to where he's going."

About a mile up the twisty river, the airboat suddenly swung a hard right, slicing into the sawgrass.

"Oh my God. They're not taking the river courses," Glenda exclaimed. "That son-of-a-bitch is cutting across the marsh."

"That's brilliant," Harry exclaimed, joining Glenda by the large screen. "He's cutting off miles. He knows the airboat can plow through the sawgrass like it wasn't there."

The small group of agents watched as Marvin guided the small craft through the deep grass, like a combine plowing through a corn field.

"What would happen if the boat hits a hidden log or something?" Matt asked.

"If the log were lying on the ground, the boat would sail over it," Harry surmised. "If it was suspended two or three feet above the mud that would be a different story."

"I wonder how he knows where he's going," Glenda said.

"Has to be pure luck," Lisa answered. "He can't see a damn thing . . . Oh, my God. Look at their course. They're about to pop out onto the Wilmington River and there's a shrimper heading their way."

With bated breath, the four watched as the small airboat surged out of the sawgrass into the direct path of the larger shrimp boat. Because of its size, the shrimper couldn't maneuver quick enough to avoid a collision, nor could the shrimp boat stop on a dime. Captain Al, with a sick feeling in the pit of his stomach, could do nothing but stare in disbelief at the assholes about to plow into him. Marvin's survival instincts kicked in the second he caught sight of the *Starfish* out of the corner of his eye. Jerking the 'stick' forward, as far as it would go, the airboat almost flew out of the water. Jerking the 'stick' hard to the right at the same moment caused the airboat to tilt dangerously to starboard, spinning like a top, throwing spray and water across the bow and wheelhouse of the *Starfish*.

"Goddamn you, Marvin," Al screamed, knowing full well

Marvin couldn't hear him.

After a few breathtaking seconds, Marvin pulled the 'stick' back halfway and the airboat, still tilting dangerously to starboard, shot off downstream, missing the *Starfish* by a hair. It reminded Matt of those stuntmen who drive cars tilted on two wheels. A hundred feet past the *Starfish*, the airboat slammed back onto its bottom, zigging and zagging until Marvin gained control. Those in the room couldn't hear Captain Al laughing and cursing, blasting his air-horn half a dozen times. Those in the room couldn't see Marvin smiling, pitching his old friend a finger. The airboat swerved and disappeared into the sawgrass.

"God, I like that man driving that airboat," Lisa said. "He has balls."

"Does anybody know where's he going?" Glenda asked.

"I bet back to a dock called AJs. That's where Special Agent Mulder says it's normally moored."

"And then what?" Glenda asked. Lisa shrugged her shoulders.

"Have the drone get back on the trawler."

"You know, we're missing a person here," Harry said, intently watching the screen.

"Who?"

"Has anyone seen Frank lately?" All shook their heads.

***

Marvin turned the engine off on the airboat, and stood up in his seat, scanning the surroundings.

"I almost crapped my pants back there," Ray said.

"I think I did," Marvin laughed.

"You seem nervous?" Ray asked. "Are we lost?"

"No. Just not sure of our whereabouts."

"Isn't that the same thing?"

"No. Lost means you have no idea where you are. I know where I am. I'm in the middle of the marsh. East is over there. I'm just not sure if we need to go that way, or that way."

"Where are we wanting to go?" Ray asked.

"Back to AJs," Marvin yelled. "We'll take my Chevy and head to the end of the island. We should get there before they do."

"And what will we do when we get there?"

Marvin said something, but it was drowned out by the engine firing up.

Chapter 40

Pulling up to AJ's, Marvin tied his airboat to the Tybee Police Department's boat, to keep it from floating away.

"Don't dilly-dally, Ray," Marvin said, running up the wooden, inclined walkway. Ray wasn't a young man, and spending a night on a small, cramped airboat hadn't helped his weary bones or his attitude. Smiling, laughing, happy, sickening people were already making their way down to their rentals, carrying fishing equipment and coolers full of food and beer, forcing Ray to sidestep and dodge to get around them.

Old person here, he wanted to scream. *Get out of the damn way. I'm a Sheriff, for Christ's sake.*

A college kid whispered something smart under his breath as Ray sideswiped him. Ray stopped and grabbed the kid's arm. "You just say something?" Ray exclaimed, frowning, patting the gun hanging on his belt.

"Come on Ray," Marvin yelled from the swinging door onto the dock. "Quit messing with the tourists."

"Today's your lucky day, Bub," Ray said, releasing the boy, who said something else under his breath as he walked away. Ray shook his head and turned to the kid, about to continue his one-sided conversation.

"Damnit Ray," Marvin yelled. "Get a move on."

By the time Ray slowly climbed into Marvin's Chevy, it was already running. Marvin slammed it into gear and spun out of the parking lot turning south onto Chatham Avenue. Chatham Avenue runs alongside the Tybee River, and at a slight bend, Chatham Avenue became 18th street. At the four-way stop on Highway 80,

Marvin goosed the Chevy through the intersection. Cars sitting at the intersection, cars which had the right-of-way, laid on their horns.

"Where're we going?" Ray asked, hoping it wasn't far and they'd get there alive.

"Pelican Point," Marvin said, not taking his eyes off the road.

"Holy shit," Ray screamed, as a large moving van backed out onto the narrow street.

Without missing a beat, Marvin jerked the steering wheel hard to the right, jumping over the curb and onto the sidewalk heading to the ocean.

"Shit," Marvin whispered, as he took out a section of white picket fence. Passing the moving van, Marvin bounced back onto the street. "The Chief is going to be pissed, and that will probably come out of my paycheck."

Pelican Point, located at the intersection of 18th Street and Strand Avenue, is the last public access to the beach. Every day, crowds from the surrounding condos poured through an opening between the sand dunes to one of the prettiest stretches of sand on the island. Marvin parked his truck on the "No Parking" concrete walkway beside the sandy trail leading out to the beach. From there they had a clear view of the shoreline.

"You think they beat us here?" Ray asked.

"Don't think so," Marvin replied. "Ray, we know FJ's on the boat. How do we get him off?"

"You mean, FJ and Charlotte."

"We don't know that, for sure. That still doesn't answer the question. How do we get him off?"

"I'm afraid we're going to have to storm the boat," Ray replied, eyeing Marvin's deer rifle hanging from a red plastic gun rack attached to the rear window.

"You're suggesting we storm a boat with a hydrogen bomb lying on its main deck?"

"Dumb I know, but at some point, it will come to that . . . Where are they? The wait is killing me."

"I know."

"I noticed your rifle," Ray commented, killing time. "It's sweet."

"It should be. It set me back two grand. You heard of the Beanfield Sniper Remington Sendero?"

"No," Ray replied, smiling.

"Why are you smiling?"

"I used to be a sniper, in another life."

"Vietnam? (Ray nodded his head.) This Beanfield has a heavy 26-inch barrel. Not as long as your sniper rifles. With the scope, it probably weighs ten pounds or more. It fires a 7mm Mag made for flat shooting, which helps for long and accurate shots. Out here along the marsh, you can't get close to the deer, they're too jumpy."

"What kind of scope did you mount?"

"It's a VX-6. I like it for its crystal-clear image. It stays clear throughout the entire magnification range. This one's max magnification is 42.00x."

"Wow. That's more than the scopes we used in Vietnam."

"Like I said, out here along the marsh, you can't get close to the deer. This baby makes the farthest target seem like you can reach out and touch it."

"Is there someone we could call, knowing that the FBI is out of the question?" Ray asked, getting jumpy.

"I have an idea," Marvin said, reaching for his cell phone.

While Marvin made his call, Ray climbed out of the Chevy and walked out toward the beach. Already people were staking out their spots near the water. Parents were applying sunscreen to their kids. Four people were throwing a Frisbee around in a circle. A guy, up near the pier, was catching the early morning breezes by flying a bright red kite in the shape of a dragon. A large container ship was on the horizon. Ray couldn't tell if it was coming into port or heading out. *Early morning, probably going out.* Toward the southern end of the island, Ray spotted a dark form making its way north. Ray's stomach jumped. *It has to be,* he thought. Soon the rust-bucket came into view. *Gotcha.*

"They're coming," Ray exclaimed, climbing back into the Chevy.

"You sure?"

Ray nodded.

"Ray, I just got off the phone with a friend of mine, Homer Gibbs, who's a captain in the Coast Guard. I brought him up to date on our predicament. And, as you could guess, he's a little pissed the FBI hadn't informed them. He said he'd call his commander."

"Look, there it is," Ray said, pointing.

"Son-of-a-bitch."

Bubba's boat was cruising about one hundred and fifty yards from the beach, making a beeline to the Savannah River. Ray could see Bubba and Pete in the wheelhouse, but nothing of Frank. Ray could also see the bomb lashed to the main deck.

"We need to stop them," Ray said, looking at Marvin. "Can we call them somehow?"

"I don't have shortwave," Marvin replied. "But I have a bullhorn."

"Can they hear us from here?"

"No, too far away."

"Then what?"

"Hang on Ray. I know just the spot."

Marvin started the engine and threw the truck in gear, throwing Ray against the back of the seat. Dodging oncoming cars and jaywalkers on Strand Avenue, Marvin made his way north on the south bound street, along the beach to the Tybee Pier. Slamming on the brakes, Marvin slid to a stop at the entrance to the Pavilion. Ray almost crashed into the windshield.

"Next time remind me to put on my seatbelt," Ray stated, rubbing his shoulder.

With the engine running, both men jumped out of the cab leaving the doors open. Ray had a small lead on Marvin because Marvin had to come around the front of the truck, but within seconds Marvin had passed him. In Marvin's hand was a red bullhorn.

Ray's breathing was labored when he caught up with Marvin at the end of the pier. He had to steady himself by hanging on to the railing. "Where are they?" he wheezed.

"There, just south of us, about fifty yards off."

"Are they close enough?"

"Just about," Marvin replied, switching on the bullhorn.

***

Pete stared at the bright red dragon floating in the sky, and at the partiers on the beach. He wished he was with them. They were innocent; he would never be innocent. He had blood on his hands. But it would be over soon, thank God. If he had known what would happen this week, he would have never come. Maybe, after time, he would be able to forgive himself. No, that would never happen.

"Hey, on the boat," a voice yelled from shore, bringing Pete out of his daze.

"Hey, on the boat," the voice yelled again.

Pete searched for the source and found it on the pier.

"Who's that?" Bubba asked from inside the wheelhouse.

"It's the Deputy with the Sheriff that was staying in the blue condo," Pete replied.

"We need to talk," Deputy Brown yelled through the bullhorn. "Pull over."

"Screw you," Bubba spat, through a handset and a speaker mounted on the wheelhouse.

Bubba's voice was loud and threatening.

FJ and Charlotte, from within the hold, heard the conversation.

"Charlotte, help me back up the vent," FJ whispered. "I need to see what's going on."

As before, FJ climbed up the narrow funnel and poked his head out, making sure no one was looking. From his position, he could see Pete and Bubba standing on the wheelhouse deck, looking toward the pier. He could also see Ray and the Deputy on the pier. *It's now or never*, he thought.

Grabbing the sides of the vent, FJ swung his body sideways and out, dropping softy to the deck. Ducking, FJ quickly stepped to the side, putting the vent tower between him and the two above. They hadn't noticed him; they were too focused on Ray and Marvin. Watching Bubba and Pete, FJ made his way around the crew quarters to the bow of the boat, beside the hatch. He started waving his arms wild and crazy, pointing toward Bubba and Pete and the pier.

"Holy crap," Ray exclaimed. "That's FJ. What the hell is he doing?"

"He's trying to get our attention," Marvin replied.

"No. He knows he has our attention, why does he keep waving?"

"He wants us to keep Bubba and Pete distracted," Marvin replied, catching on. "Hey guys, slow down. Give us a minute. Why won't you talk with us?"

FJ bent over the hatch, waiting. Bubba went into this great spill about – It's none of your damn business what we're doing, yada, yada, yada. His voice, through the speaker, filled the air, drowning out everything. As softy as he could, FJ slid the latch back and opened the hatch cover. Looking up at Bubba and Pete, FJ saw they hadn't heard the hatch being opened. Bubba was still busy cursing at the Deputy. FJ motioned for Charlotte to come up and hide behind the crew quarter, on the opposite side from the two men.

"I saw her. I just saw her," Ray exclaimed with tears starting to fill his eyes. "Thank you, Jesus."

"Amen," Marvin added.

When Bubba quit his caterwauling, Ray took the bullhorn.

"Guys, you need to get your asses over here, or I'm going to SWIM out there!"

"You better keep your asses away from us," Bubba shrieked. "I know my rights."

"I'm not kidding," Ray yelled. "I will SWIM out there and kick your asses."

Bubba pitched him a finger. Ray pitched him a finger, twice. FJ nodded his head and ducked behind the crew quarter where Charlotte waited.

"Did you hear Ray?" FJ asked. "He wants us to swim for

it. The shore's not that far away. (Charlotte shook her head.) Charlotte, it's the only way. (Charlotte nodded her head.) After what you've been through, do you think you could make it?"

Before Charlotte could answer the boat lunged forward. Peeking around the corner, FJ saw they were moving up the coast again. Pete and Bubba were back in the wheelhouse.

Marvin and Ray, surrounded by a crowd drawn to the noise, watched as the boat made its way north.

"What's that on the back of the boat?" someone asked.

"It looks like a bomb," another answered. "I bet AJ's doing some kind of publicity stunt."

"Son-bitch," Ray spat. "They're moving."

"Do you think your friend understood your message?"

"We should see in a minute. They need to get off that boat before they reach the river . . . Come on guys, get off the damn boat."

***

"You ready Charlotte?" FJ asked, staring at her swollen face. "You sure you're up to this?"

"Nothing's going to keep me on this boat another minute," she replied, smiling.

"Good, you go first, and I'll follow you," FJ said, helping her to her feet.

FJ looked around and up toward the wheelhouse. "They're both inside. Now's the time. Charlotte, go for it."

Charlotte looked up at the men, took a deep breath, and ran to the portside railing. Leaping up, she bellied her way over the rail, dropping into the sea. The ocean engulfed her; its cool water chilled her; the idea of escape thrilled her. She broke the surface, got her bearings and headed toward shore. FJ stood near the rail, out of sight of the men above, watching Charlotte swimming away. He hadn't followed her, as he told her he would. The plain fact – he couldn't swim. If he had told her, she would not have gone. FJ turned and went over to the hatch and began climbing down.

Someone would come for him, hopefully a friend.

"Pete, look there," Bubba yelled, pointing. "That's Charlotte. How in the hell did she get loose?"

"How in the hell should I know," Pete said, starting to exit the wheelhouse. "It doesn't matter now. You keep heading to Port. They'll give you your money and help you get out of the country."

"Pete, that sounds like goodbye."

"It is. Bubba, this has been the worst week of my life, but I wish you well. May God forgive us for what we have done, and for what we may have to do." With that Pete disappeared, knowing full well he would never see Bubba again, but that was okay with him.

Standing by the lower deck rail, Pete watched Charlotte making good progress toward shore. Reaching behind, Pete made sure his revolver was tucked in his waistband. With one hand on the rail, Pete jumped sideways, swinging his legs overboard, hitting the water feet first.

"Did you see that?" Marvin asked. "Charlotte's swimming to shore, but one of the men is right behind her."

"Get us down there," Ray said, already forcing his way through the crowd on the pier.

Back in Marvin's Chevy, they made their way over to Highway 80 and turned north.

"Charlotte jumped almost at your condo. Let's stop there," Marvin said, dodging slower moving cars and golf carts.

Sliding to a stop beside Mike's van, the two men ran through the breezeway to the ocean. Ray stopped when they came to the payphone and looked south, back toward the pier. The boat wasn't there. Looking north, Ray saw the trawler about a quarter mile from them.

"Raymond," Margaret said coming out of the condo, followed by Mike and Stephanie. "Where in the hell have you been?"

"Not now Margaret. Look," Ray said pointing.

"Oh my God, is that Charlotte?"

"Yeah, we better do something, or he's going to catch her. Margaret, you guys, stay here."

Marvin and Ray started for the spot Charlotte would come to ground, but was stopped by Special Agent Mulder, who had been watching everything play out. The small hover drone passed over head.

"You two need to stop right here, right now," he said. "We'll take it from here."

"Shit," Ray exclaimed, turning back to his condo. "Come on Marvin."

"You didn't put up much of a fight," Marvin said, once they were out of hearing.

"What could we do? They're the fucking FBI."

Chapter 41

Charlotte's legs and arms were getting tired, and she was having trouble catching her breath. Seemed, she couldn't keep the ocean out of her mouth. She could hear someone splashing behind her, and she prayed it was FJ. If not, she prayed she'd get to shore before her pursuer. A few minutes passed before she felt sand beneath her toes. Another few strokes and she stood flatfooted in the sand. She began battling her way through the surf, which kept trying to drag her back to sea. Exhausted, she fell to her hands and knees in the sand. Soon, Pete was lying beside her on the sand, breathing hard.

"How did you escape?" he asked. "Never mine. You can tell me later. You did it Charlotte, and it's over. You're free to go."

"Really? Just like that?"

"I needed an excuse to get off the boat. Charlotte, I'm sorry for all you've been through."

"Pete, I know it wasn't you that caused all of this. You're not responsible for the deaths. Frank wasn't responsible. Pete listen to me. If not for you, I'd be dead right now. But what are we going to do about FJ?"

"FJ?"

"My friend. The little guy. He's on the boat. He helped me escape."

Pete smiled and helped Charlotte stand; both of them stood there watching the trawler as it moved away. Pete wiped the water from his eyes. "Maybe we should go over to -"

"Hold it right there," a deep voice said behind them. "FBI."

Pete took a step behind Charlotte, holding her close, drawing his revolver.

"Stand back," he said. "I won't hesitate using this."

"Pete, please," Charlotte whispered. "You've got to let me go."

"Shut up, Charlotte," he whispered back. "I know what I'm doing."

"No, you don't. You have no frickin idea. Pete, they will kill you."

"Stand back," Pete yelled at the FBI man. Pointing his gun at Charlotte's head, Pete exclaimed, "I will shoot her."

"No, he won't," Charlotte yelled. "No, he won't. Don't shoot him."

***

"Damnit," Ray said, pacing in the parking lot. "The FBI is going to screw this up. They're going to get Charlotte killed, and they don't even know FJ's on the boat. Do they know the bomb's there as well? Sure they do. It's right there like the nose on Mulder's face. We need to do something."

"Like what?" Marvin asked.

"We need to get higher," Ray said, looking at the high risers.

"Why?"

"So, I can use your deer rifle."

"My deer rifle?"

"Are you a sniper?" Ray asked.

"Hell no."

"Well, I am. And it just may take one to save Charlotte and FJ. If the FBI screws up, we could have a lot of people hurt. Look around. People are gathering with their cell phones. This will be live on Facebook in minutes. We need to get somewhere higher."

"Come with me," Marvin said, grabbing Ray by the arm.

Backing out onto Highway 80, Marvin threw the truck into forward, peeling off and smoking rubber.

"You're going west, away from the beach. Why?"

"Hang on. You'll see."

At the light at the intersection of Highway 80 and S. Campbell Ave., beside *Bowie's Seafood,* Marvin took a right.

"Where in the hell are we going?" Ray yelled, above the engine roar.

"You'll see."

At the "T" with Van Horne, Marvin took a left and a right onto Meddin Drive.

"We need to hurry," Ray pleaded. "We don't know what's going on at the beach."

"We're almost there."

Rounding a short curve to the left, the Tybee Island Lighthouse came into view.

"You're kidding," Ray whispered.

"You said you needed a high place. There's none higher on the island than the lighthouse. You'll be able to see the beach and the river from up there."

Slamming the brakes at the lighthouse parking lot, the Chevy threw gravel and dirt in the air, making those standing in the parking lot cover their faces. Tourists stopped what they were doing to gawk. Marvin reached into the glovebox and removed a box of shells.

"Take these," he said. "I'll carry the rifle."

"Hi Marvin," an old African American attendant, who gave out tickets, said as they passed. "What's up?"

"Hey Jesse. We need to use the lighthouse."

"If you say so," Jesse said, rising from his chair.

The climb was agonizing, and Ray was glad he wasn't packing the heavy rifle. Out of breath, Ray stepped out onto the catwalk surrounding the upper level of the lighthouse.

"Excuse me, people," Marvin said to a couple of tourists. "You'll have to go on back down. This is police business, and we need the lighthouse."

"What's going on?" one asked.

"Police business," Marvin assured them, pointing to the stairwell leading down.

The couple excused themselves as they passed Ray. It had been five years since Ray had climbed the lighthouse. Marvin was right. Ray had the perfect view of the shoreline all the way up to the river. From this distance, those on the beach looked like ants.

"Let me have the rifle," Ray said, holding out his hand. Taking the rifle, Ray threw it against his shoulder and looked through the scope. Adjusting the viewfinder, everything on the beach became larger and in focus. Ray could see several FBI agents standing on the beach, surrounding Pete and Charlotte in a semicircle. Pete had Charlotte pulled up close, using her as a shield. If an agent took a step toward him, Pete would point his gun in their direction, forcing him to step back. *That won't last forever*, Ray thought. Opening the box of bullets, Ray removed one round. Pulling back the bolt, Ray slid the round into the chamber. Slamming the bolt home, Ray made sure the rifle was on safety. Suddenly the silence was broken by sirens.

All of those on the shore turned to look up the beach. Ray and Marvin turned to their left and saw four Coast Guard Cutters, side by side, making their way from the river out onto the ocean. In tandem, the four cutters turned south toward the rusty trawler.

***

Bubba killed the engine. As Pete had told him the other day, they couldn't outrun them and they sure as hell couldn't outshoot them. But he wasn't giving up. He had the bigger bang. He had a hydrogen bomb; they didn't. The two middle cutters cut their engines, letting their boats drift, coming to a stop in front of Bubba. The two outer boats cut their engines and drifted up alongside of the trawler.

"How's it going?' the captain from the other day asked. Before Bubba could reply, the captain continued. "The name's Homer. It's good seeing you again. Where're your friends?"

"They're not on board."

"It's just you?" Bubba nodded his head.

"How about the little person?"

"I have no idea what you're talking about?"

"Then you won't mind us coming aboard."

"I didn't say you could," Bubba spat, placing his hidden hand on his AK-47.

"What's that over there," Captain Homer asked. "O.M.G. Looks like you guys found her," he said after a few seconds. "Now what are you going to do with it?"

"That's none of your business . . . Wait. Back up a minute. What did you mean by 'little person'?"

"You really don't know?"

Bubba shook his head.

"I think we need to come aboard."

"No," Bubba said coolly, aiming his gun at Homer. "Not one foot."

"You think you stand a chance against us?" Homer asked.

"No. But what happens if I put several rounds through that?" he replied, swinging the AK-47 toward the bomb.

"You really don't want to do that, do you?" Homer asked. "You'll be killing a lot of people, including yourself."

"I'm dead already."

"No, you're not. You don't have to die. No one does. Not today. Let us come aboard, and we'll talk about it."

"Not one foot. If I don't die today, I will later."

"What do you mean by that?"

"I did some bad things."

"What things?"

"Bad things."

FJ had been hiding in the hold all this time, but when the engine shutdown, he stuck his head out. He smiled to himself when he saw the shiny white and red striped boats. *The Cavalry finally comes to the rescue. About damn time.* Silently making his way up the steps on the opposite side of the boat from Bubba, FJ listened to all that was being said. From the tone of Bubba's voice, FJ knew Bubba was losing it. Bubba was a murderer and a maniac that would not hesitate carrying out his threat. He had to be stopped. Reaching down, FJ withdrew his knife, testing its balance.

"You guys need to back off and give me room. Give me time to think," Bubba screamed. "By God, I mean it. I'll blow us to hell if you try and board my boat."

"Now sir, you don't want to do anything crazy," Homer said softy, raising one hand. Bubba noticed the machine-gunners aiming their weapons at him.

"I said I meant it," Bubba spat, flicking off the safety and aiming his gun at the bomb. He would not let them take him alive. Even if they didn't give him a death sentence, he would not spend the rest of his life in prison. It had all come down to this.

"Fuck you all," Bubba screamed.

Suddenly, there was sharp pain in Bubba's neck. Blood began to pump from his severed carotid artery. *What just happened?* Within four seconds Bubba was feeling dizzy, his head was spinning, and his eyes were blurring. Lightheaded, he grabbed the doorway opening to steady himself and pressed the trigger of the AK-47. Three rounds flew across the deck, inches above the bomb. Slowly Bubba sat down on the steel catwalk with his back against the rail. "No," he whispered. It wasn't supposed to end like this. He was going to live like a king. The AK-47 slipped from his numb fingers. With blood flowing from his mouth, Bubba tried to say something else, but nothing but bloody bubbles escaped. Slowly, his head slumped over onto his chest. Slowly he closed his eyes. Slowly he took his last breath.

FJ stood there staring at what he had done. His hands were shaking, and he felt lightheaded.

"That was one hell of a throw," Homer said, walking up beside FJ. "I doubt anyone could have hit his carotid artery with the way the boat is bobbing in the water."

"I was aiming at his heart," FJ said, putting his head through the railing, sucking in air, trying not to puke.

"Well, good job anyway, just like David killing Goliath," Homer laughed. "Let's get you back to your friends."

Chapter 42

All on the beach could see the trawler surrounded by the Coast Guard Cutters, and all heard the shots. Pete was wondering about Bubba and the little man. Pete pulled Charlotte closer. Agent Mulder wondered who in the hell called the Coast Guard. That wasn't part of the plan.

"Okay. Here are my demands," Pete said sternly. "First, you'll bring a -"

"No demands," Mulder interrupted. "This ends here and now. You will drop your weapon, turn loose of the woman and step away."

"The hell I will."

"Pete, please," Charlotte whispered. "They're going to kill you. You know that. Please drop your gun."

"No way Charlotte. I'm not going to prison . . . God Damnit, everyone back off."

Ray wondered how FJ was fending. Looking through the rifle scope, Ray smiled. He could see FJ, wearing a life-vest, being lowered onto the Cutter inflatable. Ray took a deep breath and turned his undivided attention to Charlotte. Looking through the scope, he had a clear and up-close image of both Pete and Charlotte. He couldn't hear what was being said, but by body language, he knew the situation wasn't good. Ray switched off the safety. The boy, at some point, would lose it, getting himself killed and maybe Charlotte as well. Ray guessed at the distance, watched the palm trees swaying in the breeze trying to determine wind direction, trying to judge the difference in elevation. Reaching up, he adjusted the scopes settings, fine tuning the scope.

"Ray, are you sure you can do this? Charlotte's too close to him, and the only clear shot is to his head. If you miss by a few inches, you'll kill Charlotte."

"You're not helping Marvin. And no, I don't know if I can do this." Setting the barrel of the rifle on the lighthouse railing, Ray took another deep breath and waited. "Marvin, if it looks like he's about to kill her, I will pull the trigger."

Pete was sweating, but not from the rising temperature. It was coming down to the wire. The thoughts of prison life filled his mind. That was not going to happen. He remembered Frank asking him if they still hung people down here. At the time, he thought it was funny. Now he wasn't sure. How do they execute people down here? His dream came back to him. No. Charlotte was his hostage, and he was going to use it to the hilt.

"You guys listen close. I'm leaving here and Charlotte is going with me. You will furnish a car and a flight out of here."

"And where are you going?" Mulder asked.

"I don't know yet, but I'll think of something."

"No. That's not how it's going to be. There'll be no car, no plane. You will hand over your weapon now, and you will let Charlotte go. You don't have to die today. It's your choice."

"Please Pete, listen to him," Charlotte pleaded.

"I'm sorry Charlotte," Pete whispered in her ear.

In one fluid motion, Pete pushed Charlotte away, and stepped to the side, leaving a couple of feet between them. Raising his weapon, he fired three rapid shots, each inches above the agent's heads. Before they could return fire, the back of Pete's head exploded, spraying the ocean with blood and brains. His lifeless body crumbled in the surf face up. For a moment, Charlotte stood there in shock. Kneeling, she took Pete's hand. Tears began flowing from her eyes, dropping on his cheek. Pete's dead eyes stared back at her.

Ray sat down heavily on the catwalk and placed his head against the cool concrete surface of the lighthouse. His eyes were closed. His hands were shaking.

"Here, take this Marvin," Ray said, offering the rifle.

"A hell of a shot, Sheriff," Marvin whispered, taking the rifle. "A hell of a shot."

"It wasn't much," Ray responded. "Anyone could have done it."

"I doubt that."

"The more I think about it, the odder it seems."

"What's that, Ray?"

"Pete knew what he was going to do, and he knew what they would do. He didn't want Charlotte hurt. That's why he pushed her out of the way. Pete wanted to die, and I just helped him."

Epilogue

Ray, Margaret, Mike, Stephanie, FJ and Charlotte found themselves in the same conference room, sitting around the same table the three men used the night Mulder and McIntire brought them in for questioning. Both agents were there, sitting on either side of the six.

"Lisa is calling in. It'll only be a few min -"

The large screen, on the wall, flickered once and the smiling face of Lisa Clark appeared.

"Hello, everyone. Mrs. Knott, I'm glad to meet you finally. You had us all worried. (FJ rolled his eyes.) How are you feeling?"

"I met with a surgeon yesterday, here in Savannah. He says I'm going to need some cosmetic surgery to fix the broken bones in my cheek. We're hoping that will help the blurriness of my left eye. I'm going to get a second opinion from my own doctor when we get back home. There's nothing, I'm afraid, that will help the scar. So, I guess it's a souvenir. At times, I can still smell the boat's interior, I see all the blood, and the alligator attacking Frank. It turns my stomach. I'm having recurring nightmares about the whole ordeal. My head and face ache when I'm not on pain pills. Let's see, other than that, I'm feeling peachy."

"You've been through a lot, I know," Lisa admitted. "A weaker person would have given up. If it's any consolation, you've been a great help in clearing up a few things. We contacted the Fish and Wildlife Department, and they're out looking for the killer croc. We wouldn't want it hurting kayakers or canoers. They tell me, they're probably never going to find the remains of Frank Beasley. It's been too many days since he was taken. Your information on the whereabouts of the other two missing persons helped. The Coast Guard located the sunken boat and the remains of Preston Mullins and his son-in-law, Parker Davis. Sara Sinclair's parents are relieved their daughter's murderer has been brought to justice.

"The story we're telling the Sinclair family members is this: Sara Sinclair saw an illegal transaction between some drug runners on the Savannah River. That cost her, her life. A lead led us to the assailants, which ended in a shootout with the FBI. There were no survivors. Case closed. The story we're telling the families of Mullins and his son-in-law, Parker Davis – there was a collision at sea involving a rusty trawler and an oyster boat. All aboard both boats died. Luckily, we were able to retrieve all the bodies but one. Case closed."

"Do you think there won't be any questions about bullet holes in the bodies?" Ray asked.

"There are no bullet holes, Mr. Harris. After our surgeons got through with them, the bodies appear horribly eaten by marine animals: fish, sharks, crabs, star fish, etc., etc. There are no bullet holes, and we recommended closed caskets. That's our story and yours as well. Anything different, won't bring back the dead.

"Now I'm speaking to Mike, Ray and Fredric. What you did was highly illegal, stupid, idiotic, and dangerous. You knowingly and willfully interfered with an ongoing Federal Investigation. I don't think you know the trouble you could be in right now. (Why isn't Deputy Brown here getting his ass rimmed? FJ thought.) All of you could have been killed. I can't stress that enough. But, you did it because you all love Charlotte. I hope I have friends that would do that for me . . . I think that wraps it up. I want to thank you all for coming in today."

"Excuse me," FJ said, raising his hand. "But that doesn't wrap things up."

"What do you mean, Frederic?" Lisa asked.

"The bomb, what happened to the bomb?"

Lisa sat there a long time thinking how she was going to answer FJ's question. "Okay, this is what I'm going to do. Agent McIntire will get six copies of our confidentiality forms. Once you've signed them, I will let you in on what happened to the hydrogen bomb."

Agent McIntire left the room. "While she's getting the forms," Lisa continued, "let me tell you what the confidentiality form means. It means you will not talk with anyone outside this room about the bomb or anything else that's said here today. If you do, you will most definitely be sent to prison for a very long time. Understood?" Everyone nodded.

It took five minutes for Agent McIntire to return with six forms, and after all signatures had been doubled checked, Lisa continued.

"The Coast Guard by their seizure of the boat, and Frederic's killing of Mr. Henry screwed our plans for catching the buyer in the Port of Savannah. But, with some quick thinking on the part of Special Agent Mulder, we were able to come up with an alternate plan. We have an African-American agent in Savannah the same height and build as Mr. Henry. This agent took Mr. Henry's place on the boat. We also have a demolition expert at Hunter Air Force Base. While the boat made its way up the Savannah River, we airlifted him to the boat. He removed the trigger."

"What about the rest of the explosive material?" Ray asked.

"Waterlogged. Useless," Lisa replied.

"But, would Wally recognize your agent?" Charlotte asked.

"Special Agent," FJ stated. "They like to be called Special Agents."

"Mr. Wilkins wasn't at the dock that day. We found him murdered in his house the morning of the raid. It appears the buyer wanted to take care of some loose ends. Luckily, our plan went off without one shot being fired. With access to the trawler, we had our agents in the wheelhouse, crew quarters and lying on the deck. When the boat came into port, our men sprang from the water, along the dock and from the boat. Sean's men were completely outnumbered and outgunned. After it was over, one of the buyer's men told us – the three men on the trawler were targeted as well. So, it seems Bubba, Pete and Frank were destined to die when they pulled into port that day." In the darkened room, no one saw the tears forming in Charlotte's eyes. *Pete was doomed the day he came to Tybee.*

"Where's the bomb now," Mike asked.

"It's in a secret government facility and will never be a problem again."

"Probably alongside the Lost Ark of the Covenant," FJ whispered to Ray.

"And what are you going to tell the public?" Ray asked, ignoring FJ.

"Nothing. As far as the public's concerned – if you believe in the legend, the bomb is still out there somewhere. If you don't, who cares?"

"But -" Ray started.

The screen went black.

About the Author

Kentucky has always been my home. I was born in Owensboro and raised in Daviess County. Life was simple back then. I grew up with outhouses, hand-pumps, and coal stoves. If you wanted hot water, you heated it on the stove. Both of my parents have passed on. I have a half-brother, Danny, but most of our younger lives he lived with his father, so we didn't get to see each other often. Looking back, sadly, it was like being an only child. My closest friends were the cows, chickens, pigs, goats, sheep, turkeys, geese, ducks, and horses my dad kept on our small farm. I hope I didn't leave anyone out. Farm animals can be so jealous. Our grocery store - mason jars of mom's canned vegetables and the occasional trip into town to the IGA.

My dad was a woodsman. You could give him a shotgun, a box of shells and a book of matches, and he could disappear into the forest for weeks. I used to hunt with him, but I was never the woodsman. I can't tell you how many deer, squirrels, rabbits, raccoons and ground hogs I've eaten.

My wife, Stephanie, and I have five kids (three boys and two girls) and eight grandchildren (five boys and three girls). All but one son live here in town. You should see Christmas day at our house.

I've had several jobs during my lifetime. When I was thirteen, I had a summer job. I was a soda-jerk at the Utica Junior High School playground. The school is now defunct. It is not my fault the school went defunct. As an adult, I started out as a janitor. Loved the work, but not the pay. Mapping came next. In other words, I was a draftsman who created maps from surveys. I did that for over twenty years. Mapping fulltime and going to Brescia College (It's now a University) at night, I got a BS in Computer Science. Career change. I was a Computer Analyst for over twenty years. There came a day when I realized I was the dinosaur of Computer Science. Technology had passed me by. So, I up and retired. That was in 2014, and I haven't missed working a day. Truth be known, I do miss the people I worked with. Notice, I've said nothing about writing. I could tell you a pretty good story, but putting it on paper was another thing. Stephanie, my wife, asked, "And why not?" I had no answer.

I should keep this short, so, I will tease you with two important events that happened in my life; two events that I haven't already discussed. When we meet each other, don't hesitate to ask me about them.

Monday, September 6, 1965, was a Labor Day, and I was out of school. On that day, I came in contact with a high voltage powerline. Seven thousand two hundred volts entered my hand and exited my head and my feet. That's not a typo. It was seven thousand two hundred volts. I was given up for dead for three days. There is a "rest of the story" as Paul Harvey used to say. Ask me about it when we meet.

The second event: September 17, 2017, I was ordained a Permanent Deacon in the Catholic Church. It keeps me busy these days. If you're not sure what a Permanent Deacon does, Goggle "Permanent Deacon of the Catholic Church."

There you have it. My life story summed up in 1000 words

or less. It sounds like a writing contest doesn't it. There's so much I left out. I could tell you about riding the rails, or the time I hung myself. But, those will have to wait until we meet.